DARKENED TRUTHS

KINGS OF POINTEBREAK BOOK 1

CARA WADE

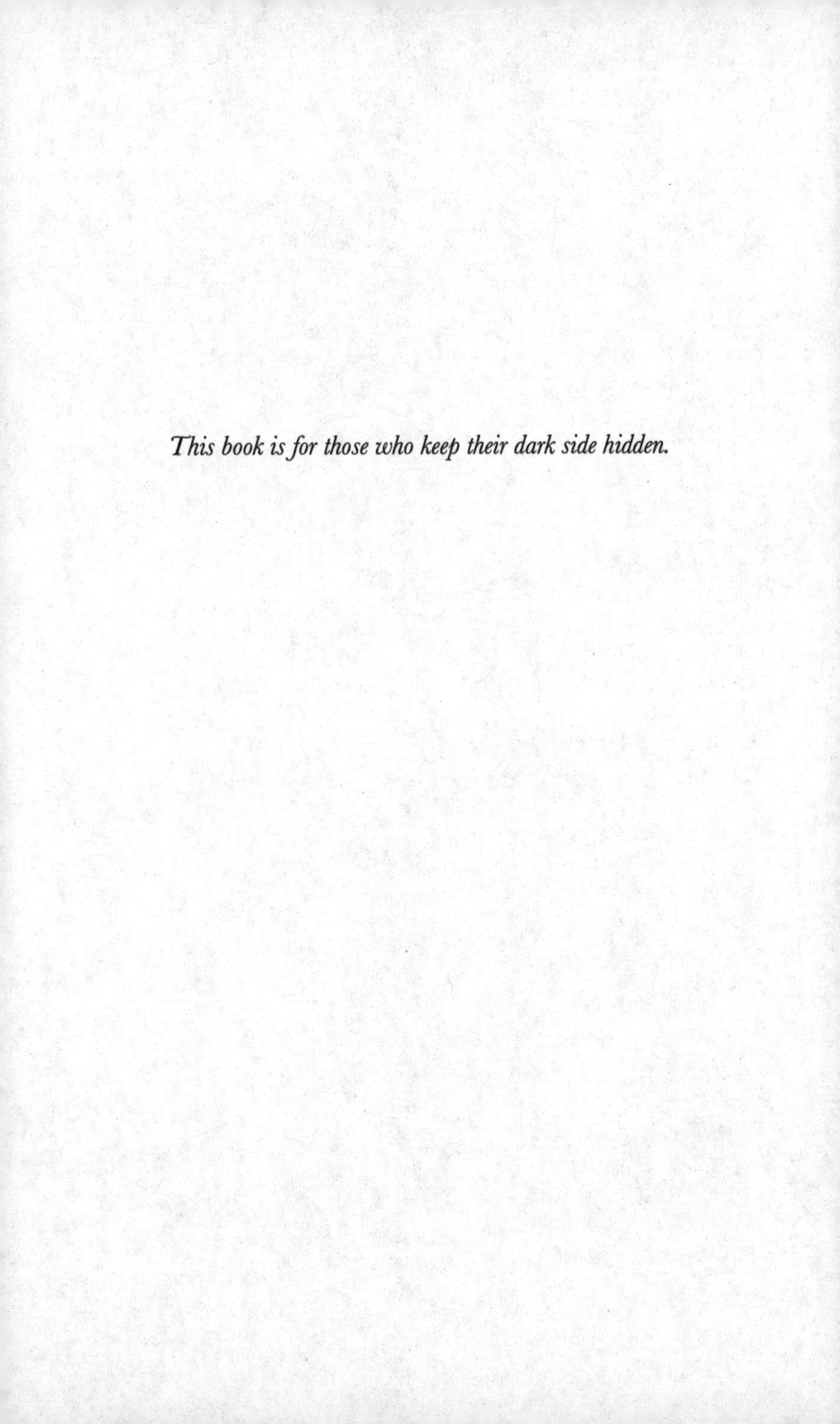

This book is for those who keep their dark side hidden.

ONE

RILEY

Daddy dearest used to be the man I looked up to for everything. Now I can't stand the *bastard*. Michael Whittier has been called several colorful names throughout his career, but I've never believed them more than I do now.

"You can't be serious about this! Pointebreak's for criminals! What about Dartmouth, huh? We agreed I was going. I worked hard to secure my spot there." He snorts, and I ignore the jab he insinuates as my crossed leg bounces a mile a minute. Rubbing my forehead, I strive to wrap my head around the bomb he dropped on me an hour ago…while on a stage…in front of five thousand people. All the while, a strained smile masked the rage that simmered beneath the surface. As soon as he said it, the blood drained from my face and my heart pumped wildly in my chest, threatening to break free. The inevitable panic attack only kept at bay because of the crowd surrounding the stage. I'm sure some people watching caught my moment of shock as I forced myself to keep my expression as neutral as I could.

He can't do this to me. Why is he doing this? The thoughts played on an endless loop as I went through the motions, not even cognizant of what I was doing. My silent rage erupted as soon as the limo doors were closed, continuing non-stop until we reached his massive, opulent home office. It's everything you'd expect and more.

An organized, large mahogany desk sits proudly in the middle of the room, a beautiful blue and white Turkish rug underneath, complete with a dark leather chair. Dad has two chairs in front of it, wooden, not meant for comfortable long visits, which is his way of forcing people to leave sooner than they might have otherwise. A large picture window is behind him, showing off the beautiful backyard and pool. Built-in shelves cover the wall to the left, which includes a few priceless first editions. On the right wall, he has a large framed Claude Monet that he will tell anyone who listens that it is real and costs a fortune, along with awards and diplomas. This room screams "look at me" and I hate it.

"It's not for criminals. It's a prestigious academy and I'm not joking, Riley. I submitted the transfer papers this morning. You're going to Pointebreak. End. Of. Discussion. It's for your own good."

My stomach sours at his words and my shoulders tighten as the stress of his decree settles deep, locking my muscles. I keep rolling my neck and pushing them away from my ears as I wrap my arms tight around my midsection, willing my body to not shake and the traitorous tears to stay put.

How could he do this to me?

"For my own good? My own good would be Dartmouth. Get an Ivy League education and find a respectful job. Not go to an institution that turns people into killers!" I scream, a tear sliding down my cheek. I wipe it on my shoulder, pretending it didn't happen.

Crimson floods his face; his neck muscles tighten, threatening to unleash a torrent of angry words and saliva. I've heard about my dad's anger issues, but this is the first time in my life I can remember it being directed at me. Sure, we've had disagreements and arguments, what family hasn't, but nothing compares to this. I want for the sting of words to slap me but they never come.

"This discussion is over. Start packing your bags. You need to be on campus in two days. Only bring essentials. I'll have everything else shipped to you. The school has your uniforms, and your class schedule is here." He jabs his index finger on a glossy folder covered in promotional photos of Pointebreak and slides it across the pristine desktop, stopping it in front of me.

I open the folder, unable to help myself. I need to know what my future is going to look like. Flipping through a few pages, I land on a rules section and scan the text in front of me. I only register every few words, but it's enough to know they have made Pointebreak as close to a prison as possible.

I stand on shaky legs, trying hard to meet his height. Even in my three-inch heels, he towers over my petite frame. It can't end like this. I soften my voice. "Dad, please reconsider. This is *me* we're talking about. I'm your only daughter. I'm the only one you have—"

"Don't you *dare* say another word," he hisses, knowing what I was going to say. The sound is so alien that I step back. He murmurs so softly, barely above a breath, that I have to lean in close to understand him. "You'll go and that's final." Then he steps around me toward the door. Without giving me a backwards glance, he adds, "Sign the contract, or so help me, I'll forge your signature myself." Then storms out, leaving me standing there stunned.

I try to keep calm, but my heart rate kicks up and my breathing shallows. My blood rushes through my ears, making it impossible to hear anything else. It feels like I can't get enough air in my lungs and I sink to the floor, my legs unable to hold my weight any longer. My dress pools around me as I rest my head on my knees, gasping. I run my clammy hands over the soft material and then wipe my damp forehead with the back of my hand.

This will pass. I need to breathe. Focus on the feel of my lungs expanding and contracting. Deep breath in, hold and release. Over and over. I look around the office and see a curtain billowing under the air conditioner vent. Then close my eyes and rock gently as I listen, forcing my attack back. There's noise of people in the hallway, the birds are chirping happily outside, and my breathing is slowing. Next, I wiggle my toes and shake out my legs. Then I shake my fingers and arms to get the blood flowing freely again. Once I feel semi-normal, I drop my head back against the wall.

God, it's been years since I've had a panic attack this bad. The room still spins, so I keep myself on the floor and continue my deep breathing until I feel the rest of my panic attack fade.

Blinking back tears, I stare at the spot my dad vacated. He's never spoken to me like that.

Ever.

I don't know what caused his reaction. I look down at the god forsaken folder that contains the contract for me to sign. I'm eighteen, a legal adult. Running away sounds like a good option, and I could make it on my own. Take my car, flee the state, and get a job. Start my life now. But deep down, I know Michael Whittier would never let that happen. He's a master at getting *exactly* what he wants. He would find me and drag me back kicking and screaming, and then still send me to Pointebreak. I'm his to control, to use and contort to whatever he needs. That man who walked out the door isn't my father. That man isn't the one who kissed my scrapes as a little girl, or dressed as Santa to keep the magic of Christmas alive.

No. I haven't seen hide nor hair of that man in years. No matter how many excuses I've made over the years, the man I knew growing up died years ago.

I don't know why this is so important to him. Everything I have worked hard for—all the studying and extra-curricular activities were for nothing. *My future is gone.* With a snap of daddy's fingers, it all disappears.

I open the glossy folder and stare at the information. The words jumble around the page as I try to focus on them. Maybe if I stare at it long enough, it will burst into flames and put a stop to this madness. Dad had to have gotten himself mixed up in something bad. There is no other reasonable explanation for him shredding my life into pieces.

My phone buzzes and I put it up to my ear without even looking at the ID.

"Riley, what the hell is going on? Why didn't you tell me you weren't going to Dartmouth? I thought we were besties! And why would you choose Pointebreak of all places? Does Troy know?" Leah practically screams through the receiver.

"I, um." I clear my throat, trying to dislodge the ball stuck there. It still burns from holding the tears back, regardless. "I didn't know. It was a surprise to me too. And I haven't had the chance to call him yet."

Troy is my boyfriend. He's handsome, and I like him, but his dad works with mine and it was almost like they played matchmaker. His family has a lot of money and is one of my dad's top campaign contributors.

There's silence as my best friend breathes, no doubt trying to come up with some infinite wisdom or advice to make this situation feel better. In. Out. In. Out. I sync mine with hers, but it does little to calm my frayed nerves. I hold the phone with my shoulder and shake my hands before wiping the dampness on my dress so the phone doesn't slip through my fingers. Even though I can't see her, I know her well enough to know exactly the face she is making. "Daddy sprung this on me today at the rally. I'm as surprised as you are." I finally get my feet to move and walk to my bedroom, leaving the unsigned contract on his desk. Closing my door, I quietly flip the lock, the metallic click of the latch echoing in the room's stillness. "I was trying to make him see reason, but he won't." A heavy stuttering sigh escapes. "I'm expected to be packed and on campus in two days."

"What the hell, Riles. How could he do this to you?"

A dull ache pulses in my temples as I press my palms against my burning eyes, attempting to stop the tears. Fat lot of luck it does. They still spill over and down my cheeks.

"I wish I knew, Leah." I take a deep breath and let out a shaky laugh, looking for some semblance of humor in this fucked up situation.

She keeps talking, but everything goes in one ear and out the other. I can't focus on anything she says. Then she gasps suddenly. "Riles, you can write an expose on the place. This could be it!"

What? Her enthusiasm does little to make me feel better. "Yeah, except I'm not the writer. That's you. Remember?" The "duh" is on the tip of my tongue, but I rein it in. No need to be bitchy to her. She did nothing wrong.

"So?" she counters with an excited squeal. "O-M-G, I got it. You go undercover, get the goods, and I'll write it. We'll sell the story to a national paper or write a book. It's genius! There's been no one who has released this type of information. No one's gonna stop you from writing about your experience." She takes a deep breath. "Riles, this could be huge for us!" Her enthusiasm is palpable. I know Leah well enough to know she's already making her bestseller list speech.

Thinking about it, she is making a few good points. There's something going on at Pointebreak, and getting to experience it first-hand could give us an enormous advantage. Most of the country doesn't know of its existence, but those in New England do. It's almost like a mythical place. No one has ever seen it, even though the people in town know it's there like a secret stitched into the town's foundation, kept quiet by generations who know better than to ask. I perk up for the first time today. She *is* making some valid points. I could sell my story, fight to make it headline news nationwide. Maybe Pointebreak could come crashing down. There are too many secrets surrounding that school. It's always astounded me that no one's come forward to quash the rumors.

I always assumed I would go into politics to help dad get further in his career, and boost mine. That seems to be what most politician kids do. They get some sort of powerful position to help boost their parents along with their own. But after today I'm not so sure what I want…

"Maybe." I offer noncommittally as I rub my forehead, hoping for some relief from this blasted headache. "I don't know." My mind and body are numb, and I'm seeing everything through a haze. It's like I'm having an out-of-body experience. I'm here, but not at the same time. Leah is still talking, but I can't keep up with her. My mind is bouncing around from one scenario to another, conjuring up nightmares of what being a Pointebreak student will mean.

I cut her off, not able to keep up with her train of thought anymore. "Leah, I gotta go. I'll call you later." We say goodbye and gently toss my phone on my bed.

There's a stupid no off-campus rule for the first years. Same thing with a car. It's a privilege granted to older students. The only chance to get away will be during Christmas break, if I'm even going to be allowed to.

Summers are probably gone too. If daddy's willing to throw me in here, what's stopping him from keeping me there year round? If I'm a betting woman, and today I sure as hell am, I would say my summers will be on campus, or locked up somewhere else where I can't escape. Something's going on. There's a reason he doesn't want me going to Dartmouth, and I intend to find out why.

Mystery shrouds Pointebreak. The good people of Barrington, New Hampshire, don't talk about it, and most pretend the school doesn't exist. The townspeople stay away from it, and the students keep themselves scarce around town. I know, because I've seen campus up close once. One of Governor Whittier's campaign tours was in Barrington. I could only look through the gates, though. One rumor is the mafia runs it and it's a training ground for the armies. That seems far-fetched to me. But then again, people also say it's owned by the government and they use it to produce super soldiers, so who really knows? All I know is I won't be taking literature this year like I assumed. And if I wanted to go out for a sorority—forget it. The school doesn't offer extra-curricular activities.

Pointebreak will be my prison for the next foreseeable future.

I slump, no longer able to stand straight—the weight of my fate is pulling me down. I ignore the suitcase that's found its way into my bedroom and search the school online. The grounds are beautiful. The vivid colored flowers throughout the pictures bring a touch of a smile to my face. But that's the trap, isn't it? Lure unsuspecting students like me into its death trap only to consume me and spit me back out as something else.

Jesus, I need to lay off the horror movies and mystery books. Dad wouldn't send me anywhere where I wouldn't be safe. But even as I think about it, I'm wondering how true that is. I scroll through several pages featuring pictures of smiling students in uniforms, before clicking on the about us page.

"Founded in 1936 by the Genovese family, the campus started off as a small private school for underprivileged students forging for a better life," I murmur. *How philanthropic...* "Students who choose to study at Pointebreak will obtain the finest all-encompassing experience between academic and extracurricular." I contort my face in confusion. "What the hell does that mean?" I sigh heavily. "Such pretty words for a prison," I mumble.

I scroll each page and read the entire website from top to bottom but nothing jumps out urging me to run far and fast. *Although, why would it?* The website showcases how most students graduate and gain acceptance into high-level jobs and positions. Something just seems...off. I don't know what it is, but something isn't right with this. It sounds too perfect.

What school makes you sign a contract? Well, I guess every college when you accept their offer, but still. And a uniform? I sigh and fall back against my headboard. I should have grabbed the folder of information so I could read through it. The last thing I want is to leave the sanctuary of my room. I glare at the suitcase again and decide I'd better pack and get a list together to buy last-minute items.

Such a good girl, doing just what daddy wants. Like always.

I'm disgusted with myself, but can't resist, and I rummage through clothes. I put my hand over my stomach, bile trying to find a way up. My earlier panic attack returns, but I quickly use my rule of three to stop it before it overwhelms me again.

I wasn't always like this—the panic attacks. They started shortly after my mom died, and things...changed. Mom was my safe place. The love she showered on me was unmatched, and when she died, I lost that. My dad loves me, I know that, or knew that, but it's not the same as with her. They started slowly. My heart would race when I was in an uncomfortable situation and my palms would sweat. But I could usually breathe through it until it passed. I didn't know what it was and when I told my dad I didn't feel right; he blamed it on hormones or anxiety like it was a normal thing.

It wasn't until I was about sixteen that the attacks got terrible. Not until after him. I shake my head. No. I'm not going down that road right now. I've got too many other things to focus on. Nothing good ever comes from thinking of him.

What has dad gotten himself into? The question snakes its way into my thoughts again. I've heard him behind closed doors enough times to know he doesn't always make deals with the kind of people you'd want to owe a favor to. Powerful men. Men who can make or break you, exposing all your dirty secrets. But dad always seemed to have people's best interests at heart even through all of that. I know he made a lot of improvements in our own town when he started off as the Town Manager. But as his political career grew, so did his attitude and need for power.

I've noticed the change slowly over the years. First, it was with some of his staff. He switched kind hearted employees out for more cutthroat people who offered smiles but rarely made me feel comfortable, and stares that made shivers run down my spine. Next were the security measures he added around the house. No longer was an alarm enough. He felt he needed to add a gate with a guard at the end, along with security cameras and alarms.

A lot of these changes happened so long ago I hardly remember a time when we didn't have them in place. I guess I figured every politician lived like that. I've heard of others having bodyguards and tight security around them, but figured it was normal protocol, especially as his popularity grew.

Plus, my world wasn't being turned upside down.

Could Leah be right? She used to joke about my dad being mixed up in some shady shit, and I always laughed it off and told her it wasn't possible. My body heats as anger simmers just below the surface. I clench my teeth and breathe deeply through my nose, willing myself to calm down for the umpteenth time today. I've been at dad's beck and call my whole life. The core of his campaign is the death of his wife and his dedication to his only daughter and the bright future he wants to give everyone.

I bite my thumb, thinking through everything that has happened today. Needing to see what's in that contract, I get off my bed and pull open the door, only to be met by the man of the hour, his hand poised to knock. I bristle as I look at him, and for a moment, his eyes soften and he gazes at me like the man—the dad I've always known. The urge to hug him is strong, but I keep my feet planted firmly and cross my arms over my chest, standing as tall as I can.

"I love you, Riley. I wouldn't make you do this if I didn't think it was best for you. Trust me. Please." His voice is soft and kind. My bottom lip trembles as I listen to him and I pull it between my teeth, biting hard to stop it.

"Why, Dad? I had plans, and they didn't involve spending the next four years of my life trapped in some sort of boot camp."

I'm not sure if I'm seeing things or not, but I swear his eyes darken and the uncaring man from earlier tries to break through, but in the same second he shuts it down and opens his arms to pull me into a hug. I step into his embrace and his chest rumbles under my cheek as he speaks again.

"You'll be safe there. I've made all the arrangements and you'll get a better education there than any college you could attend. You'll leave Pointebreak with a network of professionals anyone would dream of and can do anything you want."

I raise my head, brushing away the fresh tears that have begun to fall. "And what about you? What are you getting out of this?"

After a long pause, he finally answers. "Everything we've ever wanted."

TWO
RILEY

The sun shines through my open curtains, but I'm too tired to move. My limbs feel heavy, like I was dragged through hell and barely spit out in time to wake up. My ruined future haunted me all night, each thought bringing a fresh torrent of tears; I cried until I was so exhausted I all but passed out for a few hours. I can't believe he did this to me. I still don't understand what he meant by thinking this was best for me. Dartmouth, and an Ivy league education is what's best for me.

To add insult to injury, Troy came by last night to break up with me. According to him, he can't date someone who will slum it with criminals. How charming, right? I will say, I'm proud of myself, though. I didn't cry or beg with him there, although I couldn't keep my chin from quivering before James, our driver and bodyguard, personally escorted him to the door and removed from the standing list of invited guests. Since his dad is the one who told him to break it off with me, I'm sure he doesn't care.

Our parents threw us together for political reasons, but somehow we clicked. We were kindred spirits shaped by the same pressures of living our lives under the microscope of the public. We were always trying to be the perfect son and daughter, so the media had nothing unfavorable to report. Plus, Troy is easy on the eyes.

We got together after one of my dad's parties last summer. I was playing the perfect hostess, and Troy attended with his parents. It was love at first sight—or I guess lust would be a better way to describe it. We hit it off great. I took him on a tour of the house, and then we snuck a few glasses of champagne and hung out in the pool house, away from prying eyes.

We spent the afternoon talking and laughing and because I was a little drunk, and a horny teenager, I went down on him and he fingered me. I felt like such a bad girl. I was sure dad would take one look at me and *know*. Troy's arm was casually slung around my waist, but nothing about what we did felt casual. My face was burning, my pulse was a drum-beat of guilt and thrill. I didn't dare look my father in the eye. I had never done anything like that in my life, but had never felt so happy before. Plus, I knew daddy would approve of him, a rare feat in itself. Usually I was alone, surrounded by adults at these events, so it was a welcome distraction to have a cute boy my age there. Those parties are a way for my dad to rub shoulders with donors and act like he cares. Which, judging by the way he's sending me away, is probably another facade.

My reputation at school was that of a perpetually uptight virgin, a label whispered in hushed tones from some assholes I turned down. They didn't know I had a boyfriend because they didn't need to know about my love life. I didn't want to draw attention to myself. And I'm not, for the record, a virgin. Although Troy was constantly trying to get me to sleep with him, I refused. Third base was as far as it ever went, and I know that used to upset him. I would make some excuse why I couldn't sleep with him, and those conversations always ended in an argument.

I often wondered if he kept dating me because his dad wanted him to, or because he wanted to add another notch to his belt. Now don't get me wrong, he was a gentleman, and I was happy dating him. And most times I genuinely thought he liked me, but there were times I wondered just how much. I suppose this breakup was just a matter of time.

Tears stream down my face, hitting the pillow under my head as I think about it. No Dartmouth, no boyfriend, no life. Everything is unraveling in the blink of an eye.

I lie there, feeling sorry for myself when someone knocks on the door.

"Riley?"

"What?" I call out, hearing my best friend's voice.

I've known Leah since elementary school. Her parents aren't in the same social circles as mine, and maybe that's why we get along so well. She shows me how normal people live. We've been inseparable since we were in the same summer camp when we were eight. She's been there for it all and always without judgement. I don't know what I would have done without her. I'm not sure I would be here today if it weren't for her.

I wasn't suicidal or anything, but Leah and her family were my haven. She won a full-ride scholarship to attend Stonewall, so I was lucky enough that we got to go through high school together.

She opens the door and looks at my sad state. I texted her "over" last night and with that one word, she knew exactly what I meant. She sent a few hug GIFs, and a promise of a visit, so it's no surprise she's here today. "I'm going to assume you're newly single and ready to mingle." *I am most definitely not ready to mingle.* "He was an ass, anyway. Get up. We're going out." *That sounds miserable.* I want to sit here in my room and wallow for the day. "It's your last day of freedom and you're not spending it cooped up in your room."

She goes to my closet and rummages through, looking for something for me to wear. She spots the large suitcase in the corner of my room and shakes her head. "I still can't believe he's making you go." I sit on the bed and watch her push hangers around until she comes back with a cute pair of shorts and a flowy top and tosses them to me.

"Get up, shower, and put these on. We're going on an adventure." I go to argue with her and she places her index finger over my mouth. "Nope. You're not arguing. We're going to start our research project today."

Barrington is a quaint town with some cute shops and cafes along the main road. Nestled close to the White Mountains, Leah and I play tourist for the day. We shop at some of the small boutique stores on Main Street and wander down the sunny streets and then through the park. I'm glad she got me away from the house. I feel marginally better being in the fresh air with my best friend.

"You said you wanted to start research. What did you have in mind?" I ask as we take a rest on a bench overlooking a small pond with ducks milling around.

"I want to go to campus, and talk to people. Or maybe stop people along the way to ask questions."

"I've been to the campus before, but they locked the gates with a guard at the end. No one is getting in or out of there without their permission."

She shrugs like it's no big deal. "So let's take a drive and see if the guards will talk. I may have a twenty I can bribe them with." She smirks, and we both laugh at the ridiculousness of it. "Come on, let's see what we can dig up."

Fat lot of nothing is the answer. There are no signs to follow to get to campus and GPS ran us in circles. We stopped an elderly couple to ask for directions, and after a horrified look, the man yelled at us to leave them alone and he knew nothing. So that was a lovely experience. Even something more exciting to look forward to for the next few years. I didn't even mention I was Riley Whittier because I don't think that would have helped matters.

We finally pulled a map up online and I navigated the route shown as she drove. When we arrived in front of the school, the guard scowled at us and told us to leave. I explained I was a new student, and I was to be on campus tomorrow, but he informed us of the strict move in hours, with no exceptions.

So, now we are sitting in a booth at a small diner at the edge of town talking quietly amongst ourselves. Leah tried to ask the waitress questions about the school, but she turned her nose up and said to stop asking or she would kick us out. For a supposedly friendly town, the people here are kind of rude.

My phone keeps ringing with new messages from Dad and James, but I've been ignoring them. I responded once, saying I'm out with Leah. And I'm not stupid enough to think they don't know my whereabouts. My location tracking is on, and both have access to it. While James is my dad's guard and driver, when needed, he's mine, too. I've grown close to him over the few years he's been with us. He's more of a father to me than my own is sometimes. I almost feel bad for ignoring him. He had nothing to do with my dad's decision, and I know he only wants to ensure I'm safe. I'm glad he found his way into my dad's circle.

"Well, this was a bust," Leah says, dipping a fry in ketchup and popping the piece into her mouth. "No one wants to talk about it, not even rumors they've heard. Who doesn't like to spread rumors?"

I laugh despite myself, "A lot of people don't." I take a bite of my onion ring and hum in appreciation. The beer battered, perfectly fried vegetable is like a mini pick-me-up. There's nothing like greasy food when you're feeling down.

A group of people enter and I feel the shift in the air. Conversations die down, almost to a whisper. Heads turn down, and nobody dares to look at those who walk through the door. It's a man, a woman, and what appears to be their son and daughter. The girl is quiet, but has a smile plastered to her face as she slides into the booth, her dark brown curls bouncing with the motion, and places the paper napkin on her lap. Their son, who appears older, motions for her to slide further into the booth. He sports dark brown hair, in a messy, yet perfectly style quaff, and a blank expression. A chill runs down my spine as my gaze connects with his before he sits down, facing me. I look away, his gaze too intense to keep looking at him.

This diner is too casual for their outfits. The dad is wearing a nice pair of chinos, a button down, and an expensive-looking pair of slip-ons, while the mom is wearing a floral a-line dress with flats and pearls. It's almost comical to see them sitting on the red plastic bench, with the smell of fried food hanging in the air. The girl is in a pair of chino shorts with a button down top. It's chic as hell, and I'm woman enough to admit I'm jealous of her style, even though I know I don similar looks often. And then him. He's wearing dark wash jeans and a black button down with the sleeves rolled to his elbows showing off a slew of tattoos.

I've never seen so many decorating someone's skin before, and I hate to admit that heat spreads through me as I squirm in my seat. Averting my gaze, I look down at my plate and pretend I haven't seen a thing. I hear the waitresses talking in hushed tones off to the side until finally one of them says, "fine" and walks to the table.

I watch out of the corner of my eyes at the interaction. They are pleasant and don't give her a hard time; but she's not comfortable serving them. Which means the kids probably attend Pointebreak.

"Leah, I think those two might be students." I keep my voice down so I'm not overheard, and Leah turns to get a better view. Never one to be subtle, she stares head on and I know he's watching our table with interest.

"Well shit, sign me up," she says, drinking the guy in. "I'm gonna be jealous as hell if all the men there are that sexy. You'd better get laid, girl." She takes another bite of a fry and then adds, "heaven knows you need it."

I scoff, only slightly offended, and shake my head as a smile creeps across my face. My sex life is nonexistent. And the thought of having it with anyone else seems…wrong. I gave my V-card to a special boy who I spent a few summers with. Well, someone I thought was special. Even now, the memories of those two summers are my favorite. I was thirteen, and he was fifteen when we met. It was a fluke, but we were fast friends and we spent as much time as we could together. He is James's nephew, Rhys. Rhys told me his parents died and James was his guardian, and my dad let him come over to hang out. That summer, we laughed, snuck sweet treats, and found random hiding spots all over the property. Days when I couldn't spend them with Leah, it was a treat for Rhys to be there to hang out with.

But then the school year started again, and Rhys was nowhere to be found. Which makes sense because James doesn't live in town, but I remember wishing he would show up again so we could hang out. Then the following summer, he didn't show up with James. He was enrolled in a summer camp. I was heartbroken that year. I'd sent letters back with James, but they always went unanswered. So, I gave up, and moved on after a while. No need to force something that clearly wasn't supposed to be. Square peg, round hole.

Rhys found his way back, though. I was sixteen, and he was still seventeen, nearly eighteen. And it's like he had never left. The simple crush that started when I was thirteen had blossomed into more. He had filled out in the two years since I had seen him. No longer a lanky kid, and boy did he fill out a suit nicely. He came to one of dad's yearly events—a masquerade. It's my favorite party of the year. Everyone shows up in elegant dresses and suits, along with intricately designed masks to shield their identities. I couldn't keep my eyes off him that night. He was my knight, and I felt like a princess. We danced and laughed like he had never left. We couldn't keep our hands off one another. A stolen kiss in an empty hallway made butterflies erupt in my belly and when he took my hand, leading me away from prying eyes, I went willingly. I would follow him anywhere. I had dreams he would come back and ask me to be his girlfriend, and that we would be together forever. A stupid teenage fantasy, but one I clung to when I felt lonely.

That's how we ended up finding our way into the pool house. God, I was so inexperienced, but he put me at ease and made me feel so beautiful as he took the last part of my innocence. It hurt all the more when he disappeared again without a trace. We had fallen asleep; me sated in his muscular arms, and when I woke from a frantic call from my dad, Rhys was nowhere to be found. When I asked James how to reach him, he told me to forget about Rhys because he was going to a boarding school.

"Earth to Riley." Leah waves her hand in front of my face, snapping me out of my thoughts. I hadn't thought about Rhys in almost a year and now the memories have rolled through my mind like waves in the ocean, never ending. Some memories hit harder than others, but they always recede back with the change of the subject.

"Yeah, sorry. What were you saying?"

She rolls her eyes and shakes her head, but smiles nonetheless, so I know she's not annoyed. "I'm going to talk to the waitstaff, and then do you want to get out of here?"

"Sounds good." I take a sip of my coke and feel my face flame when I see Mr. Sexy is looking my way again.

If I get to see him again, maybe the school year won't be so bad after all.

THREE

RILEY

The car pulls up to the gate at the end of the road and I stare up at the open wrought iron with its intricate design. The school crest bends and swirls as it stands boldly in the middle. Yesterday the gates were closed when Leah and I tried to enter, but this must be easier for the move-in days. The guard lets us pass after checking for my name on his list of students and tells James where to go. I glance around at the sprawling landscape and lush grass. It's still warm, but the nights in northern New Hampshire are cooling quickly. Winter will be here before we know it. We drive further and further up the road and it's apparent this place doesn't allow just anyone to walk around the campus. Unless you belong here, you're not coming in.

Aside from going out with Leah, I spent my last night of my freedom scrolling through Reddit, searching for information, but I only found more rumors. Threads were closed shortly after being opened, and the newest one was from two years ago. No one seems to have any clear-cut answers as to what this school is, or how the acceptance process works. No graduates have offered the information either. There's not an online application, yet this place is always full, with a waiting list.

I reached out to the administration using a fake name and email address inquiring about applying, but I received a blanket statement back stating they were not accepting new students for this year and to reach out next year for more information. Fat lot of good that did me. I looked through the contract I had to sign and nothing seemed out of the ordinary except for the line that read, students willingly enter into this contract and agree to complete the entire academic process. No exceptions.

What if I flunk out of my classes? What would they do then? Or what if I *die*? Are they planning on raising my dead body from the grave to make me come back? My lips twitched up in a smirk, imagining me coming back as a zombie.

The only good thing is there was no NDA clause, so Leah's brilliant plan of revealing the inner workings of this place seems like a genuine possibility. But it still begs to differ; why isn't anyone else talking about it if there are no rules against it? I guess I have a lot of work to do. Acting won't be in my future, and my poker face needs work, but I have a solid personality. I need to make friends and start casually asking questions.

"Riley, we're here," James says as he puts the car into park.

Yes, good ole dad couldn't take the time to drive me to my first day in my new *prison*. He gave me some bullshit line about not wanting to be recognized and to not cause a PR frenzy. Although, if I'm being truthful, I'm kind of happy it's James here instead. Things aren't much better between dad and me at home, and we avoided each other my last two days at home. I stare out the window, looking at the large dark stone building next to me. Students are milling around, laughing and watching as fresh blood gets dropped off. Maybe if I just sit here, James will take me back home and I can pretend this isn't happening.

"Riley?" He asks quietly, a touch of sadness to his voice as he turns to look at me. "Are you going to get out?"

I look out the window again and notice a tall boy with dark hair glaring at me. No, he's no boy, he's all man. He looks nothing like the boys from Stonewall Academy—where they're awkward; he appears so sure of himself—confidence radiating off him as he stands unwavering. Muscles strain against his dark collared shirt, and inky tattoos run up and around his forearms in an intricate pattern. He crosses his arms over his chest and my heart picks up a notch.

What would those muscles feel like wrapped around me? Gentle or aggressive? I don't even know why that thought hits, but I can feel my face flush.

I lick my lips, tucking my bottom one in and biting on it, then take an unsteady breath as his stare lingers. Goosebumps pebble my skin as I drag my gaze over his body and back up into his eyes. From this distance, I can't tell what color they are, but I know, without a doubt, he's not someone I want to cross. I can't stop looking at him. Finally, I pull my gaze from his and glance at the two guys on either side of him who are staring at me as well. One has light hair, and the other has dark. Both are as menacing and strong as the first. Looking closer at the one with dark hair, I'm not one-hundred percent sure, but I think that's the guy from the diner. *I guess Mr. Sexy is off the list of potentials.* I'll have to let Leah know. The three of us locked in a stare down until James touches my knee, causing me to jerk and look away.

I take a deep breath, closing my eyes for a moment to restart my heart. When I open my eyes, I see his concern etched across his features. He presses his lips into a thin line, almost as if he's keeping himself from saying something he shouldn't. I nod at his earlier question and he slides out from the driver's seat to get my bag out of the trunk. I push open the door to get a good look at my new home for the next four years. Stone buildings, a beautiful landscape that must cost a fortune, and secrets waiting to be unveiled. If I didn't know any better, I'd say this was a prestigious university.

I risk a glance back to the spot where the boys were moments before, but they're gone. After a split second of disappointment, relief floods me and I let out a shaky breath.

What was that all about?

There is a large sign for orientation check in to the right and James hands me my single suitcase before pulling me into a hug, and placing a kiss on the top of my head.

"Be good, Riley. And stay out of trouble. Keep your head down and do what's asked of you and you'll be fine."

"James, do you know something I don't know about this place?"

He offers a sad smile, then kisses the top of my head, and places his hands on my shoulders. "Don't trust too easily."

If that's not a little cryptic, I don't know what is. I open my mouth to ask more and he gives a subtle shake of his head. He points to the small line of new students and when I turn to get in line, he slides back into the car and drives off. I watch him until he's down the hill and out of sight.

"Next," the girl sitting at a desk calls out to me.

I drag my bag behind me as I step up to the table. "Hi. I'm Riley Whittier."

"Hi, Riley," she smiles at me. "I need your signed contract and identification, please."

I dig both items out of my messenger bag and hand them to her. She flips through the pages until she reaches the last page and when she's satisfied that the signature belongs to me, she hands me back my ID, along with a stack of papers.

"Welcome to Pointebreak," she starts, and the rest of

what she says hardly registers. The hairs on the back of my neck stand at attention. Subtly, I look out of my peripherals to see the same three watching me with disdain. I literally just arrived. What could I have possibly done to piss these three off?

Fingers snap in front of my face, and I blink as she comes into focus again. "Earth to Riley," the girl says. She follows my line of sight and smiles widely, wiggling her fingers at the guys in greeting. They give her a courtesy glance, but otherwise pretend they haven't seen her. "Girlfriend, let me tell you they are *way* out of your league. That's Julien Azarian, Zander Fedorov, and Wesley Bastian. The Kings of Pointebreak. They're in their third year, and don't have time for anyone. Julien's in big with Zander and Wesley. He has his sights set on the prize. He doesn't date." She pauses, and a smile splits her face. "But what I wouldn't give to be tag teamed between the three of them." She says it almost to herself, a wistful look in her eyes.

And what prize is that? The question sits on the tip of my tongue, but I'm not sure I want the answer. "He doesn't seem to be ignoring me, does he?" I mumble.

She shrugs like it's nothing. "New meat. Shiny toy. Whatever euphemism you wanna use."

I look all around me and casually gesture at the other students checking in. "So are all these people. Yet they're ignoring them."

"You're one who most wouldn't expect at a place like this." She shrugs one shoulder and looks past me. "Next." And just like that, I'm dismissed. Does she mean because of who my father is? Does everyone know who I am?

I drag my suitcase behind me, trying hard to ignore the eyes glued to my back as I search for my dorm building. She handed me a map of campus with the path to the dorms clearly marked. Tension has me wound tight. My shoulders and back ache as I wander with my heavy bag. Campus is much bigger than I imagined and the lush grass, trees, and stoned pathways make it appear inviting. I'll have to walk around later today after I find my dorm and unpack. Not knowing the weekend dress code prior made it difficult to pack clothes, but I made sure I had enough to get by for the first semester, anyway. Plus, dad said he would have items shipped. I'm sure if I reached out to him or James, they could put together a care box for me of more of my stuff.

Suddenly it occurs to me I should have asked that girl more questions about the Kings, as she called them, or really about anything at Pointebreak. I literally have no clue what I'm walking into. I pass other students, most not paying attention to me as they talk with friends, or in one case that has my face burning up—a couple in a very public, private moment together that includes her on her knees in front of him. He glances up at me and winks before threading his fingers through her hair, pulling her closer to him. She's only partially hidden behind the bushes, and it doesn't take a genius to know what's happening. I quicken my step and rub my cheeks, willing the red staining to disappear. *Oh, my God! I can't believe I just saw that!* There's no way that's a normal occurrence around here. And where are the teachers or staff to stop that?

The sign for Belknap Hall is straight ahead. I give a cursory glance around me to make sure I'm not being followed by the three grumps before I climb the steps to the building. When I'm satisfied I'm alone, I glance down at the paper for my room number and make my way up the few flights of stairs.

Jesus, I'm going to die before I get to my room. My muscles are straining from the exertion of trying to pull my heavy bag up the steps. One step. Pull. One step. Pull. On and on, as I slowly ascend the stairs. I stop on the landing between the second and third floor, looking up while stretching and rubbing my arm before I attempt the last flight.

"Hey, let me help you with that," a male voice says cheerfully from behind me.

I spin on my heel with an automatic smile on my face in appreciation. Another thing that was ingrained in me. Always be grateful for help from anyone. But in this case, I really am thankful. I didn't think I packed that much, but I know I filled this thing to the brim and it easily weighs half of me.

My smile dwindles as my mouth pops open in surprise. *Are all the guys here just flat out gorgeous?* I quickly close my mouth and clear my throat. "Um…thank you. The help would be great. I'm on the third floor." I gesture up the stairs to the next landing.

"No problem. Hi, I'm Nick Halpin." He extends his hand out in front of him for me to shake. I place my much smaller one in his and warmth floods through me. It's a strange feeling. Almost like my body recognizes him as a friend, or someone who is genuine. I glance down at our hands and swallow. Lightly tugging mine back until he releases it.

"I'm Riley Whittier. Nice to meet you."

Completely unfazed, he continues, "I live on the fourth floor. You a first year? I haven't seen you before."

He grabs my bag as I nod and we climb the stairs as he continues. "I'm a second-year student. I'm learning everything so I can take over my father's business. It's an excellent school, but hard." He glances at the paper in my hand and stops down the hall in front of my door. "You'll catch on quick. It's not so bad here."

Not so bad. Now that sounds like a winning argument for Pointebreak.

A thought dawns on me as I observe him. "Did you want to come here, Nick?"

He narrows his eyes, confusion written on his face, but nods absentmindedly, a scoff leaving his mouth. "Of course. Both my parents graduated from Pointebreak. There was never another option. I'm hoping to follow in their foot-steps," he says proudly.

I nod my head, not wanting to pry too much yet. I can't tip my hand on the first day. "Thanks for the help, Nick. I appreciate it."

His face brightens with my words. "There's a bonfire tonight as a welcome for all the new students. Wanna go with me?"

I lick my bottom lip and pull it between my teeth as I think about what James told me about not trusting people here.

It's a school event. What's the worst that can happen?

My lips curved into a relaxed, comfortable smile. "Sure. I'd like that."

He grins from ear to ear. "Good. I'll pick you up here at seven."

I wave as he walks away and slide the key into the lock, pushing open the door to my new life. I don't know what I expected, but what's here is definitely not it. It's, dare I say, stunning? I enter the room and let the door swing closed behind me as I stare at the paintings on one side and the freshly made bed. Two beds, two desks with a chair, large windows that span the length of one wall, and an armoire that fills the length of the other wall. The only thing missing is the bath-room, and I'm sure I passed that on the way to my room. I do wish there was a private bathroom, but I suppose this will make it feel more like a true college experience. The space is much bigger than I thought he would be, but I have a roommate. I've never had to share a room before. Even going to Dartmouth, I had a single room guaranteed. This should be interesting. I hope I like her. I can't imagine being stuck here with a room-mate I can't stand. *Please let me like her.* I send a silent prayer up.

Glancing to my side, I see two boxes sitting on the bed. One has the Pointebreak emblem on it, so I assume those are my uniforms, but as I walk closer to the other box, I see it came from home. I dig a pen out of my purse and jab it through the tape, dragging it down so I can pull the box open. On top is an envelope with dad's writing. I ignore it for a moment, not wanting to read his loving words when he couldn't even be bothered to drop me off. I rub my hand over my chest, trying to ward off the pang of sadness that lands there as a lump forms in my burning throat.

The unread note lands on the bed, and I unpack a new pair of sheets, comforter, and pillow. I look at the bare twin sized bed and I'm thankful because I didn't even think about bedding in my haste to pack. I glance at the letter again and sigh, taking a seat on the edge of the mattress. The kind gesture makes me warm and I pull the pillow out of the box and smash it to my chest, hugging it tight as I pick up the letter. My finger works its way under the sealed corner and I pull the note free.

Riley,

I hate how we left things. I'm sorry I couldn't be there to help you move in, but I couldn't move these meetings. Pointebreak will be an excellent choice for you. I'm sorry it had to be this way, but you will find out soon enough why it was necessary. Make friends and study hard. I'll see you for Christmas break. I love you.

Dad

I just wish it was a choice *I* made and not a choice I had

made for me. If I had wanted to come here, I might have felt a thrill of excitement, instead of the dread that settles deep in my stomach. The door clicks open and a girl around my height with brown curly hair steps through. "Oh, you're here!" Her smile is infectious and I can't help when my own spreads widely as I stand and offer my hand to her.

"Hi, I'm Riley Whittier." She takes my hand and bats it away, pulling me into a hug instead. She looks so familiar but I can't place her.

"I'm so excited to meet you, Riley." She pushes out from the hug, holding on to my upper arms to look at my face. "I'm Ava Fedorov. Where are you from? Why did you decide to come here? What kind of music do you like?"

She fires questions at me without taking a moment to breathe between them, and I laugh. The first genuine laugh I've had with anyone besides Leah. Things around the house were tense, and I hardly saw dad before I left today. It's like he was avoiding me. Leah saw me off this morning, and I tried hard not to cry when it was time to leave. A few errant tears escaped and slid down my cheeks as James pulled away from the house, but I channeled that energy as quickly as I could to prepare for today.

It's been very emotional, and right now I am grateful to have someone to be excited and happy to be here. Her personality is bubbly and my anxiety eases for the first time since I've arrived.

"Um," I try to think of the questions she asked in what order so I can answer them for her. "I'm from around here. My dad forced me to come, and I listen to anything but rap."

Her smile fades and her brows pinch together as she mulls over my words. "He forced you to come here?" I nod. "Why?"

I attempt to give her a small smile, but miss my mark. "That's the million dollar question, isn't it?" She stares at me as I shift my weight under her gaze, my face warming. All I have are more questions and no answers. Finally, when I can't take the silence anymore, I change the subject. "Did you paint these?" I motion to the paintings hung around her side of the room. Her gaze follows mine and her face brightens again with a smile.

"Yes, do you like them? I can take them down if you don't. They make me happy. Painting is the escape I have when things can become too…much. Do you know what I mean?"

I give her a small shrug and nod my head. I know what it's like to have an outlet, but I've never described it as when things become too much. "Yeah, makes sense. Listen, I know nothing about Pointebreak. Will you give me the lowdown so I know what I'm walking into? My day has been…odd so far, and I would appreciate any insight. If you know, that is."

Her smile lights her face. "You and I are gonna be good friends, Riley. Let's get your room set up."

FOUR

RILEY

Jesus, what did my dad sign me up for? According to what Ava has told me, this place is basically a training ground. Not her words, though. Along with academics, they teach self-defense, gun shooting, torture tactics, and anything else one might need in an unorthodox event. I guess it would have helped if I actually looked at my class schedule. That was sitting on my desk when I walked in. What the hell kind of place is this? Who would need to know half of these things to become stand-up citizens when they get out of here?

Torture tactics? What the hell am I in for? Images of ripped off toenails and waterboarding fill my mind as disgust fills me. This place isn't for me. Nope. One time at gymnastics, I broke my arm. The pain was so intense that I almost passed out, and I think I threw up. And that was when my gymnastics career ended. I was too afraid to try again.

Dad would never associate himself with people who would use torture. Mind games, sure. That's part of politics, but never physical harm…right? I wring my hands together, struggling to wash the thoughts away.

Ava must notice my mind whirling, and she pats my fore-arm. "Come on, let's go find the cafeteria and get something to eat. You look like you could use some chocolate." *Or a stiff drink...* "Maybe some vodka," she smirks, reading my mind.

"Ava, why would you want to go to a school like this? Self-defense? Cool. Fine. Torturing people? Firing weapons? In what world would you need to use this kinda stuff?"

"Always be prepared." She throws up her three middle fingers and smirks, but I don't reciprocate. "Girl scout," she offers, as a way of explanation.

We leave, locking the door behind us and walk toward the cafeteria and it dawns on me that I haven't mentioned the bonfire to Ava. "I got invited to a bonfire tonight by um," what was his name again, "Nick Harper, or something. Are you going too?"

She pulls up short and slaps her hand down on my arm. Ow. "Wait, do you mean Nick Halpin?"

I snap my fingers and point at her, recognizing the name, and my eyes light up. "Yes! That's his name. He helped me get my bag up to our room. He seems like a nice guy. Lives up on the fourth floor. Do you know him? He said he was a second year here."

A blush creeps up her neck and stains her cheeks and she stammers. "Y-Yeah, I know him. He lives in our building?" Her voice goes up an octave as she lets out a tiny squeak of surprise.

Hmm. In the brief time I've known Ava, she's seemed so sure of herself, so confident. Yet, she's blushing and averting her gaze away from me. Looks like crushes make us all do funny things.

I try to hide my smile. "How do you know him?" I ask, unable to help myself.

"My parents know his parents and he's a year behind my brother here." She bites her lip and looks past me like he might come bounding down the stairs at the mere mention of his name.

"Obviously you've called dibs. I won't go with him tonight. He was just nice to me when I was trying to get my suitcase upstairs. That's all. I don't want to step on any toes."

Ava gives me a small smile and quietly says, "Thanks. But it's okay. He doesn't even know I exist." She gives a heavy sigh and her shoulders drop. "I've always been Zander's younger sister, and not worthy of his time."

I stop dead in my tracks as she moves on without me. How many Zanders could possibly be in this school? There's only about one hundred students per year, so that's four hundred total. Zander isn't an overly common name. I swallow harshly; the hairs standing on the back of my neck again and I look around for signs of the three being close by, only to come up empty. "Did you say Zander?" I whisper. Shit shit, what was the last name that girl said at check in? I was so overwhelmed that I hardly remember. I think it started with an F.

She stops walking when she notices I'm no longer next to her and she turns, tilting her head as she furrows her brow. "Yeah. He's a third-year student. I'm sure you'll see him lurking around here somewhere. He didn't want me to come to Pointebreak. He's always trying to protect me, but I made a compelling argument that my parents couldn't turn down."

Ignoring her explanation, I continue wearily. "Ava, what does your brother look like? I, um, I might have met him already."

Her eyes light up. "Oh! I have a picture on my phone. Hang on." She pulls her phone out of her pocket, swipes a few times and shows me her screen. My heart beats wildly in my chest when I look at the same handsome man with dark hair who was staring at me earlier today, and yesterday, at the diner. I instinctively step away from her, my pulse pounding, when she smiles brightly and waves at someone behind me. Spinning on my heel, I come face to chest with a hard as stone body blocking my view. Drawing my eyes up to see the devil himself, Julien Azarian, and his crew of cronies.

"Hey Zan, I was just telling my new friend about you." Ava pulls me back to her side and I willingly go. Any way to get away from him. My arms break out in a new set of goosebumps and I can hardly hear anything over the blood rushing through my ears. My body begs me to flee like my life depends on it, because maybe it does, but Ava's grip is punishment and protection all at once. I'm trapped. "Hi Julien, Hi Wesley," she waves at them, but they never take their eyes off me.

The three continue to glare without saying a word.

Tension, meet knife.

Does Ava not feel it? How could she not? It's suffocating. We are in a silent standoff, and I don't know the reason. For fuck's sake, this is ridiculous. I have done nothing to them. I literally showed up on campus, against my will, mind you, and somehow got locked into a staring contest with these brooding brutes. Pushing a heavy sigh past my lips, I decide now is as good a time as any to make new friends.

I wipe my clammy hands on my shorts and straighten my spine, sticking my hand out to shake theirs. "Hi, I'm Riley Whittier."

Julien looks down at my hand, and his lips turn up in a grimace. Like my touch is something filthy. Like I've crossed some invisible line I was too stupid to see. The anger rolling off him is palpable. He's a feral animal waiting for any sign of weakness to strike. And it looks like I'm his unwilling prey. I will my breathing to stay steady as a panic attack looms close by. I will not show weakness to this asshole.

"You shouldn't be here." He replies gruffly.

I know it shouldn't, but his gravelly voice draws me in.

My body sways a little as I keep myself from leaning in toward him. The sound of someone's voice has never been so intoxicating before. It's deep, gruff, and holds the promise of darkness. My tongue darts out to lick my dry lips, his eyes zeroing in on the movement. There is something so familiar about him, but I can't place it. Maybe I've seen him before in passing, and my neurons are firing to place him. When it's obvious Julien, or the others, aren't going to shake it, I pull my hand back, placing it on my hip with a small, defiant pop, jutting it out a little. "If I had a choice, I wouldn't be here, but thanks for the warm welcome." I plaster a saccharine smile to my face.

He quirks an eyebrow in surprise, and I catch Wesley and Zander smirking beside him. Ah, so they're not made of stone after all.

"Don't be rude to my friend, Zan. She's nice, and she doesn't know the ropes around here. Knows nothing about Pointebreak, actually."

I stare at Ava with wide eyes and give a barely noticeable shake of my head, needing her to shut up. Nobody else needs to know that I have no clue what I've gotten myself into. *Thanks for nothing, dad.* Julien rubs his index and middle finger slowly along his bottom lip and inspects me like I'm an animal on display again. He cocks his head to the side, studying me from different angles. I glance at Wesley. His hands are on his hips as he stares me down, but at least there's a smile on his face, even if it isn't all too friendly looking. Then I focus on Zander. He has his arms crossed over his broad chest, his lips pulled down in a frown. It takes everything in me not to scream in frustration.

But no, I can't. That's what they want, what *he* wants. Julien wants me to show my hand—my weakness—to use in whatever sick game he's playing. Julien takes a step closer, and the others move in tandem with him. He plants his feet shoulder-width apart, arms crossed over his wide chest, his muscular forearms bulging beneath his black shirt. It's an intimidation tactic, but I won't tuck my tail. I plant my feet firmly on the ground and wait.

He bends at the waist and puts his face directly in front of mine.

Green.

From this close distance, I can see the anger simmering in his vibrant green eyes, like a storm brewing behind a calm facade. I inhale a sharp breath, not expecting to feel my stomach drop and warmth to flood through me. It's more than anger though, there's something else I can't put my finger on and it makes my heart pump wildly. I take a small step back, but his hand clamps down on my hip, a firm grip keeping me in place.

Images flash through my mind of him walking me backward against a wall and pressing his lips against mine with brutal force. I stifle the groan, threatening to escape. He leans in a hairsbreadth closer and for a brief second I think he might actually do it. Kiss me. If I puckered, I could brush my lips against his. Why am I even thinking this? He's done nothing but try to intimidate me since I arrived here. My pulse flutters wildly as I blink rapidly as I wait for him to say or do something—anything. This moment in limbo seems to go on forever, and I feel his warm breath tickle my face.

"Run, Riley."

He lets me go with a shove and I stumble back, blinking up at him in confusion. That is *not* what I was expecting! He barely brought his voice above a whisper, but he may as well have screamed the words. I take Ava's arm and pull her with me, walking backwards to keep them in my line of sight, putting some much needed distance between us. She looks to her brother for an explanation, clearly confused by what just happened between us, but he gives her a barely noticeable headshake. If I wasn't so tuned in to them right now, I may not have noticed it.

Never turn your back on an enemy. It gives them more reason to shoot you, but I don't have a choice. I need to see where I'm headed. Eventually, I turn and move as fast as my legs will carry me, with Ava in tow. I see her out of the corner of my eye, brows drawn, and lips turned down in a frown. The same look her brother gave me minutes ago.

"What?" I ask as I push open the doors to the cafeteria.

"Why did he tell you to run? Do you know him? You said you didn't know anyone here."

I shake my head. "I've never met him in my life, but apparently he has something against me. Or maybe it's against my father. I really haven't got a clue. My dad hasn't always played nice, so it's entirely possible something happened and now I'm the target." I told her a little about my dad and who he is in our room, so she has a general understanding of the powerful position he's in.

She drops it for now, but I know she has more questions. Questions I haven't got a clue on how to answer. I don't even know what's going on. There's no way I can even begin to explain it to her. We grab a tray and fill it with a little of everything.

Surprisingly, the food here is good, and they have a lot of options to choose from. They offer a pasta station with various sauces, a salad bar with everything you could ever want, a stir-fry station, and even a main course option. There is literally something for everyone. I hope breakfast is just as good. After we eat, and both of us are full, Ava gives me a tour of campus like she's been here for years and not just a first year herself. She told me she helped Zander move in his first year here and wandered campus. Plus, she's studied the map and, according to her, knows this place inside and out. Which will come in handy because I have no idea where I'm going. I have until Monday to figure out where I'm going for my classes.

We get back to our room and I sit down on my freshly made bed. Ava had helped me unpack my bag and put everything away in my space. Since I brought nothing to decorate my side, she hung one of her artwork pieces over my bed to make it cozy. I'm already grateful to have her as my roommate.

I pull my schedule from my packet of information and study the list of my classes. I didn't have a choice in the matter, the academy picked for me. Some classes seem basic enough, not what I would have studied at Dartmouth, such as economics and business management. But others are just unconventional for a school. Survival? Seriously?

What does survival mean? They aren't going to use us as science experiments, are they? Or is this going to be the torture classes Ava confirmed aren't just rumors? My head spins with worst-case scenarios, and I'm hoping what I come up with is a lot worse than what the class actually is.

"Riles, you okay? You look a little green over there."

Nope. Not at all. I breathe through my nose and try to push the thoughts out of my head. "I think I'm okay. Do you know much about the survival class?"

She shakes her head; her face drops. "No. Zan doesn't talk about his classes and no one asks at home. My dad came here, but doesn't talk about it. He told me I'd find out soon enough, and there's no point in dwelling on what I won't be able to change. That's the only one I've been worried about, but they can't kill students, so I figure it'll be fine."

Well, if that isn't a winning statement, I don't know what is. Why is everything so nonchalant with Ava? Nothing seems to bother her.

"I think I want to walk around campus some more to get

the lay of the land before the bonfire tonight. Want to come?"

"No. I want to take a little nap, and then get ready. Are you gonna be fine by yourself?"

I smile and nod. "Sure. See ya in a bit." I wave as I walk out the door, taking my phone with me. I need to write everything Ava has told me for Leah, but I don't want it to seem too suspicious. Hopefully, I can find a quiet spot and jot down a few bullet points, and then I can come back to it later for more details. I've already taken a few pictures, including one of my schedule to send to her, but the campus photos are all online anyway, so that's nothing new. Day one and I've only uncovered the tip of the iceberg. There is an enormous story here waiting for me to tell. I know it. The thought has me spiraling. I need a familiar and warm voice to ease the tension. Without hesitation, I pull Leah's name up on my phone and she answers on the second ring.

"Hey bestie, how goes it? Have you met the head of the mafia yet?"

I smile despite myself. "Not funny, and no. But this place is insane, Leah." I keep my voice low and glance around to make sure no one's within earshot. "They really teach torture classes, and gun shooting, though. What the fuck? We may not be too far off thinking Pointebreak is some sort of training ground."

Her gasp is answer enough. Neither of us believed the rumors and laughed about it, but I'm not laughing now. Not when I have to take these classes. I'm still having a hard time wrapping my head around what my life is going to be like and I'm going to have to live it for the next four years. This is going to be…challenging. I'm so far out of my element. Dartmouth was going to be easy. I knew exactly what was in store for me. Mainly rich assholes who think they are better than the person next to them, with some tough classes thrown into the mix. But, this. I don't know if I can do this. My only options are to try, or get left behind. And I don't think the school takes too kindly to students who don't try.

"Where are you right now? Are you stuck in your uniform yet?"

"Walking around campus and no. I don't have to wear it until Monday, and on weekends it's not required."

"How does it look?" she asks.

"Basically like Stonewall, but less blue and silver and more red and black. Probably to hide blood stains if they happen." I scoff at my grim joke and groan. "Leah, I don't know if I can do this. My roommate is nice, but her brother and his friends...I somehow pissed them off." I take a deep breath in and push it out of my nose, shaking my head, trying to dislodge the negative thoughts taking up residence in my mind.

"What do you mean?" She asks wearily.

"I don't know. I got to campus, and they were staring at me like I killed their puppy and they are going to go all John Wick on me. All I did was step out of the car." I take a deep breath and release it. "I'm going to email you some stuff tonight. You remember the guy from the diner?"

"Mr. Sexy that I told you to tap?" She smiles through the phone and I can't help doing the same, even though she can't see me.

"He's one of them."

"Oh damn. Looks like you won't be getting lucky with him." She sucks in a sharp breath, "Or maybe you will and it will be some awesome hate sex!"

"What?" I laugh. "Maybe it's you who needs to get laid, girl."

"Yeah, that too. Battery operated toys aren't doing it for me anymore."

I snort and shake my head in disbelief. I don't make it

much further before I see Julien walk around a corner. Why is he lurking everywhere? Does he not have anything better to do with his time?

"Leah, I gotta go." I don't give her a chance to answer before hanging up. My phone rings in my hand and I silence it, wishing I hadn't turned the ringer up in the dorm. I was secretly hoping dad would call, and I didn't want to miss it. Now I realize how stupid that was. If he even cared, he would have found time to bring me. Or hell, checked in on me since arriving. Campus isn't that far from home. I assume James has been back for hours now and told him he safely dropped me off.

I turn on my heel, hoping he hasn't seen me, and duck behind a building, my back pressed flat against the cool stone as I wait and listen. Please, just go away. I don't want to deal with him right now. Once was enough, and I'm hoping I won't have to see him again since he's in his third year here. Seeing any student shouldn't scare me. Not yet anyway. I thought I'd make some headway by introducing myself and showing them I'm nice and not the monster they've somehow imagined me to be, but clearly that didn't work.

I take a deep breath and turn my head to peek around the corner when hands slam down on the stone wall on either side of my face. I yelp and slam my head back, my hair getting caught in the rough siding as I take in a shuddering breath. Fuck, that hurt. A headache worms its way through my skull and I hold in my groan of pain as I stare wide-eyed at him. This god-forsaken school must teach ninja skills! I flatten my back to make myself as flush with the wall as possible, but it doesn't matter. Julien collars his hand around my throat and I bring my hands up, holding tight to his wrist. I can't help the sudden rush of heat that blooms in my belly. I try to stand a little taller, hoping to get him to loosen his hold on me. It's not tight, I can breathe no problem, but it is dominating. I know I'm not leaving until he deems it so. My breathing is erratic as he slowly rubs his thumb up and down over my fluttering pulse. He hums as he runs his nose along my jaw, inhaling me as he goes.

Oh Jesus, Joseph, and Mary.

"W-what do you want, Julien?" I stammer, my breath coming out in shallow pants. I've never been so scared and turned on in my life. He adds pressure to his hand against my throat and my back arches away from the wall at the contact. I can still breathe, but there's no way out of his grip. Not without leaving some serious marks and getting scraped to hell from the stone at my back. He has me pinned, and from the look in his eyes, he knows it. I bite my lip to suppress the moan that wants to escape as I get a whiff of him. He smells so good. Masculine and clean with a touch of citrus.

"Stay the *fuck* away from me, Princess." His deep voice is rough in my ear.

I release the hold on his wrist and press my hands against his solid chest to push. He doesn't even register that I've touched him and presses himself flush against me instead. His strong form molding to my soft curves. The hard plains of his body under his jeans and shirt are difficult to ignore. How much time does one have to spend at the gym to get as ripped as he feels? I would be on my ass in five seconds flat if pitted against him in a fight. I push my hips up toward him, trying to buck him off. He groans, then covers it with a deep, menacing growl. My eyes flutter closed, a thrill that I've made him lose his complete and utter cool courses through me, if only for a moment. Then I snap them open again and narrow on him, remembering how he's treated me since meeting me. "I'm not the one who keeps finding you, asshole."

If I didn't know any better, I could swear his lips twitch

in amusement before he presses his groin against me one last time and pulls away. Even without glancing down, I can feel his hardness. Is he hard because this type of torment turns him on, or is he hard because I did that to him? I try not to let my mind dwell on that little tidbit, though. I cross my arms over my chest and stare at him as he backs away, his eyes firmly trained on me.

Pointebreak is going to be harder than I thought. Not only do I have to survive these crazy classes, I've made an enemy my first day and he will stop at nothing to destroy me.

FIVE

JULIEN

I can't believe she has the audacity to show her face at *my* school. Riley Whittier has no clue what she's in for and I'll take pleasure in making her life at Pointebreak hell. She should have stayed as far from me as possible. Does my little lamb know this might as well be a slaughterhouse? Pointebreak isn't for the faint of heart, and last I knew, she was a dainty flower. Based on the casual way she's been walking around, she has absolutely no idea what's in store for her.

Rule number one of Pointebreak is never be alone. Ava clearly hasn't explained the rules to her. She can't die while under the administration's care, but that doesn't mean someone can't fuck with her for fun. I pace back and forth like a caged animal in my room, fuming. Her being here threw a wrench into my plans. I live in a house at the edge of campus with Zander and Wesley—courtesy of Alec Azarian, my dad. It's been in our family for generations, but sat empty prior to me moving in. I've always received the best, and this is no exception. He wanted me to come to Pointebreak. He told me the contacts I made here would set me up for life. Along with the education they offer, I knew it was the best option for me. Plus, a traditional education has never suited me. Not when I'm an Azarian. As soon as I had my acceptance letter in hand, the house renovations started, so it would be ready for me to move in.

Tension strains my muscles as I tug at the back of my neck, trying to ease some of the pressure. I roll my shoulders and groan when I look up at Zander, who knocks on the door frame and meet his gaze. I clench my jaw, waiting for him to say something, anything, but he stares, waiting for me to talk first. He always has been good in our torture classes. Others sing like canaries, but he has this crazy ability to keep silent. The man hardly ever breaks. I gotta give him credit for it. He cracks the knuckles on his hand and blows out a breath.

"What?" I bark, unable to contain my frustration.

"Everything's set for the bonfire and students should be here within the hour," he replies, casually crossing his arms over his chest as he leans on the frame. I know there's so much more he wants to say, but Zander has always been a man of few words.

He's waiting.

Watching.

He always watches.

Dad started the bonfire when he attended Pointebreak, and I brought it back at the house instead of a random part of the woods. That's how I became friends with Wesley and Zander. I needed help, and they were willing. It didn't take long to figure out we meshed well together. Our strengths enhance one another. What one person lacks, the others make up for it. It's why we own this school. We aren't lacking people who want to get into our good graces. And each of us are working on building an empire together. Fuck everyone else. We're doing it our own way. My dad is the only one who can appreciate our plans. Wes and Zan's fathers have already made their opinion of me known and they can get bent as far as I'm concerned.

We hire a crew of ten guys to come and get everything set for tonight, along with playing bar keep and DJ. It's a good side gig for them, and we pay well. For security, we hire fourth-year students who want to earn a bit of cash. We vet those guys, but so far it's worked out well. Pointebreak doesn't host events, but we sure as hell do. And when you get this many powerful families in one location, shit is bound to go down. A few times a year, Wes, Zan, and I host a party. The bonfire and Halloween, everyone's invited to. Enemies, or allies, it doesn't matter. Since there are some classes that include all grades, it's an easy way to get to know your opponents and hopefully get some helpful information to use as dirt at a later time. The other parties are for each of our birthdays, but that's by invitation only. I don't need some asshole with a point to prove to mess with us at our own house during those.

Students don't talk about the school outside of these walls—there's an unwritten rule about it. Someone tried once…he's six feet under. Or maybe they never found his body, I'm not sure. Those who don't understand would shut Pointebreak down. Because students and alumni are so tight-lipped about what happens here, we don't take kindly to outsiders.

Riley Whittier is definitely an outsider.

For many students, tonight will significantly impact their future prospects and their ability to achieve their aspirations after graduation. People either fall in with the right crowd and make the right connections, or they're fucked the rest of their time here. Just ask our fathers.

Alec Azarian, Mikhail Fedorov, and Christos Bastian are the OG bastards at Pointebreak. They changed, molded, and shaped this academy into what it is today. The pamphlet talks about how it was a school for underprivileged students forging for a better life but that's some major bullshit to sell it to the public. The walls of this house hold a lot of secrets, and so do the academy grounds.

My mind drifts yet again to Riley. The image of holding her by the throat and feeling her reaction to my touch causes my fingers to twitch with anticipation. Who would have thought the wholesome, naïve senator's daughter was into some kinky shit? I could practically smell her arousal. I haven't been able to get her out of my mind since the moment I laid eyes on her, no matter how hard I try. And to smell her and touch her today was unreal. It shouldn't be happening like this, though. The guys don't know about my run in with her this afternoon. I know I would get the standard lecture of 'let it go', but I can't. My nostrils flare as my anger rears up again.

"Calm down. You can't let her get into your head. You know what you have to do." Zander steps into my room, directly into my line of sight.

Zander's our resident computer wiz. Need someone to hack into a system? He's the man you go to. Students pay him an ungodly amount to help them with some shady things. He doesn't ask questions, just makes sure the money is good. It's a lucrative side business and one that will go a long way to helping us after we finish here.

Zander's the reason Riley's bunking with his little sister, Ava. Originally, Ava had a private room, but when Riley was added to the roster at the last minute, he put them together to keep tabs on her. I'm not sure if Ava knew ahead of time, but she seemed excited when we ran into the two of them this afternoon. My need to control everything has made this more difficult. Since Ava is the one sharing the room, I refrained from asking him to add cameras so I could stalk her there, too. A swift kick in the nuts would have been my reward for that request. The thought of being able to watch her in various states of undress has me getting hard once again. Zander got me a copy of her schedule and I can't wait to see the pink hit her cheeks when she sees I'll be in her survival class. I'm going to make her life a living hell. It's going to be torture seeing her in that short skirt every day.

Fucking stupid uniform. The idea came around years ago when other students were being targeted for their lack of designer things. To nip it in the bud before it became a true issue, the administration provided uniforms to quash any further discrimination. Was it the best way to go about it? Probably not, but they don't seem to want to change the rules now.

"Come on, let's grab a drink and get ready for the party. Should be a doozy this year." He slaps my upper back and pulls me out of the room with him. Wesley is in the kitchen mixing up jungle juice when we walk in.

"Magical elixir?" Zander asks with this eyebrow raised in question.

Wesley grins from ear to ear as he dumps an entire bottle of rum into the large container. "My favorite kind. Makes the girls real easy to handle."

I smirk and close my eyes, shaking my head. Wesley is a man-whore. He gladly fucks anything in a skirt. Lucky for him, all the ladies at Pointebreak wear one. I've never seen him strike out, but he has the good sense to be picky about who he sticks his dick in. Most women drop their panties the moment he looks in their direction. Those big blue eyes are irresistible to the ladies. He's also smart not to get them too intoxicated. Most fathers won't take too kindly to their daughters getting fucked over. Even if a lot of them are as casual about sex as Wesley.

But his good looks aren't what make him valuable. No, his effortless charm and natural charisma make him the perfect choice to subtly gather information. That, and he makes a great bookie. He's a whiz with numbers and has a knack for calculating odds with remarkable precision. It definitely comes in handy with our side business.

I shake my head, and swipe the bottle of Macallan off the table, pour some into a tumbler, and shoot it back as I welcome the burn down my throat. The amber liquid settles in my stomach and I focus on its warmth. I need to get my head on straight. Riley being here should be the least of my problems. Her fate will come to light soon enough. Until then, I'll continue to have fun with her. Well, fun for me anyway. I pour a shot for the three of us and slide them across the table.

I clap my hands and rub them together, sliding into an effortless smile. "Alright. Eyes on the prize, boys. Have fun."

They both nod and clink their glasses before downing the shots.

More than half the school's here now. The bass of the music pouring from the speakers outside rattle the walls as Centuries from Fall Out Boy plays. Most students are out back surrounding the large fire, dancing and chatting with one another while others are inside and around the bar in the kitchen. The distinct clack of balls clanging together draws me to the game room where several students are playing pool. Zander's in deep conversation with some of the fourth-year students. We've worked with them on and off, but we've kept our distance, not entirely sure their ambitions align with ours. I'll have to check in with him later to get his opinion.

The biggest problem I have is Riley still isn't here.

Zander said he texted Ava. And they are on their way, but that was a half an hour ago. It doesn't take that long to get to the edge of campus. I should know. I've already mapped out how long it will take if I need to get to her dorm. Eighteen minutes if I'm walking, ten minutes if I run. Never know when that information will come in handy.

Unless she's not coming and Ava came alone. I know Zander would have told her to not walk alone though, so Riley should be with her. I've been monitoring the door and I haven't seen them come in. Did she walk around back and I missed her? I banish the thought from my mind as soon as it enters. It would be wise for her to stay far, far away from me; but I don't want her to. I want her in my sights as often as I can. I want her on edge, waiting for the next shoe to drop.

She's mine.

Mine to tease.

Mine to torment.

My phone buzzes with a new message, and I dig it out of my pocket to look.

WESLEY:

She's here.

Those are the two words I've been hoping to read since this party started.

ME:

Where?

WESLEY:

Kitchen. I'm being a gracious host and getting her a drink. ;)

I motion to Zander that they're here and he excuses himself to follow me. We walk into the kitchen, a smirk playing on my lips as I watch her smile and thank Wesley before sipping her drink. As soon as the alcohol hits her throat, she coughs and tries to hide it by covering her mouth with the back of her hand. Wesley grins. "It gets better the more you drink. Have a little more." He pushes the bottom of her drink toward her mouth again, but she holds her hand steady.

She shakes her head and says, "Maybe later. I want to check out the bonfire and meet some of the other students." She turns her attention to Ava and a guy she's with. "Wanna come?"

The guy in question smiles warmly at her and places his hand on the small of her back as he directs her to the back door. My nostrils flare with hatred. I take a step forward and Wesley puts his hand on my shoulder, stopping me. He has absolutely *no right* to touch her. I clench my jaw, the muscles in my neck straining against the pressure. They turn to leave, but Zander snatches the drink from Ava's hand. She gasps in surprise and when she tries to get it back, he shakes his head.

"You're underage," Zander warns.

"So is every other first year and second-year student, but you aren't stopping them," she sasses, pointing to the drink in Riley's hand. Ava is the only one who I know can talk back to Zander and will live to tell the tale. Pointebreak is the last place Zander wanted his baby sister. She's too sweet for our world. Too…innocent. She's going to get a reality check over the next four years. While Zan doesn't think she can handle it. I know she can. Under her happy-go-lucky exterior is a warrior. She's got grit, even if he doesn't want to admit it.

"They aren't my sister," he replies, his word final.

"Buzzkill," she mutters under her breath as she walks out the door with Riley and the guy.

"Who is he?" I raise my eyebrow in their retreating direction. I sip my drink, acting as nonchalant as possible, as I wait for an answer.

"That's Nick Halpin. His father is worth one point two billion and I'm planning on getting my hands on some of his fortune. His family's close to ours. Nick and I have never run in the same circles, but that's not from his lack of trying. Don't do anything stupid," Zander warns from behind me. His voice is so low that only I can hear him. I stand down and rub my jaw, easing some of the pressure. I nod once, letting him know I've heard him as I keep my eyes trained on Riley through the open door. Easy for him to say that. I bet if Nick was all over Ava, he'd feel differently about it. Riley looks around her. For a moment I think she's looking for me, but then I watch her tip the contents of her cup into a bush and I can't help but smile for real.

"Looks like she won't be as easy a target as we thought, Wes."

His eyes follow mine, as she tips her cup upright again. A barely there smile plays on his lips as he shrugs. "Good. This will make it more fun. I love a challenge."

I survey the crowd. It looks like some of our classmates are already enjoying themselves a little too much. Wes's elixir is hitting hard. Not that I'm surprised. The older students know better than to touch anything in a tub, but these first years don't know what's good for them. Drugs and alcohol aren't uncommon in most of these families, and a lot of students are looking for their next fix. The older girls who are already feeling the effects just don't care. I know several of them are hoping to warm one of our beds tonight. It's nothing new. Keep your life private and people think you're an enigma, a mystery they want to be the first to solve.

I'm too fucked up for anyone to solve my issues. And I don't need someone thinking they can fix me.

I scan the crowd and land on a familiar favorite, Stella. I don't do relationships, but I do her. She's great when I need to blow off some steam, and she's always willing. The problem is, I'm not the only one she's willing to play with and I don't enjoy sharing. I guess that's what happens when you're an only child. I've been spending less and less time in her company, and she's noticed.

"Hey handsome," she says, molding her body to my side. I keep scanning the crowd, ignoring the twitch of my cock. It knows damn well what a good time she is, even if my brain tells me it's a bad idea tonight. She drags her finger along the side of my jaw and boops my nose to gain my attention when I don't look at her.

"Not now, Stella. Go find someone else's cock to fall on."

She flushes red and digs her nails into my forearm in warning. I flick my eyes from my arm to her face, and clench my jaw, waiting for her to realize her mistake. No one touches me without consent. She knows this from the amount of times I've tied her hands behind her back to keep them there. She's starved for attention and knows I don't play her mind games.

She releases me, but doesn't move. "Julien, don't be like that. We had a good thing going. Why not take it one step further?"

I would rather slit my wrists than be involved with her in any capacity than an easy lay. "You're a distraction, and my time here's valuable."

She steps directly in front of me and runs her fingers through my hair, clasping them behind my neck, holding me against her. "It doesn't have to be anything serious. We can keep it casual like we always have. You know you're my favorite."

I reach behind me and grab both her wrists in my hands and squeeze. She flinches in my grasp, but drops her hands to her sides like an obedient girl.

"I don't do sloppy seconds. Go. Away," I growl in her face.

I brush past her in search of the one person I need to keep my eyes on—Riley. She's sticking close with Ava and chatting with other students. She smiles and laughs like everything is right in her world, when I know for a fact that's not the case. I should focus on building additional relationships, but I can't seem to stop myself from watching her instead. Every glance is a hit to the bloodstream. Sharp, sweet, and impossible to resist. I step outside the doors and the smell of smoke and burning wood fills my senses. It's a better turnout than last year. We always have some that don't attend for whatever reason.

Riley leans in to Ava and says something to her above the noise. She nods and Riley turns toward the house. She passes by several students, but most don't pay her any attention, too busy in their own conversations. And why would they? No one knows who she is yet. But her anonymity isn't long for this world. By morning, Riley's name will be on the tip of everyone's tongue.

"What are you going to do about her?" Wesley asks as he watches her get closer to us. All three of us have had eyes on her since the moment she showed up, and each for a different reason. Zander's thoughts are a mystery. He studies his subjects before deciding how to act. I know he's watching and waiting to see what her move will be. Plus, he's keeping tabs on his baby sister, so it's a win-win. Wes eyes her as if he wants to devour her, like she is the high he's craved for so long. He licks his lips as her hips sway with every step she takes.

"I haven't decided yet."

She walks inside. Then heads down the hallway and up the stairs. *Where are you headed to?* We haven't made upstairs off limits, but most know not to snoop. There's a single bathroom, and three bedrooms on the top floor, all of which have their own private ensuite. They added those rooms later during renovations to the house.

I follow behind her, but keep myself at a suitable distance so she doesn't realize I'm watching her. Riley stops at the top of the stairs, looking around, wondering which of the four closed doors to try. She starts on her right, and knocks, but someone tells her to go away. *Guess that bathroom will have to be scrubbed.* She takes a tiny step back and looks at the two doors on the left, but starts moving toward the one at the end of the hall instead.

My room.

She knocks, and when no one answers, she cracks open the door and peers into the darkness. I should have locked the door. I usually do, but tonight I was distracted. The door closes with a gentle thud as it hits the frame but doesn't latch, leaving a whisper of space between the frame and the door.

Looks like my little Riley doesn't know when to stop.

SIX

RILEY

The clean scent pulls me into the room before I know what I'm doing. It's bright, and citrusy, and reminds me of clean laundry. It's probably a dumb move because if any of them found out I was in their rooms, I'm sure they would murder me. Nerves make me giggle quietly as blood pumps loudly between my ears as my nerves dance with energy. Listening intently for approaching footsteps, I exhale slowly, shaking my hands to steady them. I know I shouldn't be here, but I can't help it. My need to know what makes the king's tick overrules my common sense. I hate surprises.

My original plan was to find the bathroom and take a few notes, but then I couldn't help that my feet took me upstairs. There are so many students milling around, I'm sure no one noticed my ascent. These three live off campus and, from what I can gather, are the only ones allowed to do so. Why? What makes them so special? This is probably the only time I'll be allowed in their house to hopefully get some answers, and I don't want to waste a moment of it. I should start writing names and ask Leah to do some digging, too. I make a mental note to shoot her an email tonight when I'm back, or tomorrow morning.

My eyes adjust to the darkened room. I don't dare turn on a light, but with the windows facing the back of the house, the bonfire supplies enough glow that I can see most of everything. I run my fingers over the king size bed—neatly made. The material is soft under my touch and I know the sheets probably feel the same. Books line the built-in book-shelves and I walk over to examine some of the titles. I don't recognize most of them, so I pick one up and start reading the back of it. Mystery. Interesting choice, considering all three are just that.

There are no personal pictures around, and while I'm not positive, I would say this is Julien's room. I wander around, drinking in everything.. Who is Julien Azarian under the hardass exterior? I stop at his desk and slowly slide open a drawer. There's nothing unusual there, just some writing materials, so I close it quietly, opening the next to find nothing of consequence. He is either good at hiding things, or he has nothing to hide. I find the second option hard to believe.

I'm too wrapped up in my thoughts to notice his pres-ence until it's too late. His hand clamps down over my mouth and he pulls me flush with his body, holding me in place. I fight against him, my heart pounding against my ribs as his fingers dig into my cheeks. He spins me around, knocking the wind out of me as he holds me against the wall, pressing his body weight into me to keep me in place. Each labored breath has me inhaling his scent. It's the same as it was earlier: masculine, clean and citrusy. Now is not the time to be focusing on how amazing he smells, but I can't help it.

"You really have a lot to learn, Princess. Who said you could come into my room?"

My shallow pants of fear make it hard for me to think

straight. *Breathe, Riley.* You're going to be a lot worse if you can't function because of a damn panic attack. My head throbs and my vision blurs. Coming in here was a bad idea; but I did it anyway. I'm the only one to blame for this, and I know it. I push against him, trying to force more room between us when he clasps both my wrists between his large one and pins them above my head. My heart is going to break out of my chest at any moment. It's beating so hard. He holds my jaw between his thumb and forefinger, forcing me to look up at him. My wild eyes struggle to focus. Julien towers over me, and is easily six-one.

It's now or never. If I show him I'm scared shitless, he'll bully me the rest of the time he's here. If I stand up to him, maybe, just *maybe*, he'll back down. I look him straight in the eye, trying to build up the confidence that I know isn't there.

"Let go of me, Julien." The words sound so sure coming out, it surprises even me.

His green eyes spark, and the corner of his mouth pulls up into a devilish grin. He slides his free hand down the side of my body, following every curve as his touch lights me up in pleasure. I shudder under his fingertips. He stops his exploration at my hip and flips me around so suddenly the air whooshes out of my lungs as my cheek hits the wall, smashing my entire front against it.

"Let go of you? You came into my personal space *uninvited*," he snarls. "I have every right to do whatever the fuck I want to you, Riley. You put this target on your back." He runs his large finger from my shoulder blades down the center of my spine and draws a small circle at the base, just above my ass. "Not me."

My whole body tingles with anticipation as wetness pools between my thighs. *What the hell is wrong with me?*

"I've done nothing to you. I don't even know you." My scared voice comes out smaller than I mean it to. Something in his tone tells me not to mess with him. Something happened to him. Why is he angry at me? I haven't met him before today.

"That's not true, now is it?" He drags his hand around to my stomach and slides it further yet. His flat palm rests on the curve of my sex before he lifts the hem of my dress and slowly rubs his fingers over my clothed slit. Oh God, that feels good, too good.

A quiet moan escapes my lips as my eyes flutter closed. *What's not true? We know one another?* I'm sure I'd remember someone who looks like him—tall, dark, and handsome. As my body takes control, reeling at his talented fingers on me, my mind struggles to keep pace. My knees buckle at his ministrations and he presses himself against me, holding me up. My too slow brain finally catches up, reminding me what a terrible idea this is, and I push back against him. The fight coming back to me after a momentary lapse in judgement. He's made it abundantly clear he's my enemy. And it doesn't matter how hot he is, I'm not sleeping with someone who has it out for me.

"I can smell you, Princess, and your panties are soaked. I never would've pegged you for a kinky one." He nips at my ear, and I gasp in surprise before biting my lip to stop the moan that wants to break free. My hips rock involuntarily into his hand, adding a delicious pressure to my already sensitive clit.

This is wrong.

So, so wrong, but I can't stop my body from moving on its own, chasing the impending release. I can't think straight, my insurmountable pleasure within reach. My sight is hazy with the impending orgasm that hovers. I've never gotten close this fast.

"S-stop calling me *Princess*," I moan as he presses a little harder and my legs begin to shake. I've never liked the nickname. People have thought it was funny over the years, but I've never laughed. I've always seen the name as a dig, an insult. I'm right on the edge, the pleasure coiled so tight in my belly I feel as if I could explode. *Please don't stop, Julien. Make me come.* He chuckles and I second guess if I said those words out loud.

"Please," he mocks. Finding his way under the thin material of my panties, he plunges two fingers inside of me over and over, finding that delicious spot. He presses his hard body against mine and his rigid cock is pressing against my ass. He grunts when I press back into him and internally I smile, knowing I pried a reaction from him.

"You gonna come for me like a good girl?" He growls in my ear before he licks the shell and bites on the lobe. I heave a breath and rock my hips, chasing the release my body desperately needs.

"Y-yes. Please, Julien."

"I love to hear a pretty girl beg."

He slows his hand and I keep rocking my hips, trying to maintain the pressure until he withdraws completely. "No," I gasp and turn around to face him. I pant and my face flames hot with embarrassment. *What did I just do?* I've done something so reckless. He sucks each long finger between his lush lips before popping it out, one digit at a time, sucking me off him. I will my body to move, to do *anything*—but I just stand there, frozen, staring at him in shock. What just happened?

He bends at the waist, bringing his face close to mine. "Next time I see you snooping where you shouldn't, a ruined orgasm will be the least of your worries. I'll find out, Princess. I've got eyes and ears all over this place. Don't do anything else stupid," he hisses, his eyes flashing with anger.

I clench my jaw and breathe deeply through my nose, not letting my anger get the best of me. I can usually control my temper, but something about Julien Azarian makes me lose my damn mind! And not having a firm grip on my control is going to get me in trouble here. He makes sure my dress is around my hips, surprisingly gently, and grabs my wrist, pulling me out of his room, slamming the door closed behind us. Shaking off the lingering daze, I yank myself free from his grasp, his scent still clinging to my clothes, and I storm off, putting some much needed distance between us.

"You'd better not touch that pussy, Riley." He hollers from the top step as I reach the bottom, making me stop dead in my tracks. "It's not punishment if you finish the job I started."

A few people look in my direction and whisper to one another. *Please, just let me die now.* My entire body feels like it's going to burst into flames at any moment—embarrassment and wrath fighting for first prize. Visions of touching myself dance in my head and when I move my arm in front of me like I'm going to do just that, he glares daggers at me.

He's won this battle. I'm woman enough to know when I've been beat. I also know the type of rumors that are likely to spread now.

Just what I need…a reputation.

I glance around for Ava, needing to hurry in my escape, but she's not close in sight. She's probably enjoying the bonfire with Nick and hopefully making a few new friends. I sure as shit can't stay here another minute. Julien tracks me like I'm his prey from the top step, his eyes glued to me. So when I narrow my eyes, give him a sarcastic smile and flip him the bird, it's no surprise a devious smirk graces his lips.

The cool night air chills my overheated skin as I slam the front door behind me, texting Ava on my way back to the dorms so she doesn't worry. I figure Nick will make sure she gets home safe, or if not her, then Zander.

SEVEN

ZANDER

Julien stands at the top of the stairs, eyes trained on Riley. I'm not sure I heard him correctly over the noise of the crowd and music that's pumping from a speaker nearby. He has a lazy, carefree smile on his face, but I notice the rigid way he's holding his body. He's angry. At himself... or at her? Julien might be a bastard sometimes, but he's not careless. He only breaks things when it serves a purpose.

You'd better not touch that pussy, Riley. It's not punishment if you finish the job I started. Her face flames as she smiles sweetly before flipping him off. Yup. I heard him correctly. What exactly went on between the two of them up there? My hand almost moves—instinct, maybe—as she brushes past. But she doesn't stop. Doesn't even look. Just keeps walking toward the door like I'm not even there.

Julien locks eyes with me, a silent agreement passing between us, and I nod, knowing he needs me to follow her. It does us no good if she ends up hurt or dead before the year even starts. Yes. *Dead.* It's a possibility. Although not one that has happened in many years—before our time here. No one needs a repeat of that situation. The student's death is the reason Pointebreak is as private as it is. I don't know the entire story, but I know the student was a first-year, when my father was a fourth-year student here. Things changed drastically after that. The administration did not allow younger students to leave campus, and they installed more barriers and cameras around campus to enhance security.

Riley tries to slam the front door behind her, but I catch it as she hurries down the steps, typing away on her phone. A few guys whistle and laugh as she walks by. Her eyes flicker toward them, then away again, choosing to ignore the catcall. When one of them tries to follow, I curl my lip in disgust as I stare daggers at them. The cocky asshole that's leading the pack holds his hands up and murmurs a pathetic "sorry" as I pass. *Don't worry, you will be once I find out who you are,* I think as I continue after her.

I follow behind, keeping enough distance that she hardly notices I'm here. She really should pay more attention to her surroundings. I assumed all women were taught that. I know my mom and I taught Ava at a young age, so she can protect herself. Riley walks fast and the skirt of her pink dress sways pleasantly around her hips. I rake my eyes down and up her form, definitely appreciating everything she offers.

Jesus, this girl is a wet dream come to life.

Not that I would ever admit that to anyone. It's better if people wonder about my sexuality. It keeps them on their toes. I can tell you, without a doubt, I am one hundred percent straight, but may have dabbled in some secret play once or twice.

She's nothing like her idiot father. He's a coward and compulsive liar, doing anything he needs to grapple his way to the top. I've never liked assholes like that. He's cocky and thinks he's untouchable; but that's what's going to fuck him over. Riley is pure. She has a strong desire to be well-liked, yet based on my limited observations, she refuses to be walked on. She's exactly the type of woman I need—*we* need. I'll watch her. It's what I'm best at.

Watching. Listening. Analyzing.

If you observe someone long enough, they always show their hand. Riley though…I don't understand. *Yet.* I know she's pissed at Julien tonight, and I'm sure he'll tell me what went down later, so we are all on the same page. But the confidence she exuded as she stormed out of there was uncanny. Full grown-ass men don't dare disrespect Julien the way she did and not piss themselves in fear. I like her. She won't let him fuck with her.

Her stride slows when she's out of sight from the house, and I do the same. She's on a path in the middle of the woods, one the students have created over the years. The dirt is soft under our footfalls, muffling the sounds of my feet. Animals rustle in the dry leaves around us and her steps falter before she stops and looks to the right and left of her. Searching. She rubs her arms despite the air still having a touch of warmth in the late summer evening. A small, involuntary smile touches my lips when I figure out what she's doing. She's listening. I can almost feel her attention on me, but I know she can't see me. Staying hidden is second nature. The shadows don't just cover me; they protect me. She knows she's not alone. *Smart girl. Trust your gut.*

The moonlight shines down on her as the clouds above us drift by. She walks again, but cocks her head slightly every few steps. The urge to grab her from behind and hold her there, chest to back, until she stops running, consumes me. Hold her…restrain her. Teach her a lesson on why she should never be alone. There are enough men in this school that will do whatever they want to a beautiful woman without a care in the world—even with rules in place that are supposed to stop that. She shouldn't trust anyone.

Especially *me*.

I'm not a safe option. When Julien told me the plan for her a year ago, I told myself I didn't have to be involved any more than necessary. Just enough to keep her in line. Then she's Julien's problem. Wesley, I'm sure will want his fun, but she's a pawn in a much bigger game.

My mind continues to wander. What would it be like to feel her against me? Her curves are unbelievable. Long light hair that's perfect for pulling, perky tits, and a nice round ass. Since she got out of the car this morning, I've been picturing the feeling of sliding past her legs and entering her heat. I growl internally at the thought that's consumed me. I can't take my eyes off the sway of her hips and I harden in my pants. My Luna needs to be taught a lesson, one only I'm fit to give. Just thinking about taking her over my knee, lifting that skirt, and smacking her bare ass until it's a beautiful red color has me losing myself to need.

I want to feel her squirm under me. I want her to beg for me and I want her to come on my cock when I finally decide to give it to her.

Suddenly, she spins and stares me down. It's easy enough to keep my face neutral, and not act surprised she caught me off guard, but damn, I'm impressed. People usually can't get a jump on me. I've had far too many years of training myself to let them, but here I stand. Fantasies of Riley under and on top of me made me forget where I am and what I'm doing. Shit. I can't be making mistakes like that. Although I'm impressed and as much as I want to smile at her and praise her, I don't react. My lips press into a tight line, and I cock my brow at her.

"What do you want, Zander?" She pulls her crossed arms tighter against her chest. I notice her hand tucked tight into a fist like she's ready to use it if she has to. Good form. At least she won't break her thumb if she were to swing at me. Not that I'd let her get that far. I'd restrain her under me before she knew it. I won't pick a fight, but I sure as hell won't stand by and let someone try to hurt me.

I cock my head to the side and look at her like the puzzle she is. "You shouldn't be alone in the dark."

"I'm not, am I? You're following me like a creep."

My lips twitch. She called me a creep like it's an insult. Like I wouldn't drag her into the dark and make her do depraved things she'd crave afterwards. She has no idea what I'm capable of.

I jerk my chin at her. "What happened at the house with Julien?"

"None of your business." She snaps as she narrows her eyes at me and turns on her heel, giving me her back, walking away.

No.

Not happening.

Only one of us is in charge here, and it sure as hell isn't Riley Whittier.

Adrenaline fuels me as I charge up behind her and grab her upper arm, spinning her to face me. She tries to jerk her arm free, but my grip tightens, no doubt leaving bruises.

"You *are* my business, Riley. Everything you do, everything you say, and everywhere you go," I say through clenched teeth, the quiet words dripping with venom. Every dirty little secret I can pull from her pretty lips is mine to use.

The moonlight highlights her angelic face. I study her, looking for any signs of the devil I've been told about, but I don't see it. The only thing Wesley and I know about Riley is what Julien has told us and the short amount of research I've completed after finding out she was coming to Pointebreak. Her life is an open book, but she keeps her nose clean. I saw no mentions of a boyfriend, so that's one less concern. Is it possible Julien's wrong about her? Riley's either a damn good actress, or she's as innocent as they come.

Innocent.

That's what she is. Untouched by the very things that have already broken me. And all I can think about is dragging her into the dark with me. Letting the part of me I keep buried sink its teeth into her. Mark her.

I've never had a longing this strong before. Fucking witch is putting me under a spell. I mentally shake the dark thoughts that are poisoning my mind. Now is *not* the time. I inhale deeply, the crisp air doing little to clear the insistent voices in my head that scream to take her. Use her. She smells like vanilla, fear, and sex. Did she have sex with Julien? Did she let him touch that pretty pussy of hers? I've never cared who Julien or Wesley fuck, but from the moment I heard those words fall from Julien's lips on the stairs, I've needed to know exactly what happened.

Her breath hitches and it's only then I realized I've backed her against a tree, pressing my body against hers. She pants, and with each shallow breath, her breasts push against my chest. I drop my face inches from hers.

"Did you let him use that pretty cunt of yours, Riley? Did you whore yourself out already?" I nestle my nose against her throat and take a deep breath. My heart hammers in my chest, a frantic drum against my ribs. I've spent my whole life keeping people at bay. Never getting too close. Yet this girl shows up and digs her way under my skin within a day. "You smell like sex."

She reaches up, attempting to slap me, but I grab her wrist and clinch it. She whimpers and I squeeze harder. I raise my eyebrow at her, a silent warning, waiting for her next move.

"Get. Off. Me," she bites out.

I hold her arm above her head and grab the other, trapping them together. She squirms and gasps when her belly brushes against my crotch.

"Try that again and I'll toss you over my knee, Luna." Do it again. Give me a reason to redden that ass of yours, beautiful. She bites her lip, staring daggers at me, but stops fighting my hold on her. "Did you let Julien fuck you?"

"No." She grits. "Let me go."

I collar her throat, rubbing my fingers over her strong pulse and drop my forehead to hers. "Why did you come here? Pointebreak isn't for you," I whisper. I need to know. I need reassurance that she won't destroy everything we're working towards.

"My dad made me. This is the last place in the entire world I want to be."

Her pulse races the moment she mentions her father. "Why?"

"I don't know," she whispers and gently shakes her head as much as I'll allow with my hold on her. "He cancelled my enrollment to Dartmouth and told me that's final. I didn't have a choice, and ever since I've gotten here, you and your gang have been up my ass. Let me go, Zander, or so help me God."

I quirk my brow. Oh, this is going to be good. "Or so help you God, what, Luna?"

"That's not my name. Stop calling me that!" She growls through clenched teeth. I tighten my hold on her throat. Her eyes widen in fear as she struggles against me, while the monstrous part of me claws for release.

Punish her.

Break her.

I notice the shift in her the moment she decides screaming is her best option. My lips crash down on hers as I hold her tight beneath me, swallowing down her cry for help. Shivers run down my spine, the sound of her fear like lightening to my dick. I want her to wrap her legs around me as I fuck up into her with my cock. I'd take her hard and fast, and then I'd drag her back to my room and tie her down to use her for days. She'd quickly become my drug of choice. I drag my hand from her throat to between her breasts and over her belly toward the apex of her thighs. Then she does the most unexpected thing. She kisses me back with a hunger that matches my own.

Riley hooks her leg around my hip and rocks herself over me, seeking more friction as her mouth opens wider. Our tongues dance as we explore one another, and I know if I don't stop kissing her, I won't. I'll claim every part of her until she's completely mine. Her inner light and goodness summon my dark and devilish side. I don't know if I'd be able to contain him if let loose. I grab her panties and pull them hard. She gasps in surprise as the stitching rips under my fingers and the fabric hangs loosely around her thighs.

We pull back from one another, both of us breathing hard, trying to catch our breaths. "Take 'em off." I command.

I release her and slide down her body, squatting in front of her, bunching her dress around her hips. I drag her ruined panties down and off her legs, then rub my scruff along the inside of her thigh. Her legs quiver and she digs her nails into my hair, positioning my face where she needs me the most, her soaked pussy. I take a deep breath and as I lean forward and swipe my tongue through her wet folds. She tastes like heaven as she tugs my hair and whimpers. I go to do it again when the sound of distant voices breaks through my lust-filled haze.

Fuck. Fuck. Fuck!

What did I almost do?

A scream of frustration builds in my chest, but I clench my jaw and hold it back. I stand, rearrange my painfully hard cock, and shove her panties in my back pocket. She scoffs and crosses her arms over her chest, but says nothing about my souvenir. Vulnerability is a weakness. Maybe that's one useful thing her dad taught her. We're doing things we shouldn't be. I'll get my chance to play with Riley. There's no mistake about that. Just not today.

"Come on. Let's get you home."

And she does the craziest thing of all.

She doesn't put up a fight.

EIGHT

RILEY

My mind's been cluttered and foggy all morning. Last night's events play on a constant loop as I try to make heads or tails of what happened. First Julien. Then Zander. What the hell is going on with me? This is *not* who I am. I'm not some sex crazed girl who plays with multiple partners. I'm the girl who wouldn't sleep with her ex because it felt like a betrayal. Or maybe because Troy wasn't right, and deep down, I knew it. I shake my head, pushing thoughts of my ex-boyfriend down deep. He's an asshole that didn't deserve me, anyway.

Both men touched me last night, did dirty things to me, and I allowed them to. I didn't even try to fight them. My mind screamed warnings about the awful idea, a cacophony of doubt, but my body? My body had full control and enjoyed every damn minute of it. Julien played me like a fiddle, and given the chance, I know I would have soaked Zander's face. That's the part I'm struggling with. I wanted it. Their touches felt good, natural. Both of them were so different, but I craved each one with the same aching intensity.

Julien touched me like he hated me—like I'd affronted him. I'll admit I shouldn't have been snooping around his room. That one's on me. But I need to know what makes him tick. I'll need every edge possible to make it here. And I'm smart enough to know my last name won't help me. From the looks of it, Michael Whittier isn't well-loved at Pointebreak. Being his daughter doesn't mean shit. But the crazy thing is, Julien wanted me as bad as I wanted him. I know he did. The way his cock was hard against his jeans, pressing against me, told me everything I needed to know. Or maybe he's crazy and has a sadistic kink. I was out of my mind in lust that I would have let him screw me. And I think that's part of why I was angry when he pushed me away. That, and the edging he gave without letting me come.

I didn't want him to stop.

Zander, though, he's dark. He has demons inside that he didn't want me to see. His rough playfulness sparked a newfound desire within me. I've never had anyone touch me or say things to me like he did. *Never.* Julien had already frustrated me by bringing me to the edge last night, and then, when Zander started talking about tossing me over his knee, I couldn't stop myself from getting wet even if I tried. It was an offhand comment, but I saw the look in his eyes. He wanted that more than anything last night. And I did too. God, did I want that. And the small taste of his mouth on mine made every nerve ending in my body crackle with electricity. I almost wished he pulled me off the trail and finished what he started.

Which is why when I got safely back to my room, courtesy of Zander, who didn't utter two words the rest of the walk, I touched myself and played until I came. Hard. I swear I blacked out for a moment. Fuck that arrogant asshole, Julien, and his rules about not touching. Like I would ever listen to him. In a sick way, though, I want to tell him that thoughts of Zander spanking me are ultimately what made me come. My ass cheeks clench at the memory, and a fresh pool of arousal floods my system.

Which brings me to my next problem. Ava. I don't even know how to start this conversation with her. Do I tell her about it? Is it something she needs to know? Her brother almost ate me out in the woods against a tree. I can't tell her that, but maybe that we had a moment? Ugh. This is all so complicated. I need to forget last night and get my head on straight. Now isn't the time for daydreams.

Classes start in the morning, so Ava and I walked around campus again, finding all our classrooms. We only have two together, unfortunately. She told me she got to choose her classes ahead of time, so that means I really was a last-minute enrollment and they gave me leftovers. I hope next semester I can choose more business type classes versus fighting ones. I'll never have a need for that in my day-to-day life. At least with business, I can do something worthwhile with it. Networking is definitely going to be a useful tool around here, and it seems a lot of students are from well-off families.

"Here's the gym," Ava says, directing my gaze to the enormous building with glass covering the front half of it. "Open twenty-four seven for all your workout needs." She smiles and waves at someone inside. Last night Ava talked with everyone. I swear now even Nick is eating out of the palm of her hand. While I spent a little time enjoying the bonfire and mingling, I wish I had spent more time talking to people instead of snooping, as that ended my night early. I'm sure I'll have plenty of time to get to know the others, but it seems like that is the event to cement yourself with a group.

"Yay," I say as I circle my finger in the air in fake enthusiasm.

"Hey, I've heard those self-defense classes are hard. It might be worth it to at least come in here once in a while."

"What's the point of those, anyway? How is that relevant? It's not like I'm going to need to know how to throat punch someone." As soon as I say the words, an image of Julien holding me by the throat against the wall invades my mind. My face flames, not for the first time today, at the thought of him bringing me to the edge and not letting me finish. I've already had to make the excuse to Ava that it's just hot outside. Not sure she's buying it anymore. Ava already told me some of the defense classes are a mix of all years because it makes for better training. First years learn a lot more from those more experienced. She seems oddly excited about this. I haven't been able to figure it out. Unless she's hoping Nick is in one of her classes.

"It's good to know, in case anything ever happens." She shrugs, like it's no big deal and a normal occurrence in her life.

I pull my brows together and watch her jerky movements. "Ava, what would happen that would make you want to learn that?"

Her laugh, sharp and strained, is a stark contrast to the easy laughter I've become accustomed to. This one is as if she's trying to convince herself. "Oh, you know, just in case. Always best to be prepared. Weren't you a Girl Scout?" She uses that silly phrase again like it explains everything.

I place my hand on her arm and force her to turn and look at me. "Prepared for what, Ava?"

Her gaze darts around my face, looking everywhere but into my eyes. She licks her lips and her throat bobs as she swallows before taking a deep breath.

"You really don't know any of the people that are here, do you?" Her voice is so low I have to strain to hear it.

The blood drains from my face and my stomach turns in

knots as I slowly shake my head no at her. My mouth, suddenly dry, feels like it is packed with cotton. The familiar fuzzy feeling of a panic attack wedging its way forward, but I catch it before it can fully develop and focus on my breathing. Breathe in for four, hold, breathe out for four.

When I have a hold of myself, I say, "Who comes to this school, Ava? Who *are* you?"

She smiles sadly at me and takes my arm, looping it through hers, making me walk with her. "Not out here. No one needs to overhear us."

We're silent on the way back to the dorm, the rest of our exploration forgotten. I can't help but look around at the other faces of students walking around us. Have I seen any of their parents in the news? I'm not stupid enough to think there aren't some famous parents of kids here. Do any of them know who I am? A few students glance in our direction, and I swear some snicker at us as we walk by. Are they looking at me or Ava? I turn my head to watch her. Her face is blank as she leads me to the stone dorm building in front of us.

We finally make it to our room and stop suddenly as Nick leans against our door, looking down at his phone. He glances up at us and smiles warmly.

"Hey, Ava. Hi, Riley. Do you ladies want to go for a walk? I can show you my favorite spots on campus."

Ava shakes her head first. "Sorry, we just got back from one. We were going to look through the class syllabus to see what we need for classes tomorrow. Maybe we can walk over to the dining room a little later for some food?"

His smile falters, but he nods his head in understanding. "Sure. You have my number. Text me later."

Their words wash over me, indistinct and unimportant, as she pushes me into our room and locks the door behind us. I sit on the edge of my bed and look up at her, waiting.

She's silent, just gnaws on her bottom lip and wrings her fingers together.

"Are you in the mafia?" The question spills past my lips before I can stop it. It wouldn't be a surprise at this point. I've always suspected that's who comes to Pointebreak. I mean, look at the men here for fuck's sake. They are built like soldiers. Dark and brutal. But why would anyone allow this many criminals into their small town? My fingers itch to get to my laptop and write anything and everything she says. I haven't been great at taking notes so far, but I'm afraid of getting caught. I jotted a few things down this morning when Ava was still sleeping and I still owe Leah that email.

She smirks and shakes her head. "Mafia's Italian." I visibly relax. Then tense with her next words.

"Bratva is the Russian term, but they're basically the same."

"Funny, Ava," I force a smile to my face, waiting for her to yell out "gotcha" or something similar, but I know. Deep down I've always known. Which means there is so much more shit my dad is in than I thought possible. Everyone here is connected to crime in one fashion or another.

She shakes her head. "I'm not laughing, Riley."

No.

No, no, no!

I scramble for the back of my bed, putting distance between us. I'm in the room with a criminal. Or a criminal's daughter...or maybe just a girl who knows way too much about organized crime? The walls are closing in around me as my breathing hitches and my palms sweat. My vision frays at the edges—a soft warning of my impending attack. The rumors are true. I'm going to school with killers—mobsters! I've never hung out with anyone who would so much as shine a negative light on our family. That's why I don't have a lot of friends to begin with. Too many students at my old school had parents with questionable motives. All well known to the media.

But that also means dad knew about this and he sent me here, regardless. Why? What's the motive behind it? I close my eyes and focus on what he told me before I left, frantically searching for any clues, but everything is hazy. I was in such shock at the time it's hard to remember anything.

I need to get out of here before this attack pulls me under. I dart my eyes around the room, looking everywhere but at her. My lungs burn with each inhale as I force them to expand, Ava's admission weighing heavy on my chest like stones. She approaches, her eyes soft, her steps quiet, careful not to startle me like I am a frightened animal. I put my hands up, stopping her in her tracks. I know I look like a crazy person, but I can't help it. Ava puts her hands in front of herself and motions for me to stay calm. Then she takes another small step forward, almost touching my bed.

I shake my head and scramble for the edge. "Don't come closer to me, Ava."

My words are just a gut punch as her face falls. "Riley, listen to me." I close my eyes, focusing on her words and not the rushing of blood through my ears. *She can't see me freak out. I need to get away from her, from here; just until I get myself under control.* My heart is still beating frantically, but as I take a few breaths, it slows. "We aren't as bad as you think. I've known my whole life my family wasn't like everyone else, but we aren't bad people. *I'm* not a bad person."

I know that. I've known that since the moment I met her, she's good. We can't help who our parents are or the situation we're born into. I should know. I've always tried to be the perfect daughter and look where that landed me—here, at Pointebreak. With the fucking mafia! I open my eyes and look at her, really look at her. She has a kind face, is friendly and clearly cares deeply for people. She's not the type of person who would go around torturing someone for information, or for fun.

"My family's involved with the Russian Bratva, but my dad will tell you he's a low man on the totem pole. I'm not stupid enough to believe it, but he's not in charge either. That's it." She reaches her hand out to me and when I don't flinch, she rests it on my knee. "Talk to me."

"So Julien, and Wesley? Also Mafia, or um, Bratva or whatever?"

"Our dads are all involved, yes. They all know one another from when they went to school here. They were more like," she pauses, purses her lips, and looks around the room before landing on me again, "enemies with benefits. My dad wasn't happy when he found out Zander fell in with Julien and Wesley." She takes a deep breath. "You asked me why I chose to come here?" I nod. "Because this way I know how to protect myself. I'm not stupid enough to think I'm free to marry who I want, or do what I want. I'm a bargaining chip. And coming to Pointebreak is the best chance I have at coming close to making my own decisions."

Listening to her reason for coming here breaks my heart. I know after I leave here I can do whatever I want. No one will pawn me off like a business deal. I can choose who I date, or who I marry. I can even choose to go to college after this if I want. Or I think so anyway. Ava, though, I can see the sadness cloud her features and I know she's not being afforded the same luxury. It doesn't change the fact that this is all a lot to take in.

"I-I think I need to go for a walk." I can't wrap my head around this with her breathing down my throat. I need a few minutes to myself to have the mental breakdown I need.

Her face falls, but she takes a step away and clasps her hands in front of her, looking to the ground. "Let me come with you."

I shake my head and all but run for the door. "No. No. I'm okay."

"You shouldn't be alone, Riley."

"I'm fine," I insist.

She sighs and nods, not believing a damn word I say. "Okay. I understand."

I practically run out of the room, down the steps and into the quad, needing a few moments to myself. There are other students milling around in the warm weather. I look closely at faces and wonder who their parents are. *Not that I'd have a clue who they were, anyway.* Mafia activity has never been my go to for some easy late night reading. I'm questioning everything I think I know. I never believed the rumors. It was always something silly Leah and I would say; but to know it's real? This is a game changer.

I have no idea where I'm going; I just keep moving. I need space. Quiet. Somewhere no one can see me fall apart. I'm surprised I've fended this attack off as long as I have. My entire body trembles as I find a shady, grassy spot behind a building and slide down the wall, tucking my head between my knees and focusing on my breathing. It's like I can feel the slow rotation of the Earth beneath me. Even sitting still, everything spins around, vertigo settling in deep. I hate this. I hate having these attacks. Why can't I control them better? It had been almost a year since my last one. I'm going to have to learn to get this in check because I can't be in the middle of class, breaking down. My vision slowly returns to normal as I focus on my breathing. When I feel the remnants of it fade, I get up and start walking, with no intended direction.

Dad had to have known. There's no way he didn't. And James. He knew. His warning to me, not to trust too easily? Yeah, that one went right over my head. I feel like a fucking idiot! The first thing I did was try to make friends and open myself up as an invitation to mess with me. And Ava? I never in my life suspected. That's because she's good, my mind reminds me. But deep down, I know she wasn't trying to fool me. She's genuine and wants to be friends. Maybe she needs a friend as much as I do?

I'm walking aimlessly, seeing everything and nothing all at once; my mind feels like it's in a blender. The hairs on the back of my neck prickle and I rub them, shaking the fog I'm caught in. *Shit.* Where am I? I don't think we came to this part of campus on either of our walks. I spin around, looking for anything that seems familiar, but nothing stands out. The building in front of me looks abandoned. Possibly a fire at some point? Black soot covers the outer stone walls. I take a step closer and reach out to touch it when a hand clamps down on my shoulder. I jump and attempt to spin around to hit my assailant, but he's faster and holds my arms down by my side.

"Riley, calm down."

I twist and turn, struggling to free myself from his grip, but it just makes him squeeze me tight against his body like a boa constrictor.

"Riley. Stop!" His booming voice leaves no room for discussion and I stop momentarily scared of the wrath that might be on the other side of the familiar voice. I twist my head to see Wesley is holding me tight.

"Let go of me." I demand, once again aiming to free myself. He waits until I stop fighting him, then slowly unwraps his arms and puts me back on my feet. I step back and face him head on. "Why are you here, Wesley?"

He gives me a languorous smile. "Looking for you. Ava texted Zander that you freaked out and ran out of the room, scared you'd get yourself into trouble." He glances over my body, quickly assessing me, and when he seems to be appeased that I'm not harmed, he says, "looks like she may have been right." His eyes dart to the building behind me before focusing on my face again.

"I needed some air."

His smile widens and his face lights up in amusement. "I heard. Guess her royal highness never thought she'd be slumming it with us lowlifes. Lucky for you, I showed up."

NINE
WESLEY

She glares at me and shakes her head. She's cute when she's angry. I'm going to have fun with her. I was outside by the fire when she left last night, but Julien told me about his tryst. Well, kind of. He told me she was snooping in his room and he taught her a lesson. He probably enjoyed that lesson just as much as she did because he's still pissy. I talked with Zander after I put our minions to work cleaning up from the party. I don't know what it is about Riley, but Julien is not himself with her. Even after talking with Zander, I know I'm missing something. I'm not sure I understand what's going on with Zander, either. He gave me an update, sure, but he wasn't…there. His mind was elsewhere, which is unlike him.

"Leave me alone, Wesley. You're the last person I wanna see." She bites her lip and gets a far off look in her eyes before focusing on me again. *I wonder where her mind jumped to.* "What is this place?" she jerks her thumb over her shoulder.

"I thought I was the last person you wanted to see?" I tease. The decrepit-looking building stands behind her and I look at it before looking back into her bright eyes. For someone who seems to be afraid of the type of people we are, she sure is nosey. Curiosity killed the cat and all that shit. Time to fuck around. "I don't know what it *used* to be used for." I wink playfully at her as she rolls her eyes. "I know what we use it for now."

"And I suppose you're not gonna tell me, right?"

With a self-satisfied smirk plastered on my face, I shrug and shake my head. She flushes, and I'm not sure if it's from the walk or from speaking with me; but she gives a humph in annoyance that's so damn cute. After a few moments of silence, she throws her hands up in defeat and turns, but I'm faster. I wrap my fingers around her wrist and drag her back to me with enough force she has to put her hands on my pecs to stop from bouncing off me. It's like she's branded me in the very spot she touches. My skin burns under her small hands, and it feels so damn good. I groan as she digs her fingers into my muscles and squeaks.

"We're not done here. You need to learn a few," I pause, thinking of the best word, "house rules. And trust me when I say I'm the best person to teach you." Julien would scare her. Although, she's been giving him a run for his money and I know defiance pisses him off. Zander is emotionally detached from people; a wall seems to exist between him and others. It makes sense with all the shit he's gone through. I don't think he would get her to listen. She needs someone who can sympathize with what she's dealing with. Pointebreak is a new world she doesn't know how to navigate—but I do. I know what it's like to have everything stacked against you.

I've known my entire life about the family I was born into. What my family expects of me. I know the role I am supposed to step into after I leave here. Riley was thrown into the lion's den without a weapon and told to survive. What kind of sick father does that? What game is Michael Whittier playing? There's so much more to this than we even realize. There has to be. But everything Julien has said about this strong-willed girl in front of me is *wrong*. He said she was weak. But that's not true. I know it deep down in my gut.. She's not a prissy princess who needs to be used as a pawn in our sick game, despite what Julien thinks. She'll need to become a warrior and fight to survive.

Survival.

Pointebreak is going to be her worst nightmare. As soon as the students learn she has no clue what she's stepped into, they're going to fuck with her just because they can. And I know a few people here would do it to get to her father. Blackmail isn't an uncommon tactic in our world. I won't let that happen—can't let it happen. We are the only ones who can mess with her. If the wrong person pushes her, she may break. She's vital to get what we need. Sometimes plans change, and we're going with the flow.

Whatever she's thinking of makes her breathing erratic. Her eyes have glossed over with a sheen of wetness. "Breathe, you're turning blue." I rub my fingers over her cheek, and she swats me away. I smile wide again, happiness bubbling inside me. What the hell is up with that?

"Alright, Hellcat, have it your way." I step back, giving her the space she seems to need.

"My name's Riley. It's five letters. Is it really that hard to remember?" The muscles in her jaw clench and she takes a deep breath through her nose.

I laugh and she narrows her eyes, clearly not as amused. "You're putting up one heck of a fight. Thought it was a suitable name." I collar the back of her neck and pull her flush to me, then dip down my face directly in front of hers. Her pulse thrums steadily along the delicate line of her neck as her lips part into an "O" shape. Images of shoving my dick between her lips and having her swallow me play like rapid fire through my mind. How's her head game? I'm sure I could teach her a few tricks. My cock grows and presses behind the zipper of my shorts as I inhale her scent. Vanilla and cherries. My own personal cherry pie is just waiting to be eaten. "You're not what I expected, Riley," I whisper.

She licks her lips and pulls the bottom one between her teeth, holding tight to it. Her breathing has picked up. She swallows hard and clears her throat. "What did you expect?" Her voice is low, sultry.

I shake my head. "Not you." I release her, pushing her away from me and take a step back, needing to distance myself from the siren in front of me.

She clears her throat and tucks a loose strand of hair behind her ear, then looks at her feet.

"What?" I ask. I can see the wheels in her head spinning. She really needs to work on that poker face of hers. She probably thinks she's good at it, but I can see through her bullshit.

"How many students here are…criminals?"

She cringes as I chuckle at her awkward question. "None." Her shoulders drop in relief and she sighs. "Just their parents. Or bosses." I shrug. "Depends on who you're talkin' to." She flops her mouth open in surprise. Is she really that surprised, though? Pointebreak is very selective about who they accept. Not everyone makes the cut. "The apple doesn't fall far from the tree, Hellcat. You're not as innocent as you think you are." I rest both hands on the top of my head, stretching my back with the groan, waiting for some sort of snarky reply that I'm sure is on the tip of her tongue. Her eyes travel to the bit of my stomach showing and I can't help the bit of warmth that spreads through me. I don't hate it. Not one bit. I resist the urge to pull my shirt up higher, giving her a better view. I know what I look like. And I know I look damn good.

"I don't get in trouble." She grits out, anger radiating off her as she clenches her fist by her side. I'm not sure if it's my words that have caused the volatile reaction or if she's pissed because she's checking me out. Let's go with the latter because I really like her sizing me up.

It's so easy to get under her skin. I rub my jaw, thinking. "No. My guess is you keep your nose squeaky clean." I tap the tip of her nose and smile as she swats my hand away in frustration. "But that doesn't mean you're not guilty by *association*."

"I'm not my father. Anything he's done isn't a reflection of me."

I shake my head, my mouth turning down into a frown. "That's not how it works. We pay for the sins of our families." *I know I sure as hell have.* "Ava's a good girl. She'll help you navigate Pointebreak. You may not know the students here, but that doesn't mean they don't already know you." Especially after last night. There are eyes and ears everywhere.

Riley shakes her head, and I watch her struggle to swallow past the lump forming in her throat. Her eyes are glassy as tears fill, threatening to spill. Then she sniffs and whispers, "I don't want to be here. I don't want any part of this life…you…these people…" An errant tear falls down her cheek, but she wipes it away quickly in anger.

I see you, Riley, and I fucking *get* it. Gently cupping her face, I tilt her head back as I gaze into her sorrowful gray eyes, then lower my lips to hers, stopping a hair's breadth away from connecting with her lush ones. I don't want to take anything else from her. She's up against a nearly impossible feat, but I need to taste her. Need to know the reason I don't feel like myself around her. It feels like an eternity before she presses up on her toes and my lips connect with her soft, supple ones. And when they do…fireworks.

Instant explosions!

It's not supposed to be like this.

I pull her flush against my body and she doesn't resist, allowing me to deepen the kiss. I explore her mouth with my tongue and nip at her bottom lip as she gasps and moans into me, effectively hardening my dick more. Her kiss is sweet but hungry as she wraps her arms around my neck, molding her body to mine. I have no option but to hold her close. The heat of her body is burning me up. It would be so easy to bring things further, to push her against the wall, or lay her down and shove my dick in her. Riley rubs against me as I tangle my fingers in her hair, holding her in place. Her breathy moans fill my ears. We're frantic for each other. I don't want to let go. She's caught me in her web, and I'm a willing victim.

I internally curse myself. *Fucking get a grip, Wes!* She's not in the right headspace, and today isn't about trying to fuck her. She'll regret anything she does now, and I don't want that. I don't want to be a regret to her. Focus on the plan. It takes everything in me to pull away. Her eyes flutter open and she licks her lips before trapping her bottom one between her teeth. *Oh, to be that lip…*

I clear my throat, pretending I'm not as affected as she looks. "Stick with Ava. Don't get caught walking alone on campus. Give me your phone."

She taps her hand against her back pocket and shrugs. "I must have left it in my room when I ran out of there."

I groan and shake my head in annoyance. "Don't go *anywhere* without your phone."

She bats her hand dismissively. "It's fine. I'm safe on campus. Imagine the headlines if I go missing at this school, or something happens to me." She flashes her hands open and closed in front of me. "Governor Whittier's daughter gets abducted at Pointebreak. The press and public would have a field day."

The smile stays on my face, but the anger's there—tight in my jaw, hot in my chest. Is she trying to be obtuse, or does she really not understand how dangerous Pointebreak is? Death may not be a common occurrence here, but that doesn't mean these forged relationships don't carry on outside of here. Make enemies with the wrong person and you can expect a target on your back after graduation.

"You really don't fucking get it, do you? I'm trying to help you *survive* in Pointebreak, Hellcat. These people... these students will stop at nothing to get what they want. Pointebreak doesn't accept just anyone, and everyone is here for a reason. Everyone has a purpose." I clench my teeth as my jaw twitches, my anger getting the better of me.

Her face reddens, and she clenches her hands at her sides as her nostrils flare in anger with each shallow breath she takes. Good. Get pissed. "You seem to have a lot of answers. Why am I here, Wesley? What reason did my dad have to send me to this godforsaken place?"

I wish I knew. God, I wish I fucking knew. Julien's been pretty quiet, but I know he'll share more when he has it. The plan was always to finish out here and take her when we were out and getting established. While here at Pointebreak, we can't do a damn thing. The other option was to ignore her, but given our status here, our names and reputations wouldn't stay hidden for long. I know why he hates Michael. Riley's just the pawn in this endgame. She's disposable. Or she was...

She knows about us now. It will not be as easy as it was before. And I feel this strange connection with her. I like how I feel around her. I don't know how to explain it.

Annoyed, she throws her hands up, then looks for a way around me. Riley tries to push past my sizable frame, but I grab her bicep in a bruising grip. "I'll walk you back to your room. Ava will give you all our numbers. Save them. Use them if you need to."

Riley gives a curt nod and pulls her arm from my grasp with a sneer. She stomps away from me and I can't help but take a moment to appreciate the way her ass sways in her jean shorts. She's disappointed I won't answer her questions, but I don't have all the answers. I don't know what compelled her dad to send her here. And while I know a bit about the vendetta Julien has with her, I won't tell her. It's not my place. I can only let her in on my story.

In only a few strides I catch up to her, and she snorts in exasperation when I sling my arm over her shoulder, tugging her against my side. There are hardly any students milling around, but that doesn't mean she should walk alone. Hell, I thought that was common sense on college campuses. This is basically the same thing. Pointebreak just houses more… dangerous students.

"I told you I'd walk you back, not walk ten paces behind you like a lost puppy."

"Maybe the lost puppy look suits you," she mumbles. I smile as she shrugs out of my grasp and crosses her arms over her chest, looking everywhere but at me. Her poker face is terrible, probably the worst I've seen. Her face is an open book, revealing every emotion through subtle shifts in her expression. Anger and confusion roll off her in waves and yet the first thing I want to do is wrap her in my arms and tell her everything is going to be fine. Hold her until the fear leaves her.

"You don't need to walk me back. I can find my dorm myself." I ignore her as we walk in silence for another minute, then she slows her steps and looks up at me. "How did you find me so fast? I haven't been gone that long, yet you seemed to walk up only minutes behind me."

"Ava gave us the general direction you walked and there

aren't many places out this way. You're very curious, and what's more thrilling than an old building that's not on any of the campus maps?" I smile at her as she narrows her eyes and glares at me. "What do you think that building is? Torture room?" I wiggle my brows and smile widely as I tease her.

She snorts. A small smile graces her lips, and for some reason, that makes me happy. "Knowing the type of people that go here, probably. But it doesn't matter. You won't tell me. I'll figure it out on my own."

I tap my lips with my index finger. "You also go here, Hellcat. Best to remember the people who are now your peers and colleagues."

"Right," she mutters quietly. "Should be an exciting four years."

TEN

RILEY

I roll over, shutting off the alarm, and throw my arm over my eyes. First day of classes and I hardly slept last night. I tried calling my dad, but he sent me straight to voicemail. *Shocking.* I wanted to call James and have him hand over the phone, but unless Dad had a speech, he would have been at home, anyway. Now, I'm more confused than ever, but one thing stuck with me all night long was something Wesley said. *I'm trying to help you survive in this place.*

Survive.

It's not the first time my stomach has dropped at the simple word since arriving here. That's what's making my skin prick up this morning. He could have phrased it in a number of different ways, but he chose those specific ones. I imagine classes are going to be harder than I originally anticipated.

Those three are a well-oiled machine. One picks up where the other left off. I've never seen anything like it. That's a dangerous combination and I need to watch my back, otherwise I'll end up with a knife in it. I wish I knew what the hell I did to warrant their attention. My goal was to fly under the radar for the next four years. *So much for that.*

My stomach grumbles in protest. After getting back last night, I refused to leave my room again, fearful of running into certain people I don't want to see, so I didn't have dinner. Ava swiped me a few small things from the cafeteria, but I wanted nothing from her. Now I wish I hadn't thrown them away. She was just trying to be nice, and I was a total bitch.

She rolls over and our eyes meet from across the room. "I'm sorry for being a bitch. You've been nothing but nice to me and I shouldn't have acted the way I did. You were only trying to make me understand." Breathing deep, I push it out. "I'm scared, Ava. I don't know how to navigate this place."

She swings her legs over the side of the bed and walks over to mine, sitting on the edge.

"I'm sorry you found out like that. I really thought you knew. I'll help you anyway I can. You have Zander, Wesley, and Julien's numbers. They'll help too."

How is she so optimistic? I scoff and scrub my hands down my face. "Julien would rather watch me drown."

She smiles and shakes her head, her curls bouncing with the motion. "You'd be surprised. I've known Julien for a few years now. Wesley too. They're my unofficial brothers and protective to a fault. If Wes told me to give you all their numbers, there's a reason."

I don't know what those three want. However, me being at Pointebreak isn't it.

"How does that work? Aren't all your families part of different gangs? How can they work together?"

Ava's laugh is melodic. "Gangs." She shakes her head and continues. "Mutual agreements. Well," she drags the word out, "sort of. Dad wasn't happy when Zander became friends with them, which I told you yesterday, but he doesn't say much about it anymore." She shrugs. I can sense there is more she wants to say, but she holds back. Rome wasn't built in a day, and she's shared more than her fair share of information. I'm thankful for that.

I inhale and nod, understanding what she's not saying. Then stand to get ready for the day. The showers are full by the time I get down there and when I finally get to hop in; the water is lukewarm at best. *I should have showered last night like Ava.* I shiver as I run back to my room, my towel wrapped tightly around me. Ava sits at her desk calmly putting on makeup. I bite my lip as I dig through my drawer for my panties and bra and wonder how I'm going to get them on with her sitting here. She watches me in her mirror and opens her mouth in an O shape when I hold my items up to show her. She closes her eyes and I dry off in record speed and pull the undergarments up.

"All set, thanks."

I blow dry my hair and the soft blown out tendrils frame my face. Another thing good 'ole dad taught me. Always look your best. Even if I wanted to look like I just rolled out of bed and threw on a potato sack, I wouldn't be able to do it. And for some reason, I don't think the other students would take kindly to me looking like a frump. Not that it should matter, but I have the impression that a certain look is to be maintained, even if it didn't specifically state that in the documents. My mind would also scream with me to go back and make myself presentable. And trust me, I thought long and hard about doing that today. But maybe if I blend in, everyone will leave me alone.

I look at myself in the full-length mirror and fidget with my hair. The uniform is like any other I've worn, but I feel like a fish out of water in it. In my other schools I'd have worn a chunky heel with it, or maybe even a cute pair of wedges, but think better of it and I opt for my red converse. I pick a piece of lint off the black button down and smooth out a wrinkle. Taking an unsteady breath, I blow it out before grabbing my bag to head out for breakfast with Ava.

"Ready?" she asks, bouncing with excitement.

"Ready as I'll ever be." I shrug and try to smile.

The cafeteria is full and buzzing with energy, but we snag some food, and my eyes are definitely bigger than my stomach, but since I didn't eat last night, I figured I could use the extra calories. Eggs, pancakes with butter and real maple syrup, along with fresh fruit, fill my plate. We sit at a table with two other girls I recognize from the bonfire but didn't catch their names, and I offer a polite smile and a hello. Ava waves at one girl as we sit and dig in.

"Darcy and Julie, this is Riley. She's my roommate," Ava introduces me. I smile warmly and shake their hands. They exchange a look with one another and Darcy forks some eggs and pops them into her mouth. Though she remains silent, the smirk playing on her lips sends a shiver down my spine, making me instantly wary.

My smile fades and I place my fork down, giving them my full attention. "What?"

"Nothing," the blonde girl, Darcy says. There's a beat of silence before she huffs and continues. "There are rumors since Saturday at the bonfire that you're off limits. The Kings deemed it so."

I furrow my brow and wait for her to elaborate. "Come again?" It seems those three are everywhere I don't want them to be. It's crystal clear who actually runs Pointebreak. And the administrators aren't it. I wait for more but when it doesn't appear she's going to elaborate I say, "Well, I don't know who told you that, but ignore whatever you've heard. No one speaks for me."

I glance at Ava, and she smiles at me, nodding in agreement. I'm thankful to have someone on my side. *That asshole.* It must be Julien. He's the only one of the three that has been out to get me. My face heats when I remember exactly how Julien brought me to the brink and then denied me. Or how I thought Zander was going to eat me out in the woods, but stopped. And then there's Wesley and his damn kiss and how, for sure, I thought he was going to push for more. I dreamed of that kiss last night. Which made it all the harder to wake and face reality this morning.

Actually, if I'm being honest, I dreamed of all of them last night. I woke several times wishing I had my very own room so I could have taken care of my frustrations; because that's exactly what they caused. Maybe I would have finally gotten a decent night's sleep. Although, with the thought of the first day of classes looming…probably not.

Ava's lucky. I'm sure everyone knows who her brother is by now and that's also why they are being so nice to her. Not that she doesn't deserve it, because she does, but it makes it easier. No one is going to mess with her and risk getting on Zander's bad side. Maybe if I play my cards right, they might take me under their wing of protection, too.

My phone burns a hole in my pocket. Finally, a school uniform skirt with pockets. Thank goodness for small miracles. I should text Julien to tell him to get bent and not to speak for me again. I should put that message out there for all of them. Stand my ground and let them know they can't screw with me. The nerve of that asshole!

"Good to know." I turn toward the male voice behind me, almost forgetting what we were talking about. He has pushed his chair back, butting it against mine. "Hey baby, I'm Derek." He offers me his hand and when I don't take it, he shakes his head with a laugh. "It ain't gonna bite you to touch it."

Is this guy serious?

I narrow my eyes and rake them up and down his body. Not bad looking, but too cocky for my taste. "I'm not your baby."

He narrows his eyes as he assesses me, then relaxes and slides into a casual smile. "Not yet, but I bet you and I could have a lot of fun." He lowers his voice and leans in closer to my ear, the heat of his breath making the hairs on my arms rise. "Heard you let Julien Azarian have a piece of you. I can guarantee I'd treat you better than that piece of shit. Plus, wouldn't it be fun to fuck with the King of Pointebreak?"

I rear back, not knowing whether to slap this sorry excuse for a man, or run out of here with my tail between my legs. Humiliation sears my skin, leaving me raw. I feel hot and cold all at the same time. While his approach is reprehensible, messing with Julien has piqued my interest. Is that the rumor spreading through this place? That I let Julien *fuck* me? I glance around at the other tables, but most students aren't paying attention, too engrossed in their own conversations. Thank God for small miracles. I assume most of the school was at the bonfire, but how many people could actually know what happened between us? Ava shrugs when I look at her for an explanation. I didn't even tell *her* what happened, so it's not like she would have known it from me. As it turns out, the rumor mill works just fine around here.

Which leaves three.

Julien Azarian, Zander Fedorov, and Wesley Bastian are dead! If they think I won't play their stupid game, they have another thing coming.

Sweat slides down the back of my neck, my collar absorbing the liquid. My legs are jittery, the urge to run is so strong that I have to wrap my feet around the chair legs to stay still; my heart pounds in my chest like a drum. I need to speak, say something, but words defy me. It's like I can't breathe and I know it's only been mere moments since Derek propositioned me.

This is not me.

Forced to defend myself like this in front of a bunch of strangers? This is a first. It was easy to ignore words thrown my way at Stonewall. As soon as they learned of it, the teachers quickly intervened to stop any bullying. I was untouchable.

Here at Pointebreak I'm bottom of the barrel.

A nobody.

I don't like it at all. Nope. But that's not how I'm going down. If I'm going to make it through here, I need to step up my game. No one knows me, knows what I'm capable of. I need to reinvent myself. I can be the bad ass bitch I've always wanted to be.

I steel my spine, push my metaphorical crown straight on my head, then clear my throat. "Interesting rumor. Guess someone wants me to be known as the campus slut." He watches intensely. "Did he also tell you he couldn't perform?" I place my hand on the side of my mouth like I'm going to whisper a secret, but keep my voice loud enough for those around me to hear. "Stage fright." I roll my eyes for emphasis. "So embarrassing." A few snickers circle around me and I can't help the surge of pride that courses through me at their reaction.

"Derek, you said?" He nods. The hairs on the back of my neck prick up. I run my hand over them and look across the cafeteria, feeling eyes on me. My gaze locks with Julien's as he stands between Zander and Wesley. And dear lord, do those three look amazing in their uniforms? Black button down collared shirts with blood red ties and dark gray pants. Julien and Wesley have their sleeves rolled to their forearms, Julien's tattoos on full display. I can see a peak of a tattoo from the top of Wesley's collar. Zander's the only one wearing the black blazer as per the uniform. Perfectly poised and quaffed.

Julien cocks his brow, and the air is sucked from my lungs, the silence deafening as he waits to see what I'll do next. I've never been skilled at chess, but he's fucking with the wrong girl and I will do *anything* to win this game—even if that means getting my hands dirty. I grab the back of Derek's neck, pull his face toward mine, and crash my lips against his. If Julien wanted me to be an obedient girl, he's got another thing coming.

Your move, your highness.

ELEVEN

JULIEN

I clench my jaw and cross my arms over my chest, the muscles in my arms straining as I hold myself back from smashing someone's face in. The tie around my neck feels like a damn noose, restricting my every breath. The room has gone quiet and most of the students are pretending to be engrossed in conversation, but secretly watching out of their peripherals. Riley's got some balls; I'll give her that. Most people around here steer clear of pissing me off, but Riley Whittier can't seem to get enough of it. She wants a target on her back. I'll give her one so big she'll come begging for me to stop.

Wesley coughs to cover his laugh. "Fuck, man. She's trouble."

When Ava texted Zander last night, I wanted to chase her, to scare her into submission, but Wes stopped me and went after her instead. I'm not sure what I would have done if I got my hands on her, anyway. In every scenario, I imagined it would have ended with her on her knees and my cock down her throat. It was best I didn't go. I need her alive and well for what we have planned for her. And scared people do stupid things. I don't need any loose screws.

According to Ava, Riley was frantic and confused after their talk. She doesn't even know half of what she's walking into. Associating with students with less than reputable families isn't wise, but the least of her problems. Wait until she finds out what her future holds.

Me.

Riley *hates* me. There's no denying that. Especially with the recent public display once she saw me standing here. And I know she did. I knew the moment she decided to make her move. She pulls away from the kiss, dropping her hand from his neck, and whispers something to him. He turns and notices us standing here…watching…waiting and he smiles. The fucker actually smiles.

"Derek Adkins. His father's George Adkins. He's known for his strip clubs, but it's money laundering cover. Deals with a lot of different clientele," Zander supplies. "Your father uses him, as does mine. He has a few clubs up and down the coastline. And his uncle is Arthur Adkins, the current headmaster here."

I know all this. I know the cocky bastard personally. Growing up, I never cared for him, but I also assumed it was because he was a bratty kid. He's only eighteen, but acts like he's twelve. I guess his dad hasn't made him grow up as fast as the rest of our families. He's untouchable, but that doesn't mean he can't earn a few broken bones.

I don't take my eyes off Riley, but she pays me no mind as she continues to flirt with Derek, lazily stroking her finger up and down his arm. She watches us out of the corner of her eye, waiting to see what I'll do. *It's not wise to fuck with the beast, Princess.* Unluckily for her, Zander's in her morning business class, and I'm in her afternoon survival class. The only one who doesn't have eyes on her is Wesley, but he's already volunteered to help get her to and from.

"Keep an eye on her. I want updates on what she does or who she's with. She's not fucking up my plans."

I need to speak with my dad. I've tried to get a hold of him, but I couldn't get through. It's not my designated time and the guards wouldn't let me talk to him. I've passed the message along. He's got ears everywhere and feet on the ground, and I'm sure he's already put a plan in motion. He'll call soon. Dad has my schedule and knows when I'm free.

She meets my gaze, and I shake my head before turning on my heel to walk out. Naughty girl. I clench my fingers into a fist as I turn and walk out of the door. Wesley and Zander stay behind to watch Riley. I know they'll keep her in check. This is the reason I didn't want her here. I wanted her completely unaware of me until the time was right to strike. I don't need her trying to make friends with students here who will help her for favors. That's a slippery slope to go down, and most people don't make it out alive when that happens. One small favor turns into five quickly.

I had it all planned out. She would have gone to college, somewhere prestigious, and I heard she got into Dartmouth —no doubt thanks to her dad. I'm not saying she's not smart, because I know better than to think that; but the massive donation to the school had more to do with an acceptance letter than her grades and extracurricular activities. I'm sure of that. She would have gotten a degree in business or political science, as most politician kids do. Then would complete an internship with her father, the *senator*. Fast track to a good life. A Husband that her father set up for her, white picket fence, dog, and two kids. Then I'd rip it all away from her just like he did…

I don't know if she remembers me or not, but I

remember her. The pretty girl in the summer dresses with an ear-splitting grin on her face. Her shrieks of laughter always brought a smile to my face. It was always few and far between, but I remember her. Our fathers used to work together once upon a time. I use the term "work" loosely. They were acquaintances, for the purpose of expanding each of their careers. My father was throwing money at Michael, helping him with his campaign and advancing his political career. In turn, Michael had the cops look the other way when there were new deliveries that had arrived. It was a win-win for everyone. Until it wasn't. I scowl, locking the horrible memories back up to focus on my task at hand.

"Zander, stop!" Ava's voice comes from behind me. "We haven't gotten to finish breakfast, and there's still time before classes start." It's then I realized I haven't made it far outside of the cafeteria. I'm distracted. *She's* a distraction. And one I can't afford. I turn to watch the scene unfold in front of me, and it's nothing less than a circus act.

Zander holds Riley firmly by the upper arm, marching her toward her class, while Ava practically runs to catch up. What's strange is Riley isn't making a fuss. She allows Zander to drag her across the quad like a rag doll, like it's no big deal, with a big smile on her face.

Not the reaction I had expected. Although, I wasn't expecting any of us to have to manhandle her, either. Zander isn't the type to interact with anyone unless he has to. So something happened that forced this reaction.

Wesley brings up the rear, his fingers flying over his phone, unaware of me several yards away.

WESLEY:

You sure you want this one?

ME:

Yes. What happened?

WESLEY:

Zan marched up to the table to take her to class, and she propositioned him in front of the entire school. I've never seen the guy flip so fast!

Zander marched up to the table? Wesley would make sense, but not Zan. Ever since the bonfire he's been acting… differently. He walked her home and then spent the rest of the night in his room; the party forgotten. Honestly, I think we all wanted to do the same; but Wes and I played host and mingled until it was time to kick everyone out. I had lost too much time in my room with her, and not enough time working on connections. I have my sights set on a few people for odd jobs here and there, so it's a good thing I stayed. Getting picked to help with tasks is an easy way into our good graces, and almost all the students know it.

"Which one of you said I was off limits?" She yells. Her anger has my head snapping in her direction. As if she can feel it, she locks on me. She doesn't even have to search for me. It's like she just knows I'm there. "Which one of you made me the school slut?" She tugs against Zander's grip, but he doesn't let go. I know how strong he is from fighting classes and from sparring with me on the mat. She's going to be bruised tomorrow. I take a few steps closer to them, stepping out of the shadows from the tall trees lining the walkway. "Let go of me," she bites out, staring daggers at Zander, struggling to free herself once again.

He leans down and whispers something in her ear that has her stopping momentarily, taking a shuddering breath. She licks her lips, a flush creeping up her neck and settling on her cheeks. Then tugs at her arm again. This time he releases her, and she rubs the spot his hand just occupied. I raise my brow in question, watching the exchange. What did he say to her?

No one challenges me. My first year here, people tried, but they only made that mistake once. It's easy to be known as the best when you are, and prove it every day. I'm cocky, but also truthful. Blood pumps through my veins quickly, making my vision cloud. I clench my jaw, muscles and veins popping as I feel like a caged bull before being set loose. She drives me insane, scrambles every thought I have. "I did." I finally answer her question, taking a few steps closer. "You don't belong here, Princess."

She laughs and shakes her head. "You say that a lot. I didn't want to come, remember? I didn't have a choice." Her voice is taking on a high pitch now. "Anyone ever tell you that you're an idiot, Julien? Or am I the first? You just gave every guy here a free pass to do what they want to me, to get to *you*! Wesley told me not to trust people around here. That they only want what's best for them." She makes a flashing motion with her hands in front of her. "News flash, asshole, you're top dog." She gives a dry chuckle, "and now they know you have a weakness."

That's where she's wrong. I don't have a weakness, especially not her. I have a plan. One that I will see through, no matter what. I step even closer now, trapping her between Zander and me. Unless she pushes past us, she has no means of escape. Even through my anger, I can register her sweet scent. She smells amazing and my body responds. I'm standing so close I can feel the heat and annoyance coming off hers as I lower my voice. "I don't have a weakness."

She narrows her eyes in challenge. "You're wrong, Julien. I am."

I clench my jaw, and my nostrils flare as I reign in my temper. Reaching my hand up, I thread it through her hair, tugging her head back to look directly into my eyes. She lets out a squeak of surprise, but flattens her lips together, keeping quiet. I like the submission a little too much. She's short to my six-one frame and too many dirty thoughts flash through my mind in a split second.

"You're mine, Riley. Mine to torment and break. I'm going to love watching you fall." She's a pawn. That's it. One that I need to get what I want. She's nothing more than a means to an end. Then why the fuck did you put a no touch rule out there? My inner thoughts betray me, which only adds to my annoyance. "Get to class, Riley, and don't do anything stupid." Then I decide to add, "Anything *else*, stupid."

I storm away from her, ignoring the whispered insult she tosses my way. Jesus, it's been three days since she's been in my orbit and I can't seem to get away from her. I also don't want to. She's the sweetest form of torture and is keeping me on my toes. Each insult that flies from her mouth only makes me want to punish her more. She needs to be brought to her knees. And if Saturday night is any indication, she wouldn't mind at all. I run my hand through my dark hair and scowl, shaking the thoughts from my head.

Stella's close by, watching the entire scene with interest. She cocks her head to the side and blinks rapidly up at me; but I brush past her. I don't have time to deal with whatever she's thinking she saw. She's not my girlfriend and never will be. She's an easy lay, and she's gotten too cocky over the past year thinking the rules don't apply to her. Stress has knotted my back muscles into a painful, rigid mass, and I'm on the verge of snapping. As soon as classes are over, I'm going to spend the night in the basement with the heavy bag, working it over until my limbs are heavy and my mind quiets down.

This weekend is the first fight night at Contend, the underground ring, and I've already put my name in. It's the first one of the school year, so it's bound to be a good crowd.

The underground world of the corrupt at its finest. There's a lot of money to make in the ring, and I know I'm a crowd favorite. The moment I saw Riley step on campus, I knew I'd use it as an outlet.

Zander never gets in the ring, but occasionally Wes needs to let off some steam and sign up for a fight or two. Usually it's after having an unpleasant conversation with his father, Christos. He doesn't talk about why he hates his father so much, but I have a few guesses. All of which I keep to myself. If he wants me to know, he'll share. Same with Zander. All three of us have our own reasons for coming together, despite their father's wishes. Alec wasn't as upset. His only advice was to make sure they were trustworthy. After the three years we've been together, I can say without a doubt they are like brothers to me and I trust them with my life. We work well together, and I'm a lucky bastard to have found them.

I step into the classroom, and the noise dies down to barely audible whispers. All eyes are on me as I take a seat in the back, dropping my bag to the floor with a plop and place my laptop on the table. Old habits die hard. I don't allow people to stay behind me for long periods of time.

I hardly concentrate in my first class of the semester, not that I care. Grades are pointless here. While we get a pass or fail, those grades only matter to those who sent them here. It's an easy way to place people within the organization. Those who are pure muscle get used as personal protection guards, or second in command. While those students with business sense get sent into mainstream jobs, less likely to get them killed.

Where the hell does Riley get off talking to us like that? Why does she get me so damn riled up? I take notes, but I'm not paying attention to anything Mr. Krativa is saying. It's all auto-pilot. This is the only class I have where I'm stuck at a desk, and I can't wait to be done with it. Studying isn't what's going to put me on top when I'm out of here. It's a tough world and the connections I've made here, along with my smarts, are what will make me reign.

I don't know how I'm going to survive this year with Riley here. The thing is, Michael has no clue who I am, or that I'm here. If he did, I'm positive he would have kept his precious daughter as far away from me as possible. I don't remember Riley being this pig-headed and combative, though. I remember the sweet smiles and shy girl who tripped over her own words. This girl, she's new. And as much as she's pissing me off, she's turning me on in equal parts. This back and forth is the best kind of foreplay. I crave more. I want to know how far I can push until she breaks.

I haven't heard from Zander yet, and his radio silence is eating me alive. It's not that I particularly care how her class is, but it's the not knowing that's killing me. I have eyes and ears around here. I have enough hungry men that are working for me in secret who would do anything to move ahead.

Me:

Update?

ZANDER:

She's fine. Made her sit next to me. Taking notes. Nothing of interest.

Me:

Make sure she doesn't go anywhere without you or Wes.

ZANDER:

Wes is taking her to her next class.

A new message pops up from an unknown number.

UNKNOWN:

Stop messaging about me like I'm not stuck right next to him. You've got a question. Ask me yourself.

I make it a point to save her number in my phone, unsure why I didn't ask Zander for it when he got back last night. Again, she's distracting me. That should have been the first thing I asked for. There are a million different questions I could ask her, but there is only one burning a hole in my brain.

ME:

Did you touch that pretty pussy of yours after the bonfire even though I told you not to?

I sent her on her way, wet and horny, knowing I'd be the cause of her discomfort. I wanted to do so much more than I did, including taking her. I replayed every second of what happened between us. Come morning, I had no choice but to take care of it in the shower, hand wrapped tight, still thinking of her. It did nothing to dispel the need I have coursing through me. And while I want to fuck her, I want to fuck with her more. She will remember me long after I forget her.

The dots appear and disappear multiple times before she finally responds.

RILEY:

Mmm, sure did, cupcake.

Cupcake? A grin tugs at my lips, not only because of the stupid nickname, but because I got her so horny she couldn't help it. She touched her needy cunt because I wouldn't let her come. I harden and tug at my pant leg, readjusting myself in my seat. I wonder if she was loud, or if she had to muffle her moans of pleasure to keep from being caught. What did she think about when she came? I know I thought of fucking her hard against the shower wall, making her come all over my dick. I roll my eyes at my thoughts. Again, she's a fucking distraction.

ME:

> Sounds like you're in need of some punishment for disobeying an order. Better not let me catch you alone.

RILEY:

> Sounds like you're annoyed I didn't listen to you. Don't worry, I wasn't thinking of you when I came so hard I blacked out. Now leave me alone. I need to get Zan to sleep with me. Can you believe he turned me down in front of a room full of people? How rude is that?

This time I can't help the smirk that takes over as I shake my head in disbelief. Has she always been this feisty? I slide my phone into my pocket and place my hands on top of my head. I'm not sure what I was expecting, but that answer sure as hell wasn't it. Even if she wasn't thinking about me when she came, that doesn't mean I wasn't the cause of it. Then another thought takes hold. I guess Wes will keep her occupied because Zander won't want to babysit Riley after today.

I find Derek after class surrounded by a few other new half wits. He stands taller as he sees me stalk toward him. "Julien Azarian, it's nice to see you again."

"A word." I say, leaving no room for discussion.

"I'll catch you guys later." He slaps one guy on the back, a wide grin splitting his face. They walk off, and I glare at their backs until I know we're alone. There are ears all over this place, and secrets don't stay that way for long when conversations are held in the open. I step into his space, inches from his face and seethe. "What the fuck do you think you're doing?"

He pushes me back and fixes a strand of hair that's fallen out of place, like the pompous asshole he truly is. "I was going with the flow. She kissed me. I reciprocated." He gives me a once over. "Looks like she's getting under your skin."

"I hired you to watch her and report back if needed. Not to stick your dick in her." I knew it was a mistake to trust him, but when he approached me at the bonfire and said he was working to get into my good graces, I figured I'd give him a simple task. How much can one screw up watching someone? I severely underestimated his stupidity.

"Didn't realize pussy was on the table."

"Not. Hers." I grit out as my molars grind together in anger.

My patience is wearing thin with this guy. He's already messed up the one task I gave him. His friends are mentally patting him on the back, thinking he's a badass for standing against me. I know we aren't one hundred percent alone, but they won't be able to hear everything. They don't know the deal we worked out at the bonfire. But this fucker needs to know his place. I put my hand on his shoulder and shove my fist in his face so hard his head snaps back and he falls to the ground with a groan. *God, that felt good!* I stare down at him, flexing my fingers, watching the blood drip down his chin. He sits on his ass, stunned, as he shakes his head, and flops his mouth open and closed like a fish. I sink to my haunches and drape my arms over my knees.

I lower my voice, knowing he's the only one who will hear me. "If she puts her hands on you again, I'll break your fucking arm." He nods his head quickly and wipes his nose on the sleeve of his jacket. "Now get up, you're coming with me. Looks like someone else needs to learn a hard lesson."

TWELVE
RILEY

Zander practically throws me in Wes's arms when he arrives and walks in the opposite direction without so much as a word. Thank goodness Wes has no problem holding me, otherwise I may have landed face first on the sidewalk. Wes wraps his arms around me with a shit-eating grin on his face.

"Ouch, Zan. No goodbye kiss?" I ask with a fake pout. Zander doesn't even give me the satisfaction of responding, just keeps walking. I smirk to myself when I see him shove his balled fists into his pants before others obstruct my view of his retreating form.

"I'll give you a kiss, Hellcat."

"I'm sure you would, Sugar Plum." He laughs and shakes his head. Out of all of them, Wes is the easiest to get along with. He's a go with the flow kind of guy and I enjoy his company. He's hot and funny. What's not to like? I'm sure if Leah were here, she would tell me to hit that, even if his buddies were trying to make my life a living hell. Well, one friend. Zander hasn't said or done much to me. It only seems to be Julien, who has a stick up his ass.

"Sugar Plum?" he asks, amused.

"Oh yes. Since you three like nicknames so much, I figured I'd give you each one of your own. Want to know Zander's?" Wiggling my eyebrows in anticipation and wait. He circles his fingers along my spine and nods, that sexy as sin smile still plastered to his face. Wriggling out of his grasp, I put a step between us. I don't need dirty thoughts to run through my mind, and his touch is affecting me. I clear my throat and focus on the conversation again. "*Daddy.* I just know he loves it." I clasp my hands behind my back, clasping my fingers and pushing my chest out proudly as I sway side to side, a big grin on my face.

The sound of Wesley's laugh—rich, deep, and undeniably sexy—sends a jolt of arousal through me, and I instinctively squeeze my thighs, trying to regain control of my body. How is that even possible? It's a laugh. It's not like he's touching me. Why can I not get a handle on my sex drive around these men? They're bullies. All three have already made it known I'm not welcome here. Yet, I keep finding myself drawn to them. This isn't normal, it can't be. There's got to be something in the air that's making me go crazy.

"I'm sure he loves that."

He drapes his arm over my shoulder and directs me away from the buildings. I stiffen under him, the playfulness from moments ago gone, and a bad feeling settles deep in my gut. My class is the other way. I remember because I mapped out where it was yesterday with Ava. Going anywhere alone with the Kings is a bad idea. I look around for some help, but no one seems interested, keeping their heads lowered or turned away instead. I push against him, but he continues to move us forward as if I were an insignificant gnat. Aside from collapsing like a sack of potatoes, I don't think I'll be able to stop him.

"Where are we going?" I ask when we step into the

parking lot. There are a handful of cars, most of which belong to the faculty, but there are some students milling around other vehicles. The flashy ones make me roll my eyes in annoyance. It doesn't surprise me that wealth loves company. I'm sure there are many spoiled brats here. So are you, my brain reminds me. I like to think I wasn't this pompous. Do you really need a bright yellow Lamborghini Revuelto in a small town close to the White Mountains? The roads can get slick, and I'm not sure a sports car is the smartest choice.

Headlights flash and it snaps my mind back to the here and now. He opens the door to a black SUV for me and leans against the door, his arm slung over the top of it, waiting for me to get in..

"A surprise." He gives me that panty dropping smile again and wiggles his brows like I did to him earlier.

Yeah right. A surprise off the side of a cliff, maybe. I'd be crazy to get in the car with him or with any of them. I can handle a babysitter walking around campus. It's unnecessary and a nuisance, but I can handle that. But, to climb willingly into a car where they can take me to God knows where? That's not happening.

"No thanks. Not big into surprises. I need to get some reading done. The life of a criminal is more studious than I imaged it to be." I step back, preparing to turn on my heel, but he grips my arm tightly, pinning me against the side of the car. The dark metal is warm on my back in the morning sun.

He lowers his head and voice, all traces of the golden boy, gone. His stare is hard, his jaw clenches as the muscles in his neck dance in tune, and he's pressing his hard body into mine, leaving no room to breathe, let alone escape. My brain yells at me to get my ass in gear, but I can't get my body to listen.

"Get in the fucking car," he demands. When I stand there blinking at him, like a deer in the headlights, he adds, "Don't make me tie you up and throw you in the trunk." His eyes turn feral as he presses the thick length of his cock against me, hard and unmistakably ready. A cruel smirk tugs at his lips when my breath catches. "Actually," he says, voice low and laced with menace, brushing a strand of hair behind my ear with disturbing gentleness—a jarring contrast to the threat still hanging in the air. "I like that idea better. Let me tie you up and throw you to the wolves, Riley. Watch what's left when they're done. How much do you think your father would pay for you? I know a lot of skin traders. Keep up this fucking attitude of yours and let's see how brave you are when you're being beaten down, drugged, and fucked in the ass."

My heart thumps wildly and my knees feel like they're going to give out at any moment. I force oxygen into my lungs, but it does little to ease the lightheadedness. Another panic attack is on the brink, and I know I have no option but to force it down. I'm going to be fine, I half heartedly tell myself. He can't know how much his threat affected me. He's joking. Right? His face is stoic, giving nothing away. I press my back into the hard surface, attempting to force space between us. This is the Wesley everyone fears. His easy going persona puts them at ease, but this version signs their death warrant.

"Now I won't ask you again. Are you going to be a good girl and get in, or are you going to be a brat and force my hand?"

He wants me to defy him so badly—and if I weren't terrified he'd follow through on his threat, I might, just to see what happens. He wants to dish out some sort of punishment and his eyes are gleeful at the prospect. I have no doubts he knows people who would use me for blackmail, or to get to my father. Despite my original thoughts of being safe on campus, I know that's not true. There are safeguards in place, sure, but nothing is one hundred percent fool-proof.

I give a jerky nod of my head. Wes gives me enough space to slide past the open door into the seat. Then, when I'm settled, he slams the door closed, making me jump out of my skin. I yelp and cover my mouth, hoping he didn't hear it. He gets into the driver's side and starts the engine without giving me a second glance.

"Where are we going?"

He doesn't answer, just shifts it into drive and peels out of the parking lot. I grasp the door handle to keep from shifting in my seat. No words pass between us. Just his death grip on the wheel, knuckles bleached with tension. *Breathe, Riley*. A rivulet of sweat drips down between my breasts and I wipe my sweaty palms on my skirt. My mind races with my thundering heart, each pulse a threat to my control. Not knowing what will break first, my sanity or my restraint, but something's about to snap. I don't like this. I never should have gotten in the car with him. Nope. I should have called his bluff. Although, deep down, I don't think he was telling complete lies. Wesley is like everyone else here. He has connections to dangerous people who do bad things.

Finally, we make it to the edge of campus when he stops the car and steps out. He whistles as he swings his keyring around his finger, catching the key fob each time it connects with the palm of his hand. Each step around the front of the car brings him closer to me. I sit there, seatbelt still on, when he stops next to me and opens the door.

"Out," he demands.

I look up at him and shake my head. "I think I'm good." A cold dread washes over me. My gut screams at me. When your brain and heart are unreliable, you can always trust your gut. And I sure as hell plan on listening to it now. Nothing good can come from getting out of the car.

With swift movements, he unbuckles the belt and drags me out, my feet getting tangled in my bag.

"No. Let go of me, Wes." I nearly fall on my butt from the force, but right myself at the last moment. I rub my upper arm to soothe the pain of his manhandling. If they keep this up, I'll have a nice collection of bruises on my upper arms from all three of them. He directs me around the back of the car, and that's when I see Julien standing there with Derek. His nose is swollen, and deep purple bruises have formed under his eyes. I don't have a lot of experience, but it looks broken. Derek is also sporting dried blood on his upper lip and scowls at us. Julien, on the other hand, looks as put together as ever. Not a dark hair out of place.

Horror rips a gasp from my lips as I worriedly shake my head. I take a step closer, but Wesley holds me in place. I jerk my gaze up to his and he shakes his head, a frown settling deep on his face. "Sorry, Hellcat. You started this."

I didn't start anything. All I did was stand up for myself from a couple of bullies who are trying to dictate my life. I'm playing the game they've forced me into, so how is this my fault?

He wraps his arms around my body and pulls my back flush with his front. He kisses my cheek, then presses his against mine. "Watch. Julien's a master at this." His deep timbre vibrates my skin, and a dread settles deep in my stomach. My eyes flutter closed, not wanting to watch.

"Tsk-tsk," he warns, and I snap them open.

My pulse pounds in my ears, a frantic drumbeat. Adrenaline surges through me, making every nerve in my body spark. I break out into goosebumps, fear fueling my body in fight or flight. "Master at what?"

"I don't appreciate you trying to fuck with the hierarchy,

Princess. There are rules, but you refuse to listen. Here's a new lesson for you." He shoves Derek forward away from him, but keeps his hand on the scruff of his neck.

My breath comes in ragged gasps as I pant and shake my head. I need to find a place to hide, to get myself under control. I won't survive this panic attack if it's in front of them. When I struggle to free myself from Wesley, he holds me tighter. His arms wrapped around me feel like a boa constrictor. "P-please let him g-go. He didn't do anything." I look at Derek and tears streaming down my face. "Please," I plead. The word meant for Julien, even though I can't look away from Derek. "I'm so sorry Derek." He smiles ruefully. I stare into Julien's darkened eyes. "Just let him go." I pull against Wesley and he grabs my face, squeezing my cheeks with one hand, forcing me to look at the scene in front of me.

"Shhh. Just watch."

Julien grabs one of Derek's fingers and snaps it back so quickly, I hear the crunch as he howls in pain before it truly registers that Julien's broken it. The blood drains from Derek's face and he turns a sheet of green and hunches over, puking in front of him. Julien takes a step behind him to avoid the spray on his legs and shoes.

"NOO!" A strangled cry tears from my throat as tears flow freely down my cheeks. "S-Stop, Julien! Let him go. He-He's innocent. This is on me," I cry out. I clench my teeth hard enough they ache and pull all my strength into my struggle to break free of Wesley's hold. I know it's futile, but I have to try something. So it's no surprise when he holds me tighter. Señor Psycho will kill him if I don't find a way to stop this.

"His blood is on your hands, Princess."

I shake my head quickly. The lump in my throat is so big it's hard to breathe. Or it could also be because I'm hyperventilating.

"Shhh, Hellcat. Be a good girl for me now. It's going to be okay," Wesley coos in my ear, rubbing his fingers in circles where he can touch me. I don't know why, but my panic attack begins to fade. Derek kicks and crawls to scramble away from Julien, but he kicks Derek hard in the stomach and climbs on top of him, straddling his chest. His fists connect with Derek's jaw in a bone crunching way. He tries to curl into himself, but Julien's weight stops him, so he covers his face and lets out a groan of pain with each hit.

A strangled cry forces its way out of me and I slump against Wesley as he supports my weight. I've never felt a desperation so deep before. Derek wasn't supposed to get hurt. I only wanted Julien to have a taste of his own medicine.

"What do you want?" I scream, pulling his attention from Derek. He turns to give me his full attention, his bloody knuckles still suspended in midair. "I'll do anything, Julien. Just let him go." I don't like this feeling of guilt that crawls through me like a bunch of spiders. It makes my skin crawl.

A sinister smile creeps over his face and my heart gallops at the sight. "Run, Princess. If I catch you, you'd better be prepared for the consequences."

Wesley releases me, and I don't hesitate before taking off into the woods. I run as fast as I can through the trees. I've made mental notes of the way we came, so I do my best to follow that trail. The dry leaves crunch under my steps and I duck under low-hanging branches. If I can make it back to campus, I can get help. Even as I think the words, I know they're not true. No one is going to help me against Julien Azarian. Derek's scream of pain in the distance slices through my thoughts and the heavily wooded area, but I don't slow down. I can't. I run as fast as my legs will carry me.

Further.

Faster.

My heart drums in my chest, and my lungs ache as I struggle to pull in enough air. I glance over my shoulder, looking for either of them, but no one is following me. My legs feel like jello as I slow my speed and finally stop, resting for a moment with my back pressed against a tree. I pant, but hold my breath, listening for any signs of movement. My heartbeat is deafening and I swear it can be heard for miles. Leaves rustle to my left and I yelp, taking off to the right.

My legs feel like dead weight, and each step is harder to take than the last. Running has never been my forte. I prefer exercises like pilates and yoga. I can't do this. My heart aches for Derek, and I stifle my cry, feeling awful for the trouble I caused him. I never meant for this to happen. *Why is this happening?*

I scream as I fall to the ground, a heavy weight presses on top of me. He pushes my cheek into the cool earth below, his hand heavy on my head. All I smell is the dirt, leaves, and *him.* My erratic breathing makes it hard to move, hard to fight, but I twist under his weight. My adrenaline kicks up another notch, and I think I might pass out from the exertion.

"Caught ya, Princess." I buck under him, aiming for a bit of space, but he won't budge. Instead, he presses himself down more. "I bet your mouth is good for some other things besides back talk." He flips me over and sits on my chest, pinning my arms above my head, holding tight to my wrists. I'm stretched out beneath him and he puts his face inches from mine. His breaths fan across my face, my body erupting in goosebumps.

"Where's Derek?" I pant, working on catching my breath.

He scowls and narrows his eyes, disapproval written over his face. *Is he mad I'm asking about Derek?* He just beat the shit out of him. Why wouldn't I ask? "With Wes. What happens to him all depends on what choices you make."

"Blackmailing me isn't how you get what you want."

"Mmm," He offers a noncommittal noise. "It is in our world."

Now that, I believe. I'm not getting out of this unscathed.

He rocks back on his haunches before standing and I scramble to sit up. The thought of getting to my feet and running tugs at the corners of my mind, but I know he'll catch me before I make it three feet. He's got height and speed on me. Maybe it's time to take up running.

Towering above me, he unbuckles his belt, letting the leather fall open, then he unbuttons and unzips his pants with a sinister grin, revealing the band of his black boxers. Shivers tingle down my spine as his hand dips down into them. The sleek stretch of his abs is interrupted only by a soft line of hair leading down, disappearing beneath his waistband like an invitation. I watch his movements, his hand jerks up and down, and my mouth salivates. "On your knees," he demands. When I shake my head, defying his order, he reaches down and pulls me to my knees by my hair, then puts his hands on his hips. He looks like a god, towering above me, but I know the devil when I see him. I place my hands on my thighs and wait, staring up into the face of a monster. Tugging my bottom lip between my teeth, I bite down, focusing on the sting.

I *hate* him.

How can he be so calm? And turned on? Is it the violence that excites him, or is it the position he has me in? I blink up at him and lick my dry lips. "Where's Wesley?"

He raises his eyebrow then finally answers. "Around. He'll break Derek's fucking arm if you don't do as you're told. We always have a choice, Riley. This is yours. Pull me out and suck my cock, Princess, or be the reason he needs more medical attention."

My nipples pebble in my bra and my face flames at his request. I pant, blinking back unshed tears. My throat burns from holding them in. His green eyes have darkened, and his menacing stare sends a ripple of shivers down my spine. I break eye contact with him and stare down at the ground, thoughts warring in my mind. If I do this, it means nothing. I'm only trying to protect someone who's innocent in a fucked up game. This whole thing is so messed up. Why isn't anyone from the school stepping in? I can tell someone, though, after this is over. I could do this to save Derek, and then I can voice my concerns with the administration. It's not the best plan, but it's all I can do right now.

"If I do this, will you leave him alone?" I risk a glance up at him. His fists, clenched at his sides, remain still. His face is stoic, but the subtle twitch of his jaw and his flared nostrils are the only signs of his impatience.

He gives a barely noticeable shake of his head. "You're in no position to make demands."

I sigh, releasing a shaky breath, and swallow hard. "You'll leave him alone, Julien. You're mad at me. Not him." I pause, knowing I'm going to regret this. "Use me instead."

"Take me out and suck it," he says through clenched teeth.

I inch closer on my knees, the twigs under the dried leaves biting into my skin. My hands shake as I reach out and pull him free of his trousers. His cock is hard, heavy and thick in my hand. My stomach flips, nerves and arousal pinging back and forth as I mentally prepare myself to do this. It's so wrong to be turned on like this. I give him a few test strokes before I lick the tip teasingly. He sucks in a sharp breath and reaches down to put his hands on my head, lacing his fingers through my hair, gripping me firmly. My scalp tingles from his manhandling and I wince. I part my lips, taking a few inches of him deep in my throat before pulling off and stroking downward with my hand. He tastes salty and some precum leaks from the tip. I lick it off before sucking him deep again.

Arousal wins over anxiety, and my panties dampen as I keep going. Even with his fingers in my hair, he allows me control. I close my eyes, breathing deeply through my nose as I pull him to the back of my throat and try to swallow around him. I cough and gag as my eyes water and I pull off him, stoking him with my hand. In the back of my mind, I register how screwed up this is; him forcing me to suck him off. But for some messed up reason, I don't mind as much as I should. My body responds to him. Each suck and thrust makes me want him more.

"Fuuuck," he groans, gripping my hair, and bats my hand off him. He holds me still as he rocks his hips forward, forcing me to take all of him. He's big, so big, and each time he hits the back of my throat, I gag more, the tears running freely down my face now. I haven't given many blow jobs, and definitely not like this. I've never allowed someone to use me without regard for what I want. And let's be honest, Julien always had the upper hand, and he knew it. I put my hands on his thighs and dig my fingers into the hard muscles, concentrating on keeping the contents in my stomach as he controls my head. I lick all around him as he fucks my mouth with abandon.

"I'm gonna come, and you're gonna swallow. Do you understand?"

I shake my head the best I can as I moan around him. Wanting to taste his salty essence. He's like an aphrodisiac, made just for me. My nipples are painful under my shirt and bra, and tingles run through my body like I've been zapped. I suck harder as he holds me in place. I want this—need this.

He bucks into me two more times before he stills and empties himself down my throat. Trying to swallow around him and start coughing instead. I shove him away; the force causing him to take a few steps back, and gasp for breath, my chest heaving. I'm aware enough to know he's tucking himself back in, but he makes no move to check if I'm okay or to help me stand. When I blink my watery eyes up at him, he glares down at me. There's no hint of remorse on his features.

"Get to class."

"Wait." I reach out to him in a desperate attempt for answers. "Will you leave Derek alone now?"

He offers that dark smile of his again, and his eyes glint with mischief. "I already sent him on his way."

His words are like a blow to the gut. They knock me down, and I sink lower on my knees as my chin trembles and my breathing hitches. I fight down a sob that wants to break free and quickly rub the water under my eyes as a frown settles deep on my face.

He tricked me.

Julien had no intention of hurting Derek more; and I played right into his hand. This was another way to knock me down, to show me he's more powerful, better at playing this wretched game than I am. How could I be such an idiot? He pulls his phone out and turns the volume up, my breathy moans filling the space between us. Then turns it around and I see myself on video sucking him deep, lost in the moment. Tiny moans of pleasure come through the speaker and his groan of pleasure makes my face flame.

He squats down into my line of sight and grabs my face roughly between his thumb and forefinger, squeezing enough to pucker my lips. "Love my souvenir. Step out of line again and I'll send it to the fucking school with a note about the services you offer. You'll have men lined up around the block to get a piece of you." He drops his hand like I'm a piece of trash and stands straight, towering over my petite frame. "And I'll charge a fee. You'll be a true whore in no time."

And then he walks away, leaving me dirty, on my knees, and sick to my stomach.

I'm not sure how long I stay like that, tears dripping on my legs as I try to keep quiet. The panic attack passed a few minutes ago, but I can't seem to get myself to move. I have my knees pulled up to my chest and my arms wrapped tightly around them. How long could I stay here until someone comes looking for me? Would anyone actually care if I went missing? IF I go back to my room, I can bury my head under my covers. I'm such a fucking fool to take them on. I should have tucked my tail and kept my head down like my plan was from the start.

After a while, I hear leaves crunching behind me, the unmistakable sound of footfalls. I don't have the will to move, so I just keep my chin tucked on my knees and pretend I don't hear him. It's not Julien. There's no way he would stick around. And Derek is long gone. I don't think he would be chivalrous enough to come find me after the crap I put him through. So that leaves Wesley.

"Riley, let me help you." Wesley says as he extends his hand in front of me.

THIRTEEN
WESLEY

She glances at my hand but ignores me and stays on the ground, looking anywhere but at me. I need to get her to class, or Julien is going to wonder what the hell happened to us. I waited and watched from a distance as she broke quietly. Her silent screams twisted my gut into knots. But I let her suffer through it alone. Riley is as messed up as the rest of us. Where we suppress everything, she lets it out in the most agonizing way. Painfully, and on full display. I wait patiently, but she doesn't move.

"Are you the start of the line?" she asks, defeated, keeping her eyes trained on the ground.

Start of the line? What's that about? "What are you talking about, Hellcat?"

She scoffs and shakes her head in disbelief. "Like you don't know."

"Pretend I don't," I deadpan, staring down at her.

"Julien made me suck his dick, and he filmed it. Said he'll release the video to the school if I don't toe the line."

The muscles in my jaw tighten as I clench down hard. My hands slowly ball into fists and I take a deep breath in, keeping myself calm. I didn't know *exactly* what he was going to do to her, but I had my suspicions. Julien wouldn't force himself on someone; he's not like that. He's fucked in the head sometimes, sure, but his thoughts on anything nonconsensual matches mine. Our world bleeds in shades of gray, and we stumble through it, numb to the difference. I know what happened today belongs in that same place—where right and wrong don't mean shit anymore, and innocence is just another thing that gets lost. Julien doesn't beg. Especially not for a blowjob. He would have a line of eager mouths, both women and men wrapped around the damn block with a snap of his fingers. Maybe I'm misunderstanding her. God, I hope I am. Because if I'm not, I don't care if he's like a brother to me, I'll bury him six-feet under.

"What do you mean, *made* you? Did he force himself?" I keep my tone even, although I'm ready to pounce, to shake the answer from her.

She glares up at me, her gray eyes painfully sad, and slowly raises her head so I can see the rest of her beautiful face. Her mascara is smudged from her crying and probably her interlude with Julien, but other than that, she seems unscathed. There's no blood, and she appears pain-free, so nothing seems broken.

"No. He gave me a choice. But it was a trick. That's all you assholes know how to do, isn't it? Lie and cheat to get what you want." She dismisses her words with a scoff and a shake of disbelief. Riley rises to her feet and steps away from me when I offer to help her get her balance. "Don't touch me, Wes." Her sullen words offer no bite.

My chest squeezes at hearing those words. It's the first time I can ever remember a girl affecting me this way. She won't push me away that easily. She can't. "Come here." I pull her to my chest and wrap her in a hug, pressing her cheek to my chest. She doesn't move. Doesn't fight. Just stands there and lets me hold her. While she's not hugging me back, she's not pushing me away, so I'll take it as a win. "What'd he say?"

"Suck his cock or he'd break Derek's arm." I feel wetness hit my tattooed arm and I pull away, tipping her face up to me, and wiping the tears from under her eyes. She closes them and takes a shuddering breath. "But he told me he let him go after the fact. He tricked me to get a blowie. He had no intentions of hurting him more, just wanted to embarrass me. Wanted to show me he's smarter than me," she bites off the last word as her anger rears its head again. She tries to shove me, but I hold her tighter. "Just leave me alone."

Julien was done with Derek the moment he told her to run. He gave him some nice parting words that almost made him shit himself. Luckily for Derek, the "no guns outside the shooting range" rule is strictly enforced. Any student found in possession of one would be disciplined harshly. And let's just say fingernails are optional. Plus, his uncle would kill us, literally. But this little run-in won't be more than a slap on the wrist. It's hard when there are so many enemies amongst families. You can only control so much, and sometimes things happen. Derek won't be fucking around with any of us anytime soon, that's sure as shit.

But for Julien to make Riley suck him, and then turn and leave her like a worthless whore, makes my blood boil. She doesn't deserve that. He's as confused as the rest of us, and the uncertainty of the situation makes her an easy target, but we need her. So no matter how he feels, a broken girl does us no good. I hold her tighter and kiss the top of her head, breathing her scent in. *It's going to be okay. I've got you.* The words are on the tip of my tongue, but I don't say them. It's pointless to; she won't believe me, anyway.

She speaks in a low voice, her voice muffled by my chest.

"I wish I'd never met you. Wish you'd all leave me the hell alone."

The words feel like a sucker punch, leaving me breathless and reeling. I huff out a breath and my lips turn down in a frown. Not that she'd know how those words truly affect me. I don't want her to hate me. I've never wanted someone the same way I want Riley. There's something about her that draws me in—I don't know what it is. She's intoxicating. Everything about her screams *mine*!

She traces the pattern of tattoos that are peaking out from under my rolled sleeves. At first it's disinterest, an involuntary tic, and then her movements become more focused. She follows the curves and hard lines of each one she can see. "How many do you have?" she asks.

"Seventeen."

The same age I was when my brother died in a horrific car accident and I became the albatross around my parents' neck. He was the prodigal son, destined to follow in our father's footsteps. He could do no wrong. I was the spare; and my father paid me no attention, especially after he uncovered my true thoughts on the family business.

I shiver and clasp my hand over hers, stopping her exploration. Then push the terrible memories aside and focus on Riley. "We need to get you back to campus."

"Why?" She looks up at me for the first time since I found her and I soften. She draws her brows down and her eyes are bright and glassy from the crying. Even through the hell she just endured, she's still beautiful.

"Because you have classes." I push an errant bunch of hair out of her face and tuck it behind her ear.

"Not that." She waves her hand in front of her face. "Why are you being nice to me? You've been out to get me since the moment I arrived. I have done nothing to you guys. I know I don't deserve to be treated like this."

I hum in reply and gather my thoughts. "No. You don't. But things are a lot bigger than you and Julien."

Without her, Julien's plan will fall apart. Julien thinks it would be best to leave her like a broken doll, but she needs to be whole. She needs to fight along with us, not being dragged behind. The entire situation changed when she came here, and like it or not, how we have her needs to change, too. She needs to learn to fight and carry her own weight. It's going to be a tough road for all of us, especially if we can pull it off; but we won't succeed without her. I can feel it deep in my gut.

She's not accustomed to this world—our world. For her, the worst thing that can happen is coming here. For most students, Pointebreak is the start of their lives. It's how they will survive the darkened world we all come from. Pointebreak hires the best of the best for a reason and she's going to find out the hard way that skipping classes aren't an option. Sick, tired, or hungover…you show up.

"I don't even know what that means, Wes."

"Listen, Riley, I know things here are a lot different from what you're used to. Your dad threw you in the deep end without a life vest, but you'll learn quickly it's sink or swim. You need to keep your head down and your mouth shut. Do as you're told and stop trying to piss Julien off."

"He—"

"No. I don't care. Stop with the self-righteousness and trying to be friends with everyone. They aren't your friends, they're your enemies and will tear you down the moment they can. Everyone here's grown up knowing exactly who they are, and who their families are." I pause and mull over my next words. "If you want, I can help you."

Let me help you.

She sighs and wipes her face, smudging a little dirt along

her cheek. I rub it off and caress her soft skin. She pushes out a harsh breath. "Help me how?"

I grin down at her. "We'll train together. Weights, cardio, agility. All of it."

"Yeah, I'm sure Julien'll love that," she says sarcastically, then licks her lips. I'm achingly aware of the movement and start to wonder what else that tongue can do. "What's in it for you?"

That's a great question and one I can't answer. Well, I fear she won't like the answer. When Riley stepped out of the car and onto Pointebreak campus, the hate radiating off Julien was palpable. The air was electrified and everyone instinctively knew to stay away. He was on high alert, and Zander and I jumped in like we always do. We're equals, the three of us, but we will always follow Julien's lead. Which is why I'm struggling to go against an order from him.

He's wrong about her, though. I just know it. He thinks she's weak, but I want to prove she's not. I want to show him what she can do, and what she's *willing* to do to get what she wants. She's already proved today she's prepared to do what she has to. If we can channel that energy to be directed with us instead of at us, we'd be unstoppable. I can almost taste victory, and it's so fucking sweet.

"The pleasure of your company, Hellcat," I respond smoothly. "Now, get your ass in gear. It's a long walk back to Hampstead Hall for your next class."

She looks behind me. "Where's the car?"

"Julien took it to get to class on time."

She rolls her eyes and crosses her arms over her chest. "What a prick. Leaving you stranded, too."

I smile and bite my lower lip to keep from laughing out loud. So. Damn. Cute. "Naw, I told him to take it. Figured I'd eventually get you to move."

"Oh yeah, and what would have happened if I hadn't?"

She cocks her eyebrow and pops her hip, a bit of her personality coming back.

Ahh, there's the sassy girl I know and like. She's much more fun when she pretends she doesn't care. "I would have flung you over my shoulder and carried you." She opens her mouth, but I cut her off, "and before you tell me, you would put up a fight. I would have smacked your ass every time you were bratty. Maybe even called Zander to redden it a bit," I add seductively with a wiggle of my eyebrows.

She squeaks and blood rushes up, staining her cheeks a pretty pink.

"Glad to see the color's returned to your face. Come on."

I push open the metal door and pull Riley through with me. The room echoes with the noise. All eyes fall on us, but I pay them no attention, looking for Julien at the back of the class instead. I nod to him once, our usual way of letting each other know we're okay, and he glances at Riley, who's looking around with big doe eyes.

"Mr. Scarboro, I have Miss Whittier here. Seems she got a bit lost on her way around campus and I helped her find her way. Please excuse the tardiness," I say, speaking to the large man at the front of the room.

"The Senator's daughter?" he asks, not even acknowledging her.

"Governor. He's running for senator," she replies.

Mr. Scarboro scoffs and smirks at her. "Right. Whatever you say, Miss Whittier."

She glances at me, her brows furrowed in question as she pulls her bottom lip between her teeth, a nervous tic I'm picking up on. I try to give her my best reassuring smile, but afraid I miss the mark when she winces.

"I don't appreciate students who waste my time. Be late again and there'll be consequences." He motions toward the rest of the class. "Join in." Some students are smirking, while others whisper to one another. She looks around the room, probably searching for someone she knows to stand with, when her eyes land on Julien and she scowls.

"Miss Whittier, I don't have all day."

"Sorry," she mutters as she offers a small wave to me and stands alone in a corner, as far from the rest of the students and Julien as possible. Julien has her bag by his feet and I know she notices with the way she keeps glancing at it.

They set up the gym with scaffolding, crates, shipping containers, and various small platforms, all on a padded floor. At first glance, it looks like a giant obstacle course. I remember this class well. Fewer spots to hide, more and more fighting as time goes on. They don't allow guns outside of the shooting range for good reason, and this class is one of them. The Hatfields and McCoys have nothing on some of these families and how deeply rooted their hate is. Survival class isn't required for third and fourth-year students. Those who sign up do so only because someone asked them to, or they find joy in it.

Mr. Scarboro asked for Julien, and Julien made damn sure Riley was with him. I wish I was in this class with her. Julien's going to go after her again and again, and she will not be ready for him…yet. Once I'm through with her, she will be unstoppable.

FOURTEEN

JULIEN

"Now, as I was saying. Welcome to survival. This class is going to get harder as the semester goes on." Mr. Scarboro starts his speech up again, but I don't listen. This class tests students' abilities, and what better way than letting upperclassmen, with more experience "help"? Mr. Scarboro asked for me specifically, and I made damn sure Riley would be here. The easiest way to break her is to constantly keep her off balance.

Mr. Scarboro and my dad work together, and I know he was placed in Pointebreak to keep tabs on me. Again, it's amazing what that man can accomplish behind bars. He's been in jail for eight years now, but he always has eyes on me. I know I'm luckier than Wesley and Zander in that department, but it doesn't mean he's always been so great. Like any man who's in his line of business, he's not always the easiest to deal with, but at the end of the day, he's my father and I need him.

I clench my jaw and mentally shake myself, not wanting to go down a dark path again. Those intrusive thoughts have been creeping in more frequently these past few days, and I know it's because of Riley.

"You need to always be on your toes and keep your wits about you. This class is going to be one of the hardest you have throughout your time here, but it's crucial to learn these skills."

I stare at Riley and she bites her bottom lip, shifting her weight uncomfortably from foot to foot. She keeps her eyes trained on the teacher, listening to him, and I know the moment she senses I'm watching. She visibly shivers and rubs her arm and turns her head toward me. I cock my eyebrow at her and lick my lips. She turns away quickly and I smirk despite myself.

"You're going to be tested on your current skills, so I know what we need to work on. Look around, think of today as a game—a little hide and seek. Don't get caught. If you are, there will be no fighting today. Let's save that for another day. The key to survival is adaptation." He looks at each of his ten newbies and I'm afraid one or two of them might shit themselves. "There are enough hiding spots if you're creative. You've got a thirty- second head start. I suggest you use it to your advantage. On my whistle."

FWEET

The other ten third and fourth-year students know damn well to leave Riley to me. I made that clear when I put the no touch rule out there. I don't need anyone else thinking they can fuck with her for fun—that's *my* job. The first-year students run, searching for a place to hide, but we stalk them, watching their every step. Some have had training, it's obvious, but my princess hasn't. She stands there, seemingly frozen in place, watching the others scramble to find a spot.

"Whittier, move!" Mr. Scarboro bellows at her. She jumps out of her skin and runs to the back of the room and behind some crates. He blows the whistle again and off we stalk to catch our targets. I'm so focused on Riley, it's like I can smell her vanilla and cherry scent as I move swiftly in the same direction.

"Come out, come out wherever you are, Princess." I tease. I slam my hand on top of a crate that I suspect she's crawled into, but there's no sound and when I look inside, it's empty.

Hmmmm…

I close my eyes and breathe deeply. The screams of the other students send goosebumps skirting over my skin as they're caught like prey and brought up to the front of the class again. I tilt my head and hear a quiet squeak of a shoe behind me. Turning quickly, I look up, down, and all around for the source of the sound.

"I know you're close, Riley. I can smell you—smell your fear. Or maybe it's arousal. Are you turned on by this little chase?"

I know I am. This cat-and-mouse game is the best kind of torture, and even though she's already sucked me off, the thought of having her on me again starts a flood of heat at the base of my spine. I would love to chase her through the woods again. My cock was so hard it was painful. It was the best type of foreplay, and I'm looking forward to getting a repeat.

"If I find you, are you gonna use that pretty little mouth on me again? Maybe this time I'll come over your face and really show this school who you belong to."

More yelling permeates around me as students are caught. If I had to guess, I'd say we're down to two. I check my watch. Three minutes to spare. This is too easy.

A metal clang in the shipping container next to me draws my attention back to the task at hand. There are no hand-holds, so I know she hasn't climbed up or on the back of it. No. She's inside. I lay my hand on the opening and pry it open slowly until her beautiful face comes into view. She's crouched down, her fingertips resting on the ground and her feet are under her, ready to pounce. She runs at me full speed, probably expecting to knock me on my ass and get away.

That would work, except I'm used to men twice the size of her attacking me. I easily grab her around the waist and hoist her over my shoulder, bringing the two of us to the ground in a body slam to the mats. She gasps and attempts to suck in some air until finally she sucks in a sharp breath, her eyes going wide in fear. I knocked the wind out of her, and I know that feeling all too well. She claws at me, trying to gain purchase and escape my grasp. I pin her, the full weight of my muscular frame pressing her into the padding beneath us.

"Caught ya," I mock, my voice low and menacing.

The final whistle blows as Mr. Scarboro walks up to us. "I said no fighting, Whittier."

She digs her short nails into my biceps as her chest presses against mine with every labored breath. Lowering my head, my breath hot against her ear, I groan, pressing my hips against hers, using them to pin her further. I want to bury myself in her tight heat. It would be so easy to push her panties aside and slide in. I'm rock hard now and I know she feels it. My dick pulses with each inhale, begging for me to take her. Her core is like liquid fire. I can feel it through her panties and my pants.

"I was trying to run past him," she pants.

I ignore Mr. Scarboro and whisper, "Do you know how easy it would be to fuck you like this, Princess?"

"Azarian, get up."

"Saved by the whistle," I taunt, and I stand, readjusting myself so only she can see. Then turn and walk to the front of the class, making her pick herself up off the floor, not for the first time today.

I loosen my tie and pull it off as I walk into the house. Zander comes into view as I round the corner into the kitchen. He has a half eaten plate of food in front of him as he focuses on his MacBook, typing away quickly.

I reach into the fridge for a drink and turn toward him, leaning against the counter.

"What is it?"

"I'm tapping into the school video feeds for her building to watch her comings and goings," he supplies without stopping his aggressive typing. He'll have access to those cameras in no time. The cameras weren't part of the original plan. That changed the moment she pulled her stunt this morning. We need eyes on her as often as we can. I'm surprised he's working down here, though, and not up in his dungeon of a room. He has multiple computers and screens, among other…things.

He drowns in work when he has something on his mind. I'm about to ask him when the front door slams open and rattles the shelves.

"Julien!" Wesley yells out in anger. I step into his line of sight and he marches into my space, toe for toe. Wesley's not a small guy. He and I match for height, but I overpower him in the muscle department. He's strong, and can hold his own against me, but I can still knock him on his ass if I have to. Out of the three of us, he's the only one who sometimes wears his heart on his sleeve. It helps keep us more human, but it's also a bitch when directed toward us, like right now.

"You took a video of her?" he seethes.

Zander's gaze dart between us, his lips drawn in a tight line.

I push him away from me and narrow my eyes. "Blackmail. She needs to watch herself, and now I have something to use." I cross my arms over my chest and stand tall. "Besides, you're the one who came up with the brilliant idea of making her suck me off. Don't walk in here all high and mighty. If I didn't know better, I'd think you're jealous."

Zander watches us closely, but knows well enough to let us solve this on our own. When you're like brothers with your best friends, it's not always smooth sailing. We have spats from time to time. Usually, a few rounds in the gym with our fists and we can work out any argument.

"Oh, that's some bullshit and you know it, Julien!" He gets in my face again, but this time pushes me. I stagger back a few steps, but regain my balance quickly. I've known Wesley for three years, and I have never once seen him *this* upset. Especially over a girl. "When I said she should suck you off, I was joking and you damn well know it. Any girl in this place would give her left tit to say she's done that to you. I never thought you'd use it as punishment, though."

I didn't know it either. "Well, now you know."

My phone buzzes in my pocket, and I look at the screen. It's dad. "I need to take this, but you and I aren't done here. Get your head out of your ass, Wes. She's a means to an end, not your fucking queen."

I accept the call as I storm up the stairs to my room.

"You've heard?" I ask as I slam the door behind me.

"I've heard. Michael's a fool for sending her there. I'm not sure what he's thinking," my dad, Alec says. "Keep her close, Julien. I'm working on a plan, but I need you to be patient with me. I've sped things up to keep the upper hand."

I sigh and rub my forehead. "I know."

"I'll be out of here before you know it. Keep up the good work. I'm proud of you, son."

My chest aches at those five brief words. It's been a long

time since I've heard them. Alec isn't big into affection, but he has his moments.

"Thanks, Dad," I murmur.

He disconnects the call before I can ask more questions. Phone calls with him are always brief on time and short on words. Too many ears tapped into each phone call. He'll send word through someone else with the updated plan. I need to hold tight for now, even if it kills me to do so.

I change into a pair of elastic waisted shorts and wrap my hands, fully intending to unleash all my anger out on the boxing bag in the basement. I'd appreciate a sparring partner, but afraid Wesley would kill me. And Zander is more of a hands-off guy, for good reason.

The doorbell rings just as I make it to the bottom step and I yank the door open to find Stella there on the other side.

"Hey, sexy. How was your first day of classes?" She walks in like she owns the place and sits down on the couch as if I invited her in.

She's more of a pain in my ass than usual. "What do you want, Stella?"

"What? I can't stop by to see my boyfriend?" she asks, inspecting her nails like I've scorned her.

"You're not my girlfriend. You're just a girl I fuck," I correct her.

She perks up and purrs, "Oh, is sex on the table?" She takes in my appearance, walks to me, and puts her hands on my bare chest, squeezing the taught muscles in my pecs and adds, "I can help you work out some of that stress, big boy."

With deft fingers, she undoes the top buttons on her blouse until I stop her.

"Leave, Stella."

She pouts, "Baby, don't be like that."

Stella wraps her hand around the back of my neck and pulls me down. She tips her head back and brushes her lips against the shell of my ear. I can smell her perfume and, for the first time in my life, it makes me want to gag. It's sickly sweet and rancid all at the same time. How did I ever find her attractive? Everything about Stella screams, "look at me" and I can't stand it anymore. She's good in bed, that much is true, but other than that, I couldn't care less about her.

"Let me suck your cock. I know how much you like it."

I grab her upper arm and drag her to the door. She gasps in shock as I all but toss her ass first onto the porch. "You're not welcome here anymore, Stella. Come here again and you'll wish you hadn't."

She tries to speak, but I slam the door in her face and lock it before heading down into the basement where we have our own personal gym set up. Weights and benches in one corner and a sparring mat with a hanging bag in another. It's simple, but everything we need. I put my head-phones in and blast rock music, drowning everything out.

I hit the bag, gently at first, warming up my muscles.

Cross. Jab.

Cross. Jab. Uppercut.

Each hit gets progressively stronger. And the more I think about Riley, the more worked up I get, hitting the bag. I can't get her out of my fucking head. I need her out. She's fucking up all my plans. My arms scream in pain, but I push harder and harder, ignoring the burning until Wesley spins me around. The satisfying thud of my fist on his jaw snapping me out of my haze.

Oh shit.

I yank my earbuds out and extend my hand out to help him stand. Red stains my hand wraps, and I feel the raw flesh burning underneath. "Sorry, man. I was in my own head."

He stretches his jaw and rubs it, glaring daggers up at me, then finally allows me to help him stand.

He motions to my bloodied knuckles. "You need your hands for this weekend's fight. Maybe use gloves next time, asshole." I snort. Yeah, probably would have been a good idea. They are going to be sore the next few days, but I'll survive. "I'm training Riley. And before you say anything, I think it's a good idea." *Doubtful.* "Look, we need her on our side and pushing her away is gonna make her fight us more. We need her willing, not scared."

I toss his words around in my mind. I liked scared Riley today. She turned me on more than anyone ever has. It's obvious she's still the same girl I knew. I'm the one who has changed and I hate to admit it. It's easier using her as the scapegoat to hide my true thoughts. Having her with us and not fighting us would make things easier, and dad said to keep her close. But I know I can't get attached to her. At some point, I'm going to have to make a hard choice, and she can't be one of them. There's no room in my life for her kind of distraction.

"Fine. Train her. Fuck her. Do whatever the hell you want with her, Wes. But do *not* tell her anything about us. That's an order."

With a slow, sly smile, he raises two fingers in the air. "Scout's honor."

FIFTEEN

RILEY

My last class of the day was an accounting class. *Yay, more numbers.* The saving grace is Ava's in that one with me, so I don't have to sit alone. It's hard being a pariah when I used to be more of a social butterfly. Guess I'm learning new lessons all around.

Trickery.

Mockery.

Lust.

I shake that last thought right out of my damn mind. It's been hard enough to concentrate today without adding thoughts of the three Kings to the mix. I can't believe Julien tricked me into sucking him off. I'm so angry with myself. Angry that he could convince me so easily, but I'm more upset over the fact that it turned me on. I tried to talk to Derek after my classes, but he ignored me. To be fair, I'd ignore me too if I had my fingers broken by a crazy man. I'm such an asshole for putting him through that. I didn't think Julien would go as far as hurting someone over a stupid kiss. Although Derek didn't have to go along with your plan initially, my inner voice chimes in.

I take my computer out of my bag, and open a new word document. Julien left my bag on the floor in survival class for me. I didn't dare try to take it until he gave me one last sneer and walked out of the doors. Even now, I'm nervous he tampered with it, but I don't have an option. I need to get some stuff out to Leah. She's been champing at the bit. I'm sitting in the library in a corner booth away from prying eyes. Who ever would have thought a place like this would have a library. It's not as large as other college type campuses, but it will do. It's quiet here and allows me a reprieve from…everything.

My phone buzzes with an incoming text. Ava added me to a group chat with Nick at some point today and the two of them have been talking. I'm pretty sure she's added me to make her feelings for him less obvious, but I don't mind. I'll take any friend I can get. Most of the girls around here seem to hate my guts, and the guys keep their distance. Like I said…pariah.

NICK:

How was the first day of classes?

AVA:

Good, but tiresome. I had shooting lessons today. My dad's made me take them already and I'm a decent marksman, so I may get to drop it or move up to a higher level.

NICK:

Well done, Ava! That's great to hear. How about you Riley? Okay day?

ME:

I survived, so that's something. Loved getting chased by my nemesis, that was a blast. :/

NICK:

Oh yeah, those survival classes can be brutal, but you'll make it through. Who do you have?

ME:

Scarboro.

NICK:

Don't be late and you'll do fine. Hang in there!

Yeah, solid advice. Just a few hours too late, unfortunately. Ignoring the insistent buzz of my phone as they text back and forth, I put it down. I need to get more information for Leah. I quickly jot what I recall from conversations with Ava this weekend and about my classes today; the chase through the woods at the forefront of my mind. Do I add that? Am I ready for Leah to know about that? I know she would freak out, and not for safety concerns. She would want all the sexy details and squeal in excitement. I know my best friend too well.

My body trembles with the memories of today. The smell of Julien, his firm muscles pinning me down, not once, but twice. Then there's that small tidbit of how he tasted, and it wasn't completely unpleasant. I've never let a guy come down my throat before. Not that I've had many opportunities, either. I rub my thighs together to ease some of the pressure building. It's a dangerous game, getting involved with them—bending to their will. But in a sick, twisted way, I want to.

What is wrong with me?

I shake my head, clearing my disoriented thoughts. Rereading what I have, I remove all traces of the chase. Leah doesn't need to know my confusing thoughts about Julien yet.

Or Zander.

Or Wesley.

I'm not ready for anyone to. I finish and save my file, then shoot it off to Leah in an email. I hit send, my heart pounding, fearing an immediate alarm and subsequent arrest. I know I'm being stupid, but with all the unofficial rules at Pointebreak, I'm sure sharing their secrets is frowned upon.

When nothing happens, I sigh in relief. Julien, Zander, and Wesley are probably the best angle for the piece. Leah could expose the school, but also the unofficial rulers. I bet the administration would turn a blind eye if one of them asked. I laugh to myself and shake my head before sighing. *Like those three would ever ask for a damn thing.* It's always a demand. I'll tell her eventually, my mind calling me a liar.

I open a new private web browser. Now, what can I learn about the Kings? Social media is always the best place to scout for information. Maybe I should start with Wesley.

He helped me today when he didn't have to. He could have left me there in the woods alone, and hell, I might not have gotten up until the sun was setting. I wanted to curl up into a ball and cry more—have a pity party, but then he showed up. When I told him Julien made me suck him off, it's like he changed for a moment. He was feral, angry. It was...*hot*! Groaning, I drop my face into my hands. I should not be thinking about how sexy it was that he helped me. I'm grateful he came to help, but I shouldn't be relying on him.

The worst I've ever had in my life is a bad date, and even then, James got me out of that when I texted him for help. I've never had to do a thing on my own, not really anyway. Stopping, I ponder that thought. I didn't even reach out to my dad that night. The man who is supposed to protect me. Did I ever tell my dad about the date after? I don't think I did. James is the only one who knows. It was never brought up in conversations, so James never told him either. My relationship with my father is more messed up than I realize. And now, I have to rely on myself. There are no white knights coming to rescue me this time.

Who are Julien Azarian, Wesley Bastian, and Zander Fedorov? Let's find out.

Nothing. After searching high and low for the better part of an hour, I can't find anything about Julien. It's like he doesn't exist. There are no pictures of him, no social accounts, and no mention of his name in any capacity. How is that possible? I thought everyone had a digital trail. I've found plenty of information about who I assume is his father, Alec Azarian. He's serving a thirty-year jail sentence. Considering the school's clientele, it's unsurprising. But it's as if Julien doesn't exist.

Wesley is easy to find. He has pictures of him living the party life plastered all over social media. Random girls, alcohol, and parties fill the dark, colorful pictures. He seems like a party boy, always up for a good time. I spot Zander in a few pictures, but like Julien, he doesn't have any of his own accounts. I started following Ava, and Zander seems to have a soft spot for her and will get in some pictures with her— always brooding, but there nonetheless.

Pictures aren't getting me answers, though. There's not enough information in these small snippets to paint an entire picture. Rubbing my forehead, I feel the dull throb behind my eyes as stress takes hold. I finish my business assignments undisturbed, but I know someone has spotted me when I hear whispers nearby. I glance around to find the source of the noise and I see two girls, heads close together but eyes trained on me. Here's the thing, there are very few of us here. Seventy-five percent of the student body is male. So there are very few women to gossip about and Darcy and Julie already filled me in on the deets this morning.

Heat travels up my neck and settles into my cheeks, and I want to tuck my tail and run. But what good is that going to do me? All that's going to do is give them more ammo to come after me, and I don't need more people trying to tear me to shreds.

"You got something you wanna say to me?"

One girl squeaks and turns, walking swiftly in the opposite direction.

I stare at the other one, who won't take her eyes off me.

"Stay away from him, bitch." She flips her blonde hair over her shoulder and leaves.

"Nice chatting with you," I call out, knowing she can't hear me.

Which "him" is she referring to, though? My guess would be Julien, although with Wesley's playboy persona, it could be him. For some reason, I don't think Zander's the target. I pack up my items and walk to the cafeteria to get something to eat. It's been a long day, and I missed lunch so I'm starving. I text Ava and she said she'd meet me there. I'm sure she'll have a lot to talk about. She's generally pretty chatty. I don't even know how I'd explain my day. She knows a bit because of the group messages, but that was strictly about classes.

"There you are, Hellcat." Wesley jogs up beside me and scoops my hand into his, twining our fingers together. "Good news. I'm gonna be training you."

I tug, attempting to untangle our hands, but when he grips tighter, I give in and let him hold it. "I never said I wanted you to. You only offered."

That ear splitting grin is back. "True, true. But I'm gonna do it anyway. You can thank me later."

"Your master gave you permission?" I dig, smiling to myself.

He pulls us up short, stopping me, and I look into his darkened eyes. His jaw ticks and he swallows hard. All playfulness from moments ago, gone. This is the man the other students fear. "Watch what you say about him, Riley. He's like a brother to me. We're equals, do you hear me?" His bitter voice holds no room for arguments.

I nod my head quickly, a little afraid of the man standing in front of me. "Yes. I understand."

In the blink of an eye the playboy Wesley's back, grinning like we just shared a funny exchange. I'm going to end up with whiplash with his personality changes.

"I'm starving. Let's eat."

We load our plates up; I opt for salad and lasagna, and grab a table in the back of the room. Ava and Nick join us a few minutes later and the conversation flows easily. Well, Ava and Wes keep the conversation going. Nick and I sit quietly and listen intently. Ava tells me about her classes and how excited she is about things ramping up. Nick asks her questions here and there, and she beams every time he does. I notice Wesley watching them closely, and I know he's going to report back to Zander. I open a new text to him.

ME:

> Don't make this a big deal. Ava likes him, and he's nice. They're friends.

WESLEY:

> Not sure what you're talking about.

Sure he doesn't. "Where are the others?" I ask Wes.

"Home. They don't eat here. I usually don't either, but figured we could talk about your training schedule."

"Oh, you two are training together?" Ava asks, taking a bite of her food, a glint of humor in her eyes.

That bastard. "Oh, um, n-no. Well, maybe. I don't know." I shrug, avoiding eye contact, then spear a bit of pasta on my plate but don't lift it to my mouth. Why am I so damn tongue tied over this? It should be a simple no. N-O.

"Yup. Figured I could help Riley get up to speed around here."

I roll my eyes, needing to get away from him and all these conflicting emotions he draws from me. I push away from the table and excuse myself, gathering my things and heading to the door. Wesley follows and steps in front of me.

"Riley, stop. I told you not to walk around campus alone. That's twice now I've caught you disobeying."

"Third time's the charm." My sarcasm has really leveled up since I got here.

"There won't be a third time. Do it again and there will be consequences."

The argument is on the tip of my tongue, but I let it die, knowing I won't win this fight.

I'm unable to sleep. My mind races, a whirlwind of images and sensations from the day, replaying like a broken record. As soon as I shut one thought down, another pops up to take its place. Around and around I go. I want off this merry-go-round before I get sick.

I showered before bed so I can hopefully spend a little more time in bed. I'm tired, but full of energy—a damn oxymoron. So when the door handle jiggles at four in the morning, I sit straight up and pull the blankets to my chin. A scream is on the tip of my tongue, but it's frozen there.

Maybe it's just someone going to pee in the middle of the night and is at the wrong door. No one tries to pound on the door or break it down, but the door swings open slowly. A large figure steps into the room and when he sees I'm sitting up, smiles.

"Training starts now, Hellcat."

SIXTEEN

ZANDER

I heard Wesley leave the house and got up to watch the events unfold. He wants to train her, teach her how to fight and be strong. He told me his plan after his visit to Julien in the gym, where he came back with a nice red mark on his jaw. I want to train her too, but for entirely different reasons.

It doesn't take long for him to make it to her dorm, and even less time to walk out with her. Wesley and Riley step out of her room after a few minutes and she's in a sports bra, tank top and leggings. It's a little chilly this early in the morning, but if I know Wes, he's going to give her a good workout.

"How did you get into my room?" her muffled voice comes through my speakers and I shiver. She does it to me every damn time she talks. Her voice is a melody that seduces even the darkest parts of me.

The cameras don't have audio attached to them, but I put spyware on her phone. When Ava texted me the other day about Riley running off, I went over and installed the program and she's been none the wiser. She really shouldn't leave her stuff lying around. Nothing of consequence has come up, but it's nice to have ears on her. Unfortunately, during classes, I can't listen to her because I'd have my earbuds tossed without a second thought. I'm still working on getting all the cameras linked to my phone, but that's an ongoing project. I'll have access to those soon enough. Until then, I have to watch her in my room, on my three screens.

He says nothing, but then she scoffs. "Really? You made a copy of my key?" she whispers as they walk down the quiet hallway. *Now that's interesting. I wasn't aware he had a key.* I promised Ava I wouldn't make one, but I guess my promise doesn't extend to my brothers. I know he did it to get to Riley, but I'm not sure how much I like him having a key to my sister's room. Wes and I are going to have a little chat about that later.

"Never know when it'll come in handy. Better than breaking down your door, don't you think?" Wes says.

There are times I wish I was more easy going like him. He's a natural with people. He always knows what to say and how to persuade them to do what he wants. Life has dealt us different hands. He grew up differently than I did, which makes him more eager to please people. I protect the few people closest to me. I shake my head, focusing on the video in front of me.

I follow their every move on the cameras, their path interrupted briefly by blind spots until the next one picks up. They don't talk and she blindly follows him. She trusts him. Deep down, that notion does strange things to me. I know about the woods, and about how Wesley came to pick up the pieces after Julien left her there alone. Dick move on his part, but I understand his thought process. Show no weakness. Kindness is a sign of weakness, and Riley was right when she said he painted a target on her back by putting her off limits. I see the way Julien looks at her, and not all looks are the same. There's a longing there. He wants her just as much as he wants to fuck with her.

Wesley starts at a light jog and she stays with him, clearly not expecting the cardio so early in the morning. When he slows his pace to match hers, I can hear a muffled conversation, most likely because of her phone being tucked in a pocket. A few words pop here and there, but I know I won't be able to hear them again until they reach the gym and she puts her phone down.

Her tits bounce with every step and I can't help but wish I could take her shirt off to play with them. They're perfect. I could tell from that damn dress she wore over the weekend where her cleavage was on display. And I still can't believe she propositioned me in front of most of the student body. Jokes on her, though. I would have gladly pinned her against the wall and fucked her brains out. I wouldn't give a shit if anyone was watching. In fact, I'd welcome it. Voyeurism is my favorite kink, not that this should come as a surprise to anyone. I watch everything, so it's a natural craving. Everyone here thinks I don't get involved because I don't want to, but it's because no one can handle my lifestyle choices. Sexually, I know what I like, and I have yet to meet anyone who enjoys the same to the full extent. I'm too…sadistic. Maybe I'm a masochist too, because what other reason do I have to watch the two of them?

When I graduate, I'm opening an exclusive club for pleasures of a more darkened nature. Most people would call it a sex club, but it would be so much more than that. It would be a true reprieve for those who are too afraid to act on their fantasies in an otherwise "normal" setting. It's also a way for me to act out my fantasies with mutual parties who are interested. Exclusive clientele with fat wallets, and willing participants. It's going to make a killing. The guys know what I'm planning and have already agreed to be partners in the business.

Images of Riley bound and gagged, looking up at me, make me stiffen in my shorts. I press my hand over my hardened cock, trying to relieve the pressure that's building. She gave me the worst nickname too, *Daddy*. It's like she fucking knew what I was into and wanted to poke the bear. But to have her call me that under different circumstances, you bet your ass I'd give her so many damn orgasms. I've always preferred Sir, but something about how the word rolled off her tongue. Longing hit too close to home and I had to get away from her. I shoved her into Wesley's waiting arms, desperate to get away from her and my primal urges. No one has ever gotten under my skin before, not like this. Not in a way that makes me want to burn the world and protect her all at the same time. I don't know how to handle these feelings. So it's best to watch from a distance like I always do.

Alone.

I catch sight of them on the camera, almost to the gym. I'm sure he plans on getting her on the mat and pinning her as often as possible. It's best to learn to fight hand-to-hand. After all, most of what she learns this year will be with fists. As she moves through each grade, she'll learn to fight with guns and knives too. Pointebreak turns its students into fighters. That was always the purpose. Learn to hurt, maim, and even kill without a second thought.

Over the years that's changed, especially by letting women into the school. Around here, the women mostly study survival, money laundering, and business. It's the reason Ava's here. I didn't like the idea of her coming to Pointebreak, not with the hardened men who attend, but the idea of her being able to fight and defend herself won me over in the end. Mikhail likes that she's here because then he doesn't have the deal with her right now. She's a pawn, like most women here. I know she's going to be married off some day and I won't be able to protect her in the same capacity. She needs to know how to do that on her own.

If I close my eyes and think back to this weekend, I swear I can still smell Riley. It could also be from the pair of panties sitting next to me. I groan when they reach the mats, just as I predicted, and know I'm going to be in for the show of a lifetime. Her lithe form is lying out on the mat, breathing hard from the exertion of the run. I bite back a groan and try to focus on the cameras and not my sexual fantasy of her tied in that position as I cut every inch of clothing off her.

"Alright, Hellcat, show me what you've got. Try to pin me," Wes says as he pats his chest. I can't see her face in the camera, but her hesitation tells me everything I need. She knows she can't win against him, but she's stubborn enough to try, anyway. She runs toward him and dips her shoulder, aiming for his gut. He easily grabs her waist and lifts her, tossing her onto his back. He gives her ass a playful slap, and I groan when she squeaks in surprise.

"Again," he announces as he places her down.

She huffs. "I'm not going to be able to knock you down, Wes. I don't even know what I'm doing. You haven't shown me anything."

"I want to see your fighting style. Pick out things you're doing well and things we can work on. Try whatever feels right."

Again and again she tries to knock him over, to no avail. I've got to give her credit, though. She tries different moves. Anything she thinks will work. Growling, she turns away from him, a hand on her waist as she lifts the top of her shirt to wipe the sweat from her brow. She's frustrated. Even through the camera, I can read her body language.

He picks up his phone, reads the message, and smiles up at the camera—at me. He knew I'd be watching, so it's no surprise.

He tosses his phone on the mat and focuses on Riley again. This time, he focuses on giving her tips and teaching her how to take down an opponent who is bigger than her. It would still be a challenge, because most men around her have at least fifty pounds, if not more, on her. Dip low, focus on the legs, and if that doesn't work, go for the eyes, nose, and throat. That's the aim. She needs to stay on foot because if she gets pinned in an actual fight, that's it. She needs to use unique skills without having the height or strength of a potential opponent. They practice over and over. She's breathing hard and I know she's going to be sore tomorrow.

My hand moves slowly up and down my aching cock. Watching her attack repeatedly has got to be one of the most erotic things to watch. She drops her shoulder and reaches out for his legs and finally pulls him down.

"Yes!" she shouts with excitement, and I can't help but smile at her.

Good job, Luna.

Wesley lifts his hand and when she tries to help him stand, he pulls her down and rolls them so she's flat on her back under him. He cradles the back of her head and brackets her legs with his own, pressing her down into the mat.

"Once your attacker is down, run, don't stick around."

She drops her head back and groans, her chest rising and falling rapidly in defeat. "What happened to your jaw?" She touches the subtle bruise Wesley got from Julien and he pins her hand down above her head to the mat, ignoring the question.

I've always enjoyed watching others, and Riley is definitely my porn of choice. I can't stand it any longer. It has been pure torture watching them. I pull my dick free from my shorts and wrap my fist tightly around the base, squeezing the tip as I slide it back down again. Over and over. The pressure rises and falls as I edge myself, not willing to give into the climax. Needing to torture myself longer. Wesley stays on top of her and when he lowers his lips to hers in a kiss, my hand speeds up. I imagine I'm there instead, on top of her, kissing her, smelling her. Those whimpered moans for me, and not for him.

Fisting her panties in my other hand, I bring them to my nose, smelling her as I jack myself. I'm out of control and I don't like it. I don't want to be like this. Her breathy moan fills my ears, and I look at the camera again, anticipating seeing them naked, but they aren't. She wraps her legs around his waist and digs her short nails into his back. He's feasting on her and her hands explore every inch she can reach. I'm recording this session and I know this won't be the only time I watch it. He dips his hips into her and I speed up when her moan of pleasure reaches my ears. I can feel my orgasm at the base of my spine growing in intensity.

He drops his head to her ear and whispers something. She turns her head to the camera and stares at me. She doesn't speak it out loud, but mouths *Daddy* at the camera. *That stupid fucking name.* The nickname that's going to be my undoing. I can't keep her close to me after that. I *want* her so damn much and I'm no good for her. Wesley bites her neck and when she bows her back, I come all over myself, her eyes never leaving mine.

SEVENTEEN

RILEY

I break out in goosebumps as I watch the camera. Wesley bites the juncture between my neck and shoulder and I writhe in pleasure, my orgasm washing over me in waves. I can't help the moan that escapes. Wesley said Zander was watching, and it's like I can feel him—his anger. Yet, that's what helped push me over the edge, knowing Zander was watching us this whole time. Wesley presses his weight on me, forcing my hips to stop undulating. I whimper, wanting more. He's still hard as a rock between my thighs. When I reach down between us, wanting to help him the way he did me, he stops me.

"Come with me this weekend," Wesley murmurs in my ear.

Furrowing my brow, I look up at him. "Where?"

"Contend. There's a fight and I want you there with me."

He gives me one more chaste kiss before extracting himself and helping me to my feet. I should be grateful that our little makeout session didn't turn into more. Although he made me come, so I guess it was a bit more than making out.

We're in a public spot and I'm sure students will get up soon enough. *And Zander's watching.* Except Zander is why I want to continue. As soon as I found out he was watching, I became soaked. Things got more heated from there, and obviously stopped with my happy ending.

What is wrong with me? Two men? Is one not enough? Maybe Julien is right, and I am becoming the campus slut. I'm not going to lie, though. I feel like the bragging rights would go a long way. The women around here fawn over the Kings, and that girl on the first day said she'd love to have all three. I shake my head at the thought. I'm being silly and need to get my hormones in check. There's no way it will happen.

My nipples are so hard that even my sports bra can't completely hide them and I know Wesley notices too. I roll my neck and ignore the dirty thoughts running through my head. I stretch my arms overhead and Wes takes one in his hand gingerly.

"You're bruised."

I look at the marks around my bicep and shrug. "What did you think was gonna happen when you three drag me around like a rag doll?"

His face softens, and he places a chaste kiss to each minor mark before interlacing his fingers with mine, leading us out of the gym. A few students walk through doors as we leave, but other than that, there isn't much activity on campus yet.

"What's Contend? I assume some sort of fighting ring, but I'm not supposed to leave campus." He strokes the back of my hand with his thumb and I have a hard time focusing on anything else. I flush as I think about where we were moments ago and how I orgasmed from a little dry humping. *What the hell is going on with me?*

He gives me a lazy smile. "As long as you're with me, you won't get in trouble. Don't worry about it. But to answer your question, it's an underground ring. Amateur fighters, but that doesn't mean it's not thrilling. Lots of cash to be made if you bet on the right fighter."

"Is it in town?" I ask. Barrington doesn't seem like the type of community to accept anything that may fall into a gray area, the current campus not included. And even then, they pretend the dark stain that is the campus doesn't exist.

"At Pointebreak, but there are ways for people other than students to find a way into the fights. You need to know the right people and have enough money for it. It's surprising who shows up at these things."

"On campus? Doesn't the administration have a problem with that?"

A slow grin stretches across his face, crinkling the corners of his eyes. "You're cute, do you know that?" I half expect him to pat the top of my head, but thankfully he refrains.

I wonder if good old dad has been spotted here before. The more I learn about this world, the more I'm convinced he's part of it in some fashion. It's like he can read my mind and offers a small nod of his head. Although maybe I'm reading too much into it.

"Can I bring Ava?"

His smile fades, and he shakes his head. "Zan wouldn't like it. He's already made it very clear we can't involve her in anything."

I roll my eyes and shake my head. "So stupid. She's a legal adult. He can't baby her forever."

"There are things about him you don't understand. Best to let him have his way." He shakes his head. "No Ava."

We walk up the steps to my dorm and he spins me around so we are chest to chest. Even though we both worked up a good sweat, he still smells great. He cups my cheek and lowers his face, brushing his lips against mine. I steady myself by holding his upper arms and press into his kiss, allowing him to control it. It's gentle at first, but then he puts power behind it and I gladly open for him, moaning into his mouth.

I trail my hand down his chest and stomach and when I brush over his length, I'm met with a guttural groan.

He pulls away and I drop my hand to my side as I flutter my eyes open. "Get ready for class. I'll meet you in the cafeteria in forty minutes for breakfast."

I nod in a daze, and find my way up to my room where Ava is awake and showered. She looks at me through her mirror and smiles warmly.

"Looks like Wes trained you after all this morning. Not gonna lie, I'm jealous. It'd be good to learn more of this stuff, so I'm prepared."

I sit on my bed, and she turns to face me. "Sorry, Ava. I had no choice. He snuck in here at four this morning and made me go with him." I yawn and stretch, wishing I could lie down and go back to bed. Although if his training is any sign of what's coming, I'm screwed. "Maybe Nick can help train you. Have you thought about asking him?"

She shakes her head. "No. I don't want to bother him with that. Plus, I'm not sure how Zander would feel about it."

"Who cares what Zander thinks?" I already know her answer before she says it, so it's no surprise when the words, "I do," come out of her mouth. Wesley said he didn't want her involved in anything, but I can't help but think that's going to hurt her more than help her.

I get ready for breakfast as quickly as I can, and I'm starving this morning. I can't wait to eat. Nick meets us in line and we fill up plates with eggs, toast, and fresh fruit. At least the food here is good. I'm not sure what I would do if I had to choke down something less than stellar. We sit down and Wesley pulls a chair up to our table and tosses his arm around me, then kisses my shoulder.

Jealousy hangs in the air like smoke—thick enough to suffocate. The student body watches our exchange along with hushed whispers. From what I've gathered from my web searches last night, Wesley is a playboy and isn't one to be tied down. That, along with the King's stupid no touch rule, and I am target number one around here. Most of the guys are staring at me like I'm some mythical beast, but the girls…they have murder in their eyes. And I'm not sure I'd put it past them to try to take me out in one of these fighting classes. Maybe my shooting class. Oops, sorry, I missed the target. Yeah, no thanks.

I brush his arm off me, embarrassed to be the center of attention, and murmur, "Everyone's staring."

He looks around and when he locks eyes with a table full of girls; he gives them a flirty wink and they all giggle and put their heads together to chat. *And my blood boils.* He can't go around flirting with other girls if he's trying to get in my pants.

"No." I say and he tilts his head. His eyes narrowed, examining me.

"No what, Hellcat?"

"I suppose you don't offer to train all the ladies here?" He shakes his head, confirming my suspicions.. "Then I assume I'm considered special to you."

"You have no idea," he offers quietly.

"Then you're not going to flirt with other girls. You put a no touch rule out there on me. Well," I pause, deciding if my next words are wise to say, "I'm putting one on you. If you want to chase someone else, stop everything with me." I'm not sure why I feel so heated about this, but I do. I refuse to be one of many side chicks. I know I'm worth more than that.

"You're putting a no touch rule on me?" He asks, amusement lacing his words. He laughs when my cheeks redden instead of offering him an answer. Turning to face me head on, he asks, "Are you jealous?"

I cross my arms over my chest and hate that I am. The conflicting emotions I feel toward the three of them leave me confused most nights. I could picture myself with Wesley. He has a way of making me feel wanted and cared for when he's not doing Julien's dirty work. Zander is a man of few words but is intense. I know he stands up for those he loves and would do anything to keep them safe. He's that way with Ava, protective of her. And I have a feeling he would be that way with me, too. The only hint of interest was when he dropped to his knees that first night in the woods and stole my panties. But yesterday's manhandling didn't feel like want. It felt like a warning.

Julien though…Julien I can't figure out. He's messed in the head. Something happened to him to make him this way. Something big. He says he hates me, but the way his body reacts to mine, I know he's lying. And mine reacts the same to his. He turns me on even when he's being a jerk to me. I don't know what draws me to him, but I wish I could carve it out of me before it becomes something I can't escape. We're in this game of tug-of-war and I'm not sure who will win.

"I don't enjoy being played with."

He leans in and whispers in my ear, "but think of how much fun we could have."

My entire body heats as I think about how easy it was for me to come with him earlier today. If it's like that when he's not even trying…what would it be like if he was?

"Orgasm after orgasm, Hellcat," he answers my unspoken question. I suck in a sharp breath and school my features. My lack of poker face is not dealing me any favors. It feels like everyone knows exactly what he's said. I stuff food in my mouth, looking for any excuse to end this conversation.

Ava and I were in class together again this morning, and I was so happy for a familiar face today. I still have weapons, shooting, and a swim class to get through. Swimming seems random, but according to Ava, everyone has to take it. I guess it's good they don't want students to drown. Zander meets me outside of my class and he spends a moment speaking with Ava quietly in what I assume is Russian before turning his stare on me.

"Bye, girl," Ava says as Nick jogs up to her. I hear her laugh and Zander growl.

I spot the moment Zander realizes Nick is trying to make a move on his sister. His stance goes rigid and his muscles flex like he's restraining himself. So I touch his upper arm, stopping him from going after them. He glances at my fingers on his right biceps and glances up into my eyes before looking away again.

"She's fine. He's nice. She said you know his family." He gives a curt nod but doesn't relax. The muscles in his neck strain under his black button down. "Zander. Let her live a little. She wants this too. How much trouble can she really get in?"

He actually looks at me this time. "That depends. Trouble seems to find *you* easily."

"Not because of my doing, *Daddy.*" I emphasize the last word for good measure, just to dig it in a little.

I walk away, feeling good about myself and my witty retort, when he catches up and collars the front of my throat, pulling me flush against the hard plains of his body. Instantly reacting to his touch, heat pools low in my belly. I press my backside against him and extract a guttural groan from his lips. I know I'm not imagining the way he also responds to me. He may be a man of few words, but this situation requires no words.

"Watch it, Luna. Keep that up and you're going to find yourself bound and gagged with no way to escape. I won't play fair, either."

I'm not sure what comes over me, but I can't stop the words that fall from my lips. "Is that a promise?"

His lips are against the shell of my ear as he caresses my throat, cutting my air off just enough to make me wheeze. I lock my hands around his wrist, but I know he won't hurt me. He would have done it by now if he was going to. "Yes," he growls quietly in my ear.

Great. And now I need new panties.

EIGHTEEN

RILEY

I causally slipped the information about the fight to Nick and he asked Ava straight away. It turns out he was going too. He holds a standing invitation and said he attends from time to time. Ava needs to have a bit of fun too, and while a fight isn't exactly my idea of a good time, it's something to do. It gets her out of the dorm and she can spend more time with Nick.

My muscles cry out in agony from my first week of classes and the extra training sessions from Wesley. Thank God Julien tried nothing else in my survival classes. Although, being partnered with one of the girls probably wasn't much better. I had whispered insults slung my way throughout our entire sparring session. I could feel Julien's eyes on me the whole time. Not missing a beat when I escaped someone's grasp. And if I'm not mistaken, I could have sworn I saw a minute smile. And I won't admit this to anyone, but I secretly loved it. I shouldn't care—I don't care, but gaining his approval did something to me. Made me feel more confident, maybe? I don't know, but I like it.

I will say I was pretty proud of myself for taking her

down and earning a "good job" from Mr. Scarboro. Julien glared at me as if I had personally offended him. I wanted to flip him the bird but thought better of it at the last minute. No need to poke the bear more.

The other women here hate me. I keep trying to make friends but I'm shut down. Darcy and Julie are the only ones who speak to me, and only when I'm with Ava. Maybe I don't need anyone else. What's that saying, quality over quantity? Leah is the only one out of my high school friends who attempts to reach. And Ava and I get along great. I'm not sure how I would have managed with a different roommate.

This morning I swatted Wesley away when he stepped into my room at four in the morning. What kind of monster doesn't sleep in on the weekends? It's Saturday and I don't need to do homework. When he extracted me from my bed himself, I went dead weight on him. I guess that works better while standing because he had no problem tossing me over his shoulder and swatted my butt. Ava woke and told me to keep it down. She needed her beauty sleep and then rolled over like I wasn't just flung around like a sack of potatoes. What ever happened to chicks before dicks?

We trained for an hour, where I pinned him twice. He told me we were going to start with weights next week before he let me go to get food. Since it's a weekend, I don't have to be in uniform and I ran straight over, thankful for the lack of a line. I've gotten used to having him eat with me, so I was a little saddened to sit alone, but since most students weren't up yet, I could eat in peace. Another thing I was grateful for. I haven't seen Wesley since then. He told me to wear something nice tonight, so I've been back and forth on whether or not I wear a cute pair of wedges.

"Just wear 'em," Ava insists, putting the last pin in her

hair to hold it up. "You've been staring at them for like ten minutes now."

I huff and nod. She's right. I'll wear them. As if on queue, there's a knock at the door. I know it's Wesley because Ava told Nick she'd text him after I was gone. Better safe than sorry.

I open the door and Wesley drinks me in. I'm wearing a pair of dark skinny jeans that hug my curves, a light purple sweater that falls off my shoulder, and my hair falls in loose curls down my back. Top it off with the sexy wedges and I feel confident, ready to face anything. Including the sexy as sin man who is standing on the other side of the door frame.

"Damn. You look good enough to eat." He leans in and places a chaste kiss to my cheek.

I blush and try to cover my smile. "Thanks."

He takes my hand and tosses a goodbye over his shoulder to Ava. I don't even think he noticed she's dressed for the evening either. He parked his SUV outside and opens the door for me. I go to climb in, but he presses me against the side of the car, holding me in place with his hips. His lips meet mine in a scorching kiss and I'm panting when he finally pulls away moments later.

"You play dirty, Sugar Plum." I blink up at him.

He laughs when I use the nickname on him. "I said something nice, not something that makes me want to fuck you against the side of the car, Hellcat."

The thought of him following through with his desire has my stomach twisted up in need. Most of our training sessions end up with a makeout and dry humping session that may or may not result in me having soaked panties. We haven't breached that line. I know he's holding back and I know I should, too. But while Julien still feels like a tormentor and Zander tries to avoid me most of the time, Wesley…doesn't. He's constantly helping me. It's unsettling how quickly he's shifted from tormentor to something dangerously close to a friend.

"Wes," I say his name in a breathy tone, but he shakes his head.

"Get in. We don't wanna be late."

I climb in and fasten my belt, sitting on my hands, an anxious gesture I do from time to time. He gets behind the wheel and starts the car, pulling out of the parking lot faster than I would have. He doesn't talk, but keeps glancing at me like I'm about to disappear. Nervous energy bubbles in my gut like a jacuzzi. He's really attractive, and it makes me feel inferior to him and the others. How is it they can make me feel this way? Desired, but unwanted at the same time.

We pull into a small parking lot with only a few cars. There aren't any buildings around and I slowly unbuckle my seat belt, unsure. The last time he brought me for a ride, I ended up getting chased through the woods by a psycho Julien and blackmailed into sucking him off. My face flames with the memory and I rub my cool hand over my cheek, hoping it goes away without Wesley noticing. He helps me out of the car and takes my hand, leading me down a path that looks vaguely familiar but also not in its darkened state. *They should really invest in more lights around.* It's only September, but campus is going to be shrouded in darkness come winter.

We stop in front of the old, burnt, abandoned building and I bite back a laugh. "Are you serious?" He grins at me. "Isn't it dilapidated or something? It's been on fire." But even as I say it, I can hear a cacophony of sounds coming from inside. I expect more people to be milling around outside, but no one is here.

"Where's everyone?"

"Inside." He ushers me in front of him and opens a heavy door for me to enter first. "Come on. I've saved us seats in the front."

The scent of bodies and booze smack me in the face. Not entirely unpleasant, but also not the best. It's warm inside, and I imagine it's from the amount of people milling around. Wesley scans a QR code on his phone and the large man nods at him once it's accepted. I'm momentarily blinded until my eyes adjust to the bright light in the center of the room, a boxing ring standing proudly in the middle.

We weave our way through the crowd and I search for anyone familiar. This school is small enough, with only four hundred students enrolled. I've gotten to know many of the faces, even if I don't know names. Men of various sizes and ages move around the space with familiarity. They are too old to be students, and none of them look like teachers I've met. Some are with beautiful women dressed to the nines, and some who seem to be with a crowd of buddies instead. There aren't many students here, so I find it interesting that it's held on campus. How many of these people are parents of the students here? How many people travel for these matches?

"Wait here. I'll be back in a few minutes. Just need to check on something." I nod, only half listening as my eyes drift from face to face. I swear I see a few glances of recognition, but none seem to care enough to investigate. In a way, I'm thankful. One less thing that will make it onto gossip sites. "I'm serious, Riley. Don't move." I hold up my hands in surrender and widen my eyes, the "okay" written across my face. With a final nod of satisfaction, he hurries down a darkened hall, leaving me alone in a crowd of strangers.

I've never seen a fight before. It's not my thing generally, but already it seems like fun. People place bets, talking, laughing, and cheering. I listen to conversations happening all around me and smile when the woman behind me tells a stupid joke. The energy in the room is electrifying. I'm giddy sitting in my seat watching everything unfold around me. A couple sit down next to me and smile politely, and I nod at them in greeting. There are whispered words around me, and I get antsy sitting here, waiting. Where's Wesley? I stand to expel some of my nervous energy and to locate my date for the night. My gaze circles the room, finally settling in the direction he left in. Glimpsing up at the ring, my stomach drops, and my heart races. I inhale on a shaky breath and lick my lips as the devil himself stares down at me.

Julien.

His bare broad chest and muscles in places I didn't think they could be, have my attention. Of course, he has a six-pack. I'm almost annoyed that he looks like a perfectly chiseled Greek god standing up there in only shorts. He continues to wrap his knuckles with white athletic tape, his green eyes staring holes into my soul. I should have known when Wesley ran off that something was up. He was going to check on his friends. He never offered the names of the fighters, but I never asked. I didn't think it was important.

My stomach flips as I think about him hitting someone tonight. And worse yet, being hit in return. I don't want Julien to get hurt, even if he is an asshole to me. He's important to Wesley, and Wesley is quickly becoming important to me. I peek behind Julien and Zander is in the ring's corner, eyes also trained on me.

Shit.

Julien shakes his head the moment Wesley finds his way back to me and circles his arms around my waist, pulling me against him, and tilting my chin up for a kiss. The one he gives me isn't short or sweet. It's demanding, and full of dark promises, and it makes my pulse quicken at the prospect of more. Even over the crowd of people, I swear I can hear Julien's low growl of displeasure. I peek at him without breaking the kiss until Wesley finally pulls away himself. Julien's jaw tightens and his chest rises and falls rapidly as he secures the gloves to his hands. So angry. And so hot. I'm getting used to his moody side, even if I don't agree with his actions. I wonder what will happen when I finally see him smile. Gasp! Does Julien even possess the ability? Or if he tries, will he drop dead of a heart attack because it finally started to beat again?

Zander doesn't look any happier as he grinds his teeth and crosses his arms over his chest. His eyes focus out on the crowd away from me as his mouth tugs down into a frown. He says something to Julien, and he focuses on whatever Zander is looking at. I pull away from Wesley and scan the crowd until I find what has his rapt attention. Ava and Nick. She's not even aware he's looking at her as she smiles up at Nick and then laughs at something he says, her curls bouncing with the motion.

Double shit.

Wesley turns his attention now as well, and I hear him growl in frustration. "What did you do, Hellcat?" He asks through clenched teeth.

"Nothing. This isn't my doing." Okay, so that may not be entirely the truth, but how much trouble can she really get in? "Why didn't you tell me Julien was fighting tonight and that Zander would also be here?" I scold, smacking Wesley playfully in the chest. He takes my hand in his and laces our fingers together, pulling us down into our seats. I didn't need to see them. It's hard enough making it through classes with them throughout the week, but I don't need my weekends filled with their hateful glares and scowls.

"Because I wanted you here with me, and Julien doesn't control everything."

The bell rings, and the referee steps into the ring to start his announcements. Julien walks to the opposite corner and lowers his head, listening to Zander. This isn't good. I bite my lower lip and play with the hem of my sweater, a wave of nervous energy coursing through me.

"Wwwwwelcome to fight night!" The announcer booms into the mic, making the crowd cheer and go wild. "In this corner," he points to a large guy with dark hair and a smattering of hair over his large muscled chest and abs, "we have Axel!" The announcer's voice booms as he drags out Axel's name. Axel gets a decent amount of excitement and whoops, but a fair amount of boos as well. It appears he may not be tonight's favorite, but from the looks of it, there have been a decent number of bets on him. The announcer turns and extends his arm in the opposite corner. "And in this corner," he pauses, allowing time for the cheers to ramp up, "Julien!" The crowd goes crazy! I look all around the stands and I can't help but be excited for him with all the people making a racket, supporting him. Clearly, he's a fan favorite, and I feel a small sense of pride because I know him.

He hates me, and the feeling is mutual, but that doesn't mean I want to see him beaten to a pulp. Even if this was his choice to fight.

"What happens if he loses?" I ask Wesley over the noise of the crowd.

"A lot of pissed off people."

That's what I'm afraid of. "Wesley, he can't lose this fight. He's already seen me and is not happy. It's going to mess with his head. Why'd you bring me here?" My voice has taken on a higher pitch. Anxiety settling low in my belly, worried about the next ten minutes.

He sighs, "because as much as he doesn't want to admit it, you light a fire under his ass. I know damn well he won't lose in front of you. And Axel is tough. Sometimes, Julien acts cocky—"

"Sometimes?" I cut him off and raise my brow in question..

He smiles and doesn't miss a beat. "And thinks he's the best, but in this fight, the odds are against him. I gave him a reason to win." He relaxes back into his seat and tosses his arm over my shoulder, stroking my bare shoulder with his thumb. Each stroke feels like a tiny fire licking across my skin. The first round bell rings and the fighters take their stance. I've seen bits of boxing matches on videos before, but it's nothing like this. Axel, Julien's opponent, comes out with a vengeance. He charges toward Julien, fists swinging, and Julien dodges every one of them with ease.

It's almost like a dance the two men are doing. Punch. Dodge. Kick. Jump back. The crowd shifts restlessly, tension crackling as they hurl scattered insults at the men. Julien glimpses at me, and that's enough of an opening that Axel clips the side of his head. The crowd groans as I let out a gasp of surprise and cover my mouth. Wesley places a kiss on my shoulder, but I can't relax. Julien shakes the punch off and focuses on Axel again, clearly pissed at himself for letting him land one on him. Around and around they circle until the bell dings and the first round is over.

Each man goes to their own corner, and I watch Julien and Zander closely. Both men seem off. And if I'm betting, I'd say Wesley is supposed to be over there in his corner, offering advice and being a supportive friend.

"You're usually over there, aren't you?" I ask, not taking my eyes off them, but leaning closer to Wesley to be heard over the boisterous crowd.

"Yeah, usually." He sounds somber with a shrug.

I knock my shoulder into his, and he turns, giving me his full attention. "Go."

His brows furrow, and he cocks his head. I nod and he smiles at me before planting a quick kiss to my lips and jogs to the other side of the ring to join his friends. Zander slaps him on the back and Julien gives a look over his shoulder at me, but Wesley drags his attention back to him, saying a few more words. If only I was good at reading lips. Maybe that's a skill they teach here at Pointebreak.

The bell rings, signaling round two, and the fighters take their stance. Julien keeps his gloves by his face and circles Axel, looking for an in. Axel charges again, but Julien is quicker and knocks him off his feet. He scurries on top, placing his weight on Axel's hips, and he lets loose. Pure rage coats his features as he lands punch after punch on him. Axel has his hands up by his face, trying to protect himself, but Julien still plows into him. I swear I hear a crunch and I wince as Axel goes lax. I gasp, my eyes widening at the scene in front of me. Is he dead? The referee blows his whistle and holds Julien's arm high in the air. Beads of sweat cling to his body and his chest rising and falling rapidly.

"Winner!" the announcer yells. I jump from my seat and scream and cheer with excitement. Axel's team rushes over to him and helps him stand, his eyes already beginning to swell shut, and his face is coated in blood. That looks painful. I wince and seek the three Kings out again. Julien still has a scowl on his face, but he accepts a half hug and a back slap from Wesley and Zander.

I turn in a slow circle to watch the crowd as I clap, looking at the audience, and the smile drops from my face.

What the hell is he doing here?

One blink, and he's gone. I track the person I think I saw as I push my way past those who are collecting their winnings and grabbing drinks at the makeshift bar, hoping to catch up to him. When I follow where he may have turned to, it's a dead end. It's not like he disappeared into thin air, so where the hell did he go? Spinning around, I looked for another juncture or hallway I missed, but there's nothing. I drag my phone out of my small bag and open a new text thread.

ME:

What are you doing at Contend?

I jiggle the handle of a random door I find, but it doesn't give, not that I expected it to. Walking around with my face in my phone, I wait for a reply when Wesley calls out for me. I glance up at the sound of my name and the instant relief on his face when he sees me has my haunches going up. He's scared. Why? I raise my brows in question and wiggle my fingers in greeting.

He pulls me into his arms and kisses the top of my head and I melt into him. I'm getting too used to his comforting touches; and the way he smells seems to have a calming effect on me as well. His warmth and touch soothe me in ways I didn't think were possible. "Jesus, Riles, you said you would stay put." His heart pounds against his chest as he hugs me tighter to him. I settle into his embrace and kiss his pecs as he takes a deep breath, his exhale moving my hair.

"Sorry. I thought I saw someone I knew." He holds me out in front of him and looks me over as if checking for injuries. "I'm fine, Wes." I shrug him off.

He spins us, pressing my back against the wall. He places his finger under my chin and drops his face inches from mine. My heart thumps wildly as I wait on bated breath for him to close the distance. Time moves agonizingly slowly and when he doesn't move, I whimper.

"Kiss me, Wes." He drops his lips to mine and I moan into him. His kiss is hard and demanding and I match him, exploring his mouth with my tongue. I run my fingers through his short hair and tug him closer to me. He wraps his hand around my waist and we are groin to groin, his hard-on prominent. I shift, needing more friction, and he groans, breaking the kiss.

"Come on, let's get out of here."

NINETEEN

WESLEY

I grab her hand and all but drag her behind me. I need her. Need to be alone with her. After Julien's win tonight, I saw her. She was beaming with excitement. She knew this was a big deal for him—hell, for all of us. We won big on this fight. Not only money but also status within this circle. And that can go a long way. Julien swaggered into the corner and Zander and I checked him over like we always do before slapping a one-armed hug on his back in congratulations. I knew it was the right move to bring Riley here. Riley's arrival at Pointebreak distracted him, and he's focused on the wrong things for too long. Distractions get people killed in our world. Axel easily could have done more damage tonight. And I'm sure he'll want a chance at a rematch sooner than later.

Julien had been nervous about fighting Axel, even if the asshole refused to admit it. Julien's a big guy, not only height but also muscles; but Axel's bigger. I knew having Riley watching him would light the fire under his ass that he needed to win. There's not a chance he would let that girl see him fail on any level. I'm glad I was right.

One moment she was there, and the next she wasn't. My stomach dropped when she wasn't where I left her. She fucking promised she would stay put. What part of that does she not understand? I rushed off in search of her, not even offering the guys an explanation of where I was going. But Zander would have noticed she wasn't where I left her. Nothing gets by him, and I'm sure he will be on high alert until I give him the all clear. Contend isn't the place to be alone, especially for her. Too many people know the claim Julien's put on her now, no doubt students slipping that tidbit of information to their guardians. Hardened men attend these fights, and I wouldn't put it past someone to put their own plan into action. What better way to bring down a king than taking his queen?

Julien Azarian may only be a student here, but his father has a lot of enemies who will do whatever it takes to bring him down.

"Wes, where are we going?" Riley asks from behind me, my hold on her hand never letting up.

"My place," I say as I push my way through the throng of people milling around. Being in the middle of a crowd has never pissed me off more than right now. I'm painfully hard thinking of the night I have planned for us. I want Riley in every position, and as many times as she'll let me. Training sessions have been torture. I'm man enough to admit I've been taking more showers than usual.

She pulls against my grasp, but I hold her tight until we make it through the doors and out into the cool night air. When we get to the car, I pin her to the side and place my forearms on either side of her head, caging her in. "This is your chance to tell me no, Hellcat. If you don't want me, tell me and I'll back off." *Not sure I have the balls to, but she doesn't need to know that.* "But if you come with me, you're *mine*," I growl, unable to contain myself.

She licks her lips and bites her lower one, pulling it between her teeth. I've gotten used to her tells. This is my favorite. It usually means she's turned on and is trying to contain it, holding herself back. I want to see the naughty girl she keeps tucked away from prying eyes.

She holds her breath and releases it with a shaky sigh. "Yes."

The corner of my lips tug up. "Good girl." I open the door and swat her ass as she gets in. She lets out a yelp of surprise before I close the door and jog to the other side, getting in. The house isn't far from Contend but even the five-minute ride will feel like a lifetime. I place my hand on her upper thigh and peel out of the parking spot. She spreads her legs and places her hand over mine, moving it up so I can graze my fingers over her clothed pussy. Riley deserves the world, and I will burn everything so she can get what she wants.

I don't want my first time with her to be in a dirty building against a brick wall. Not to say the thought didn't cross my mind when I found her in the dark hall all alone. Thank God she had the good sense to wear jeans and not a dress tonight. I'm not sure I would have been able to contain myself. Riley twists things up inside me. No one can hold a candle to her, and she doesn't even realize it.

I throw the car in park and all but jump out, racing to her side to open her door. I may be an asshole sometimes, but I know how to be a proper gentleman. She takes my hand and slides out, following me up the path. Nervous energy surrounds her as she crosses the threshold into the house and looks around. The last time she was here, Julien all but threw her out. I want to erase those crap memories and replace them with new ones tonight.

"Come on. Nothin' to fear."

"Right, just the boogeyman who lives down the hall," she murmurs.

Leading her upstairs, I push her against Zander's closed door. His room is directly across from mine, and I know he has cameras set up to watch everything that happens outside his room. He's caught me doing the walk of shame on several occasions. But this is different. We rarely invite girls back here, and when we do, they never stay. Smash and dispatch. But there's not a chance in hell Riley's going home after this. Having her once won't be enough. She's going to be my drug of choice. I've barely gotten a taste and I'm already planning the future. I place my arm above her head and lean down into her, getting a whiff of her signature cherries and vanilla. What is it that makes her smell so good?

"Text Ava and tell her you won't be back tonight."

Her throat bobs as she swallows hard, obeying without a second thought. I lick her racing pulse as she tucks her phone back into her bag.

"Good girl," I praise.

She closes her eyes and drops her head back against the door on a moan as I bite her shoulder. Her gasp of surprise, followed by the lick of her lips, tells me all I need to know. There's my girl's dark side. I fully intend on finding out just how black her desire runs.

"Tell me you want this," I say, giving her another chance to back down.

"I want you," she says without missing a beat.

My pulse throbs in time with my dick. She wants me. Those words have never sounded sweeter than from her lips. Grabbing her hand, I lead her across the hall, opening the door to my room. I don't give her time to look around before I slam the door behind us and attach my mouth to hers once again. She moans into my kiss and digs her fingers into my shirt, then pulls, almost as if she is determined to rip it off me. I can't take my hands off her. Breaking the kiss, I yank my shirt up over my head and when I bend to take her lips with mine again, she gasps. She notices the intricate designs of tattoos that adorn my arms and chest. I know she's seen some of them. She numbly traced them after Julien chased her into the woods. But this is different, and a sense of pride washes over me.

"Take your shirt off, Riley," I command. She'll have plenty of time later to get to know each design, but I need her too much to let her explore now.

She draws her eyes up to mine and does as I ask, pulling the purple sweater over her head and tosses it on the floor. She stands in front of me in a sexy black lacy bra and I salivate, needing to know if her panties match. I've been sporting a hard-on for most of the night, hell for the week, and while I'd love to know how good her mouth and hands feel on me, I know I won't last if she does. When she reaches out for me, I push her arm back toward her and shake my head. I walk backwards until I hit the side of the bed and sit down, extending my arms behind me to hold my weight.

"Strip. I wanna watch you."

Her face reddens, and she licks her lips before looking down at the ground. Her hands slowly rise as she tries to cover herself.

"No."

Her arms stop mid way up and she gradually raises her head to watch me with interest. I know she's not this timid thing. I've seen the video of her sucking Julien, and besides the fact that I jacked off to that video after seeing it, I know she needs to get out of her own head. It's the same with training. If she thinks too hard about it, she stumbles. Everything needs to be instinct with her.

"I'm about to rip those fucking jeans from your legs. So I suggest if you want to have something to go home in tomorrow, you strip for me." I give her a devilish grin. "Although seeing you parade around in my boxers would be a great way to make sure everyone knows who you belong to. Do you understand?" I lower my voice, commanding her to listen to me. Guiding her to give me what I want. What we both want. Although the more I think about it, the more I want her wearing my clothes all the time. Thoughts of her in my shirts, in my boxers, waiting patiently for me between classes flits through my mind.

Her gray eyes go wide in shock and she nods her head. She takes a deep breath and pushes it out slowly, working up the courage to do what I've asked. She bends at the waist, giving me a magnificent view of the tops of her tits, undoes the buckles on her wedges, and kicks them off before shimmying the pants down her thighs, revealing matching black boyshorts lace panties. A smile lifts my lips and I rub my fingers over them, taking in every inch of her perfect little body. She's fucking perfect.

I hold my hand out and she walks toward me, red still staining her cheeks. I pat my lap and she sits, knees on the edge of the bed and hands on my shoulders for balance before I collar her neck and drag her lips to mine.

Greed.

Hunger.

MINE.

The kiss consumes me and when she rubs herself on my hardened length; I know she's ready for more. A small, unhappy mewl escapes her as I end the kiss to help her stand. She blinks her doe eyes up at me and when I sink to the ground and grip her thighs; she gasps in surprise. I've wanted a taste of her all damn week. I've wanted to bite and suck every inch of her sexy, lithe body. Training was a challenge because my dick was doing the thinking for me. It doesn't help that she smelled like vanilla and sweet cherries, and her pussy was constantly around my arm or waist. I'm never going to be able to smell a cherry pie without thinking of Riley. Every damn morning before I went to get her, I had to give myself a mental kick in the ass to keep it in my damn pants. Zander's watched all week and I know it's turned her on. My girl likes to be watched. Any time we would start kissing, I would notice she would glance toward the camera before connecting her lips with mine.

Tonight, I'm letting my cock lead. There's no more holding back. Both of us deserve this release, but I need to make sure she's ready for me first. I know how big my dick is. I've had enough women over the years comment on the girth that I know I'm bigger than average. And I don't want to hurt her. Maybe another day she may like the sting of pain, but tonight isn't the night to find out. I attach my lips over her clothed core to suck and lick her, soaking through her already damn wet panties. Even the small taste of her is driving me insane. She digs her fingers into my hair and pulls me closer to her; her ragged breathing in my ear sends shivers down my spine.

"I wanna hear you, Hellcat. Moan for me, don't hold back."

She squeaks when I yank her panties to the side and dive in like a man starved. She tastes like everything I've ever wanted in my life. Her pussy may be my newest addiction. I slide one finger into her and stroke her g-spot as she whimpers. Her fingers dig into my scalp as if she's holding on for dear life. She's warm and tight. So fucking tight. I pump in and out as I explore her with my tongue. Adding a second finger and her body grips me, trying to suck me in deeper. My dick jumps at the thought of getting to feel her softness wrapped around it.

"Oh God, Wes," she pants, "don't stop. Please don't stop," she begs. Her fingers dig into my hair and she holds my face against her, gyrating her hips to maximize her pleasure. I love a woman who takes what she wants.

I kiss, and suck, and lick, determined to bring her to the edge, and when her legs begin to shake, and her breathing turns into labored pants, I kick it up a notch. She's milking my fingers and when I apply pressure to that sensitive spot inside her, all her muscles lock and she comes on the loudest fucking moan. I look up at her, relishing because I put that blissful look on her face. God, she looks fucking beautiful coming on my fingers like this.

I make her ride the wave of her high, slowing, but not stopping until the last of her tremors subside. Her fingers relax in my hair and she pets me, using my body to keep her balance as her knees buckled the moment her orgasm washed over her. I slide her panties down and off, tossing them with the growing pile of clothes on the floor.

Standing in front of her, I kiss her fingertips. Her eyes are dancing with mirth and I can't help the smile that spreads across my face. It doesn't last long before I kiss her, making her taste herself from my lips, and she hungrily does. I kick my jeans off and tug my boxers down, freeing myself. My dick settles between us, pulsing against her belly, begging to fuck her.

She reaches her hand down between us and stills when she can't wrap her fingers all the way around it. With hooded eyes, I examine her. I see the concern—the hesitation and a thought hits me like a freight train.

"Are you a virgin?" I blurt.

"N-no." She shakes her head, confirming her words. "But um," she pauses and bites her lip, looking away from me. "I've, um, never been with someone so…endowed." A blush rises to her cheeks as she keeps her eyes trained on me. "And it was only one time." She waves her hand in front of her face like she's batting away an old memory.

I can't help the smile. She may as well be a virgin if it was only once. I love the fact she hasn't been with many men. If I could have it my way, I'd be her last. Julien needs her for his plans. He doesn't need to fuck her. "It'll fit. But if you want to stop, tell me now."

I might die if she tells me to stop, but I'll never let her know that.

She shakes her head and unclasps her bra before crawling on the bed, and scooting her butt further up before resting on her forearms as she looks up at me in anticipation. I grab a condom from the drawer beside my bed. Before I roll it down, I swipe a bead of precum on my thumb and hold it out to her.

"Open." I command as I crawl over to her.

She does and sticks her tongue out, licking and sucking my finger as I swirl it in her warm mouth. The way she's sucking on it is driving me crazy; I'm not sure I'll last if she keeps this up. Hell, I'm not sure I'm going to last anyway, but why add fuel to the fire? Pulling my digit free, I roll the condom on and position myself on top of her. I drop my head to her breasts and take a pert nipple between my teeth, sucking hard. She moans and drops her head back on the bed, then wraps her legs around me.

I line myself up with her, slicking my dick up with her juices. She tenses as I press forward an inch, the tip of my cock barely inside her. Oh Jesus, it's going to be a tight fit. I reach down and rub her clit in tight circles until she relaxes a little. I switch to her other breast and shower it with the same attention, slowly inching my way inside of her with each thrust of my hips. When I'm fully seated, I give her a moment to breathe through it, even though I want to fuck her hard and fast. But I know I'm going to want her more than once tonight and she's not going to be able to if she's sore.

"Are you okay?" I ask through clenched teeth. She probably doesn't even realize she tightens around me with each inhale.

She nods and lifts her head, searching for my lips. "Kiss me, Wesley."

I lower my face to hers, devouring her lips like she's mine to consume, exploring her mouth as I slowly thrust in and out of her. This must be what heaven feels like, because I have never experienced something so earth shattering as having sex with Riley Whittier.

Too soon, my orgasm sits at the base of my spine. I know if I allow myself to, I'll come in two seconds flat, but I want to feel her come on my cock. I want her to milk me as I pump everything into her.

I collar her throat, adding enough pressure until her breath comes out in a wheeze and she surprises me by moaning and holding on.

"Dirty girl. I knew you would be. What else turns you on, baby?"

She sighs and sucks my finger into her mouth, exploring, enjoying, lost in the moment. When she doesn't respond, I slap her cheek, stunning her into opening her eyes. Her irises are molten lava.

"What else?" I reach my hand between us and rub her clit. I'm getting close and there's no way I'm getting there without her.

"D-dirty talk," she finally answers.

I rub her harder and faster, working her body over. "You're gonna come on my dick like a good little girl, do you understand? And one day, when you're ready for it, I'm going to fuck your tight asshole. You're mine, Riley. You feel like heaven, baby. So damn tight and perfect. Come on my cock," I demand.

Her body shakes, and she pants as I ride her harder,

slamming my aching cock deep within her. Over and over. I refuse to come before her. When her body tightens and her back bows, I know she's there.

"Come for me, Riley. Now!"

And she does. Her eyes roll back and her entire body shakes, sending my orgasm spiraling out of me. I moan her name and pump until she drains every damn drop from my body and I lay half spent on top of her, my softening dick still nestled warmly in her. She lays still on the bed, clearly as worn out as me. And then she laughs. It's small at first, but it bubbles until I can't help but laugh with her.

Yup. I'm screwed. Sex has never been like this, and I don't think anyone else will compare.

TWENTY

RILEY

Having sex with Wesley tonight was definitely not on my Pointebreak bingo card, but I couldn't have stopped it even if I tried. I like him. God, do I like him. Even over the course of a week, he's changed how he acts around me. While Zander keeps his distance and only interacts when he needs to, and Julien is still his annoying brutish self—Wesley has become someone I feel I can rely on. And that scares me. I'm falling hard and fast for him. He's the first guy since Rhys that I've felt like this with. And now I feel like a jerk for thinking of someone else after I just had the most mind blowing sex of my life.

He gets off the bed after the giggles subside to get a face cloth to clean me up. I really could use a shower, but this is a start. I lay still, my face flaming as he drags the warm cloth between my sore thighs. It's so intimate, it should be illegal. Like we've crossed some invisible line we can't uncross. He tosses it back in the bathroom, grabs some clothes from his drawer and gives me one of his large t-shirts to throw on as he pulls up a pair of boxers and lies on the bed.

I look down at it, unsure what this means. "Are you sure?

I don't mind going back to my room. I'm not sure the others would like that I'm here."

He tucks some hair behind my ear and places a kiss to my lips. "Positive. Let me deal with them. Plus, you already told Ava you wouldn't be home."

He has a point; I just don't want to cause any ripples between them. After pulling the soft fabric over my head, he pulls me against him on the bed. I curl up against his side and play with some tattoos I can reach. He has a lot of them. Most of them are black, but he has a few that are loaded with colors. It's beautiful actually. Whoever the artist is did a fantastic job.

"Tell me something real," he says.

There's something in the way he says it, quiet and unguarded, that makes my heart twist. Like he needs to hear something honest to believe this. Like he wants to tether himself to me in a way that goes deeper than skin. And for a second, I want to give him that. Something true, just for him. Not the superficial crap, or the stuff everyone's read in the newspaper or online about my family, but something specific to me. Something no one knows. After two killer orgasms, I feel like I could tell him practically anything. Orgasms must be a truth serum.

I go to speak, and James' warning comes back to haunt me. *Don't trust too easily.* Nothing about Wesley and his group of friends is easy. Nothing about my situation is easy, but he makes it bearable. And I hate the fact that I'm truly falling for this man, even though I know I shouldn't. He's going to cause nothing but heartbreak in my future. My father would never accept a man like Wesley. He doesn't fit the cookie cutter image Michael likes to highlight.

"How about I go first?" He offers as my mind races through thought after thought. If left to my own devices, I'm sure I'd stumble down a rabbit hole and start rethinking every step I've taken since arriving here.

I clear my throat. "Sure."

"As you wish," he says as he nudges my shoulder. Then waits.

I draw my brows together as I shake my head and shrug my shoulders. "Okay. Are you gonna tell me something?"

"I did."

"Huh?" I ask again, confusion clouding every feature and thought.

"Princess Bride? The movie?"

I smile warmly, realization finally clicking. "Wesley," I say with a fondness to my voice. He nods. "You're named after Wesley from The Princess Bride?" Another gleeful giggle bubbles out of me and I bury my face in his chest, inhaling him.

"My mom loved the movie. My dad promised her if they had another boy, she could name him after Wesley." His smile falters as he looks down at me.

"What about your brother?"

"Dead." He speaks the word in the same cadence. Dead. No emotion.

I kiss his chest and look up into his eyes. "I'm so sorry, Wesley."

"Yeah. Me too." He looks up at the ceiling, his hand casually running up and down my back.

Shit, that got deep fast. I need to say something to get us away from this awkwardness. I want to know more, and I'm sure if, given the time, he'll open up to me.

"My mom's dead too." I take a deep breath. "While that's well known, I have my doubts it was accidental." I shudder and he holds me tighter, so I continue. If I share, maybe he will too. "She died when I was eight. It was a car accident. Rainy night, hard to see and all that jazz." I grit my teeth to stop my chin from trembling and close my eyes, trying to remember the facts I've been told. "She was hit from behind and her car flipped a few times before landing in a ditch. Died instantly. Or that's what I was told."

"Jesus, Riley. I'm so sorry." He pulls me tighter against him.

I hold my breath, warding off the tears that want to spill over. "I haven't talked about my mom in so long, I've forgotten little things about her. Her smell, her smile, the songs she would sing me to sleep." I smile sadly at the memory. "Dad bought me a music box with the lullaby she would sing to me, and I used that every night until I was ten."

"What song?"

"Edelweiss," I snort and laugh. Just talking about her, even the little things, brings a sense of relief, like a weight has been lifted from my chest. "Sorry." I shift to sit up and he holds me against him.

"Don't you dare get up, Hellcat." So I don't and I settle back against him.

"She was everything to me. When she left us…my family changed. My dad changed. Slowly, things were different around the house. Different security came in. Guys who were meaner and angrier looking. Most of them scared me. Tighter securities went up. Gates, alarms, all that crap." I shrug. "I just assumed because he was a politician that it was normal. But the more I think about it, the more I know…it's not." I want to say so much more, but I hesitate. I've already shared so much with him, and I can't forget that at the end of the day, he's friends with Julien, who has it out for me.

He takes a deep breath. "When I was seventeen, my brother, Elias, died."

I lift my head to look at him. He turns and his icy blue eyes stare into mine. "That had to have been really hard."

He gives a heavy sigh. "Not as hard as the survivor's guilt I've had to deal with for the past four years. Doesn't help that my family blames me and has told me I should've died and not him." His body tenses under mine and he tightens his jaw, swallowing hard. "If I knew it wasn't safe for him to get me that night, I never would have called him. So maybe it is my fucking fault."

My heart breaks for him. No one should ever be told they should have died. Especially by family, the people that are supposed to love you unconditionally.

I sit up, tossing my leg over him to straddle his hips and take his face in my hands. "That's not true, Wes. I know I don't know a lot about you, but I can tell you that you are loyal to a fault, protective, and love deeply. You're a good person and," I bite my lip, hesitating on my next words, "I-I like you a lot. You've been an asshole to me, but you've also shown me a different side of you. And that side, I really like."

Wesley gives me a cocky grin. "Oh, yeah?" He flips me under him and lowers his head to mine for a kiss. I could get used to rolling around mostly with him. And that thought maybe doesn't scare me as much as it should.

The ache between my thighs is the only indication of how many times Wesley and I had sex. His breath is still deep and even on my cheek and I slide out of his bed, careful not to disturb him. I've gathered from our talks that sleep is more of a hobby than a habit with Wesley. Maybe it's the same for all the guys. I heard someone slam their bedroom door last night just as Wes brought me to another orgasm and demanded I scream his name. Oops. I hope it was Julien that heard us. The thought makes me smirk.

I freshen up in the bathroom and take a drink of water before tossing on the oversized t-shirt Wesley gave to me last night. After our last round, we were both so exhausted that we fell asleep with him holding me. There was no need for clothing. It's long enough that I can walk around without feeling too indecent. I don't want to get back into my jeans just yet.

I wander around, admiring his room. It's a little disorderly, but not dirty. Our pile of clothes is proudly on display in the middle of the room and brings a smile to my face. Five orgasms! Five. That's how many times Wes got me off. I have never had that many in one night in my life. My face flames as I think about everything we did last night and I fan myself. *Leah and Ava will never believe this.*

There's nothing too exciting in here. A dresser of drawers, desk, king sized bed, closet, and a few knickknacks. The only thing that stands out is a picture of a beautiful woman with two young boys on either side of her. She smiles brightly in the picture. I pick it up and run my finger over the three, instantly picking out Wesley—the little boy with messy hair and a shit-eating grin.

He looks so happy. He can't be older than eight or nine here.

"That's my mom."

I startle and almost drop the frame before catching it and clutching it to my chest. "Jesus, Wes, you scared me." I place it on his desk and turn to face him. "She's beautiful."

"Yeah," he gives a non-committal answer.

I know he doesn't want to talk about her. It's written all over his face. So I decide to change the subject. "I'm starving. Got anything to eat around here?"

He gets up and pulls a shirt over his head and gives me a once over. "You look good wearing my clothes, Hellcat.

Better with them off, but no need to give the guys a free show, eh?"

I smack him lightly in the chest and lean into his embrace. Then he takes my hand and leads me downstairs. The smell of freshly brewed coffee has me closing my eyes and smiling at the nutty aroma.

"I definitely need some of that coffee. The stuff in the cafeteria isn't cutting it."

"One hot cup coming right up." He opens the cabinet door, pulls out two mugs, and adds a heaping amount of cream to mine, then hands me the cup. I freeze, my fingers slowly wrapping around the mug when the air changes and I feel someone walk up behind me. The hairs on my arms stand at attention as I pull my shoulders back, waiting for the inevitable fight to happen.

"Mornin'," Wes says, looking over my shoulder.

We're greeted with a grunt from the doorway. I turn and put my mug to my lips, blowing on the hot liquid. I stare at Julien, every nerve screaming to step away and closer to Wesley; but I won't give him the satisfaction of seeing my fear.

"Good fight last night," I offer the olive branch.

"You shouldn't have been there," he says, his eyes trained on my mouth as I take a sip.

"Wes invited me." *Jesus, could this man be any less likeable?*

"Mmm." He offers and takes the mug Wesley offers to him without breaking eye contact with me. "Don't make it a habit of letting your fuck buddies spend the night, Wes."

I scoff and pop my mouth open as I stare at him in disbelief. He's joking, right? Like, there's no way he's being serious right now.

"Julien Azarian, you can kiss my ass." I blurt.

His lips draw into a sneer, as if the very thought of

touching me was so repulsive he would rather have his toenails removed. "I wouldn't kiss it, Princess. I'd smack it red and then fuck it. Hard." He steps into my space, and I press my back against the counter. "You shouldn't be here," he repeats.

I clamp my thighs together, not wanting him to know the effect he has on me. Why does that turn me on way more than I want to admit? "I'm not going anywhere, *Cupcake*."

"If you kids can't play nice, I'm going to have to lock you in a room until you learn," Wesley teases. "Julien, leave her alone."

Zander picks that moment to walk into the kitchen and looks down at my bare legs and oversized t-shirt. When he reaches my eyes again, they are dark. Darker than I've ever seen them before.

"Better yet, I'll let Zan tie you down and beat it." Julien taunts.

Zander looks at him and back at me, but I can't read his expression. That doesn't stop my mind from picturing the three of them together in a room with me. I now have images of all three of them spanking me, and let's just say it doesn't sound half bad. A breathy sigh escapes and I don't miss how quickly Zander snaps his head in my direction. I bite my lip and look at my feet, trying to hide whatever thoughts and emotions are rocking me to my very core.

Wesley comes around the counter to stand behind me, almost like my own personal bodyguard. The other men move around us, the conversation from moments ago forgotten. He kisses the top of my head and motions for me to take a seat at the counter while the three of them work in tandem to cook up some breakfast.

I've seen nothing like it. They are all perfectly coordinated. It's alarming how well the three of them can read one another, and I suddenly feel like I'm invading their personal space.

"I need to check my phone. Be back in a minute."

I find it in my jeans pocket with a new message.

JAMES:

What's Contend? I've been on the road with
Michael. We were in Portsmouth last night.

No. That's not right. I'm pretty sure it was him. I bite my lip and reread the message, then pull up a search and see James is right. My dad was in Portsmouth last night. I click on a video clip of him answering some questions from audience members.

"How's your daughter, Riley, doing at Pointebreak?"

His smile is wide as he beams at the crowd. "She's doing wonderful. She's really taken to the curriculum and is enjoying herself. We spoke just last night, in fact."

I scoff and shake my head as my heart sinks. I haven't been able to get in touch with him at all this week. He keeps sending me to voicemail. I've been pretending I don't care because I'm still mad at him, but it's actually affecting me a lot. I check my phone way more than I should, hoping for a message or email from him, but I get nothing. My few texts have also gone unanswered. The only person who has answered my calls is James, and even that was a brief conversation with him cutting me off.

ME:

NVM, guess I saw your twin.

I look up when I hear a knock on the door, and Wesley fills the frame. "Everything okay?"

"Yup." I put my phone back in my pocket and drop the pants on the floor.

"Breakfast is ready."

I lick my lips and worry my bottom one between my

teeth. "Not sure I should eat with you three. I feel like I'm intruding in your personal space."

"You're not," he assures me. "Come on, it'll be fine. His bark is worse than his bite."

"Somehow, I doubt that," I mutter as I take his hand and he leads us back downstairs. I sit at Wesley's right with Zander next to me and Julien across from me. It's all very… domesticated. And dare I say, kind of nice?

"Where are you guys from?" I ask when I can no longer stand the silence.

Three sets of eyes look at me, and when he swallows, Wesley answers first. "I grew up in Connecticut. Zander's family is from New York and Julien is from here in New Hampshire."

I sit up straighter. That's a surprise. "Oh really? Whereabouts?"

"Doesn't matter," he says.

I snort. "Of course not," I mutter, playing with the food on my plate. "Um," I clear my throat, "so why Pointebreak? I'm sure you could have gone to any school you wanted."

"Family tradition. Our fathers came here, and it was the expectation." Zander's deep timbre sends a thrill through me. He speaks so rarely that it almost always catches me off guard when he does. "Those who attend Pointebreak are more successful than those who don't."

That seems surprising to me. There are many Ivy league and highly rated schools I would think would look better on a resume than Pointebreak. "How so?"

"Think of this place as an exclusive club. Everyone here has something to offer, or some connection to make. They don't let just anyone in." Julien snorts and rolls his eyes, but Zander continues. "Even you."

"Zander," Julien warns.

Zander glares at Julien, but picks up his fork and takes a bite of his eggs. It seems like that's all I'm going to get out of them right now. Except, now I have more questions than answers.

Wesley places his arm on the door frame next to me, tilts my chin up, and places a gentle, almost loving kiss on my lips. If I could melt right now, I'd be a puddle on the floor outside of my room.

"I'll see you bright and early tomorrow morning for training, Hellcat."

I nod. "See ya later." Then I let myself into my room and lock the door behind me. Ava's not here, and I mentally send up a thank you. I need to get Leah some more information. She's been champing at the bit, waiting. It's only been a week though, so it's not like I have a lot more to share with her other than what I've already sent.

I dial her number, and she answers on the first ring. "Have you forgotten all about me since joining the mafia?" She teases.

I roll my eyes. "Funny. No, I wanted to call and tell you about my classes the rest of the week. Swim was pretty boring, nothing of interest there. Get in, do laps, blah blah. My gun class was interesting, though. I'm not allowed to shoot the damn thing until I can successfully take apart and rebuild it."

"Really?" she asks, the last bit of the word she says with a shrillness to her voice.

I laugh. "Yeah, really. Who knows if I'll even be shooting one this year! The other classes are basically business, and math, things like that. I would have loved having some sort of art or something fun, but it's not as terrible as I was imagining."

Thoughts of Wesley last night pop into my head and I can't bite back the smile that spreads across my face. I share everything with Leah and it's been killing me to not share the guys with her.

"So, um, I'm kinda seeing someone."

"Damn girl, you work quick! Who is it? Is he hot?"

This is why I love Leah. No disdain, no hate, just pure excitement. "His name is Wesley, and yes. He's wicked hot! Like book boyfriend material, hot."

She gasps and squeals. "Give me his full name. I'm going to stalk him."

My smile fades at that. And for some reason, I don't want her to. I don't want her possibly uncovering a deep, dark secret about him I haven't already tried to find. I learned a bit about him and his family last night, and I don't want to add to the heartache. And I know Leah. She won't stop until she finds something.

Just then the door unlocks and Ava comes in. *Saved by the bell.*

"Hey, I gotta go, but I'll tell you later. Talk soon."

"Okay. Bye, babe." We hang up and I plug my phone in, so the damn thing doesn't die.

"Hey." Ava waves and tries to hide the smile on her face but misses by a mile. She has a towel wrapped around her and hugs it closer as she locks the door.

"You look like you're up to no good. Tell me everything."

TWENTY-ONE

ZANDER

I can't keep my damn eyes off Riley. Ever since she slept with Wes, it's like something inside of me has cracked. I feel like a damned caged animal. Plus, that fucker knew what he was doing when he pushed her against my door and made her moan. I've watched that tape over and over and jacked to it. Fantasies of the two of them behind his closed door consume my every thought. I would have preferred if he fucked her against my door instead, at least then I could have watched instead of wondered. Now I know what a damn addict feels like.

She's nervous today. Keeps bouncing her leg and fiddling with that stupid pen I want to chuck across the room. She peeks glances at me out of the corner of her eye and her mouth is flopping like a damn fish as she tries to figure out what to say. Wesley walked her to class again today, and I was already sitting here waiting for her to take her seat next to me. I will say it was amusing watching her decide if I was worth sitting next to. Finally, on a sigh, she sat down. I ignored her all day on Monday in class, so it's no surprise she's antsy.

"Why won't you talk to me?" she finally whispers.

"We're in class. We shouldn't be talking," I reply.

"You know what I mean," she retorts. "You've been avoiding me ever since I stayed at your place."

"I'm sitting next to you. How can I be avoiding you?"

She closes her eyes and huffs out a harsh breath. A tiny, involuntary smile tugs at the corners of my mouth. I love getting her worked up.

"You know—"

"Miss Whittier, is there a problem?" Mrs. Polnick asks.

The entire class turns to look in our direction. Riley looks around and I join the class in staring at her, hoping to keep her on her toes a little longer.

"Nope. Just trying to figure out why my buddy here won't talk to me." She hitches her thumb over her shoulder at me. I lock my jaw and growl in annoyance under my breath. I should have seen that coming. Riley hasn't been one to back down from a challenge. She's vulnerable with Wes, and occasionally with me—but never with the other students here.

She refuses to show them any sort of weakness. If I'm a betting man, I would say she's like this because she didn't receive the warm welcome she was expecting. She's adapting to her surroundings. No one here is going to worship at her feet, except for maybe Wes. She's got him hook, line, and sinker. The moment he told Julien he was training her, I knew he'd do anything for her. I know, as long as she's with him, she'll be safe. And with what Julien has planned for her, it's best if Wes can be there for her. *Like I want to be there.*

"Maybe you and Mr. Fedorov should take this quarrel out of my classroom." Before Riley can open her mouth and make it worse, she adds, "that's not a request. Get out." She points to the door.

There are a few snickers throughout the room, but as soon as I make eye contact with the offenders, it stops. With a frustrated shake of my head, I jam my computer and books into my bag so hard, I'm surprised it doesn't rip at the seams. I don't need this shit right now. I walk out of the door and hear her coming up quickly behind me.

"Zander, wait."

I turn on her, and she pauses.

The beast within me is trying like hell to break free. I can feel him just below the surface, begging to be freed. It has only been a few weeks since my last play session, but it's not enough. I need more. I want to pull her over my knee and spank her until it makes both of us feel better. Even though I want her, I need to keep her away from me. I'm dangerous—the last person she needs. Wesley is good for her. Out of the three of us, he's the best with people. He knows how to play them, mold them, make them feel safe. I'm only good at hurting others. I watch from a distance because I can't do damage.

My chest rises and falls with each labored breath as I work hard to maintain my composure. "I told Julien I'd keep an eye on you. That's it, Luna. You're not my plaything, nor my buddy. You have Wes for that. There's *no* reason we need to talk at all."

"You're my—"

"I'm not your anything, Riley. Get it through your fucking head." I descend upon her and she backs until she bumps into the wall behind her, her body jarring with the impact. I place my arm above her on the rough brick and lean down so I'm in her face. Her pulse races under the pale skin on her delicate neck. I've pictured putting my hands around it far more than I'd like to admit. Watch her face redden as she struggles to breathe under my touch, then right before she passes out, give her the euphoric high of air once again. I play rough, but I think she would like it. She's already shown an interest in being tied and spanked. Maybe I can convince her to act on her fantasies.

"You're a fucking cock tease, Riley." She opens her mouth to say something and I place my finger over her lips. "Shhhh. Don't talk. Do you enjoy teasing me the way you do? Fucking Wesley against my bedroom door, or dry humping him on the mats? You know I'm watching, which means you put on a fucking show. Is it for you, or for me? What about the incessant nickname you gave me?"

"It's a—"

"Shut up and listen to me. Whatever you think I am... I'm not. Get it through your head. We aren't friends. You're my fucking ward. I'm here to make sure you stay out of trouble and out of the way."

Her eyes glisten, and her chin trembles, but she swallows and licks her lips giving me a curt nod. My eyes track every movement. My cock hardening at the thought of her lips on mine. Her tongue and mouth around my cock.

"I know that's not true," she whispers.

I narrow my eyes at her, lower my head, and press my hips against hers, pinning her to the wall. She shifts in my grasp, but when she reaches to touch me, I collar her wrists between my hand, and press them against the wall, holding her stretched and exposed to me. It doesn't matter that we both have all our clothes on. The moment feels raw. Real. More intimate than I've ever experienced with anyone naked.

My lips brush the outer shell of her ear. "You'd look beautiful with a red ass tied to my bed, Luna. Maybe I'd let the guys watch. You seem to enjoy knowing I watch you. I think it turns you on. What about if I put my hands on you?" She sucks in a deep breath, and I dip my head, smelling her intoxicating scent. My own personal cherry pie. I've never been hungrier in my life. "What if I fuck your pretty cunt?"

"Please," she whispers, grinding her hips against mine. I reach my free hand under her skirt, rubbing my fingers over her soaked panties. I want to take them from her, gather a collection so I can use them to stuff in her mouth when she's being bratty. I know she has survival next and I don't need to send her there without anything on. If Julien got his hands on her like that, I'm not sure he wouldn't do something. Or worse, someone else. I would murder anyone else who touched her. She belongs to us; Julien, Wesley, and me.

"You're fucking soaked, Riley, just like a good fucking girl."

"Yes," she moans breathlessly. When her tongue darts out to moisten her lips again, something inside of me snaps. I can't contain the beast any longer, he needs to play. I crush my mouth to hers, wanting to taste her, needing the sweet relief that my body craves.

Riley Whittier is my kryptonite, my weakness.

I coax her mouth open and she willingly submits to me, making me that much harder. I know the type of woman she is in bed. Wes hasn't told me anything, but the submission she's giving to me here tells me all I need to know. She would be perfect for me. She'd take everything I give to her and then ask for more.

She moans and tugs her arms, wanting me to free her, but I hold her tighter and wrap my other arm around her waist, clutching her to me, exactly where I need her. Her breasts are squished between us and she rubs her body against me like a bitch in heat. As I roll my hips against hers, I feel her sharp intake of breath, followed by a moan that I swallow. I don't want anyone to hear her. These moans are for me, not anyone else, not right now. I bite and suck her lower lip between my teeth before releasing it with a pop. I'm about ready to unzip my pants and take her right here in the courtyard, but the sound of students filtering out of the class-rooms makes me pause.

I pull back, both of us breathing heavily, and I release my grip on her. Her arms drop to her sides, tugging her shirt back into place. Her face is flushed, and her eyes are blown with desire. The sudden loss of her skin under me makes me burn for more. I'm so fucking screwed.

"I," I start to give her an explanation, but shake my head and walk away from her, leaving her all alone. I text Julien where he can find her to bring her to her next class, because if I can't feel any comfort, I sure as shit don't want her to. Maybe it's time to bring some toys out for fun.

This is getting out of hand. I can't control my darker urges for much longer, and if I unleash them on her, I know she will run. I open a new message.

ME:

I need you. Meet me tonight at our spot. Bring everything you have.

TWENTY-TWO
RILEY

What the hell just happened? I trace my swollen lips as I stare in the direction Zander walked in moments ago. Everything with him is so hot and cold. One minute he's basically fucking me against the wall, then the next he's running with his tail tucked between his legs. I can't keep up. He's almost as bad as Julien…almost. Does he want me, or not? Do I want him? I space out, my mind working to make sense of everything that's been happening.

I'm so confused about this whole thing.

"What the fuck did you do this time?" Julien roars as he descends upon me. A few students slow and turn their heads to look in our direction, but hurry along when Julien glares at them.

I mentally take a moment to prepare for this conversation. Clearly he woke up on the wrong side of the bed today and needs to get his head out of his ass. He doesn't take well to being ignored. Which makes pushing him just a little further, even more satisfying.

"Wow, you really are turning into a whore."

I snap my attention to his; my eyes flare with anger.

Excuse me? He did *not* just call me that. My entire body feels hot, and I narrow my eyes at him. I despise him with every fiber of my being. I hate the fact that he's so damn good looking, because his personality ruins that. There are moments I almost feel bad for him, but then he does stupid crap like this and the animosity returns with a vengeance.

"I'm not a whore, Julien. And fuck you for saying that." I spit out, anger lacing my words. I pick up my bag, pushing past him to get to the class we share. His dark chuckle behind me makes me walk that much faster trying to get away from him. It's not my fault Zander kissed me. It's not my fault Wes pulled me under his wing to protect me. I didn't choose that. In fact, I wanted to stay as far from the Kings as I could. They're the ones who wouldn't let me. Each one dragged me to the center of their inner circle.

"You know, we've all had our fill of women to fuck around here. No one can say they've had all three Kings though. We should give you a fucking medal for it."

Oh. My. God. I'm going to murder this man before the day is through. I turn on him and shove my finger into his chest. He looks down at it, and with his head lowered, looks up at me through his thick lashes. It's dark—menacing. He's a wolf and I'm the lamb he's going to slaughter. I won't go down like this. I will not cower in a dark, musty corner and tremble in fear. Julien swats my hand away but doesn't move. He just grinds his teeth, his jaw muscles twitching like crazy. I hope he chips a fucking tooth.

"I haven't been with all three of you. I've been with Wes. You're the one that made me suck your cock, buddy. And Zander's the one who kissed me." Someone whistles from behind me and I get a few cat calls that are less than pleasant. *I shouldn't have said that out loud.* I close my eyes and rub my forehead, a stress headache taking hold.

"You make it sound as though you didn't enjoy sucking

me off. If I remember correctly, you were all but set to rub that little pink clit of yours and find your own release. You were soaked for me in the woods. So don't kid yourself." He leans into me and takes a deep inhale. "Now move. We've got class and I don't want to be late." He walks backwards, keeping me in his line of sight until finally he turns and walks away. *Asshole.* I hate the fact that I have to follow him like a lost puppy.

As usual, I stand as far away from Julien as possible as we wait for class to begin. And once again, the other students keep their distance. It doesn't bother me that the others stay away. In fact, I'm thankful for it. I don't want to be associated with the kinds of people who go here. Except…I guess I'm one of them now. I may not be a mafia princess, but my father still sent me here to mingle amongst them.

In a class of twenty, ten students are upperclassmen, and out of the rest of us there are only three girls in this class. A girl named Chloe, who I think feels like an outcast like myself. And there's Chastity, who seems to be the opposite of her name. In every class, she keeps her eyes glued to Julien like he's a prized heifer at an auction. She's constantly surrounded by the men in the class and I have to keep from gagging every time I hear her giggle.

"Julien, do you want to be my partner today?" She asks loud enough for me to hear.

Please say yes. Please say yes. It would get him away from me for a while, a welcomed reprieve.

I'll give him some credit. He doesn't turn her down right away. He drifts his gaze over her body, her long legs on full display in a skirt that is a few inches shorter than my own. She must have made a few alterations in her free time. She pops her hip and twirls her strawberry blonde hair around her finger, as she waits for him to respond.

"No."

The sweet smile she has plastered to her face drops quickly as she turns back to the circle of guys and one of them, Bruno, offers to be her partner today. A wave of satisfaction washes over me, and I can't help but give myself an internal fist pump. I may not want him to be *my* partner, but it's oddly comforting that he doesn't want to be hers.

I take a chance and stand next to Chloe. "Hey," I say.

"Hi." She keeps her eyes on Chastity and her group of goons.

"I'm Riley. You're Chloe, right?" I ask, pretending I don't know.

"Yeah."

Not much of a conversationalist, I see. Okay. I guess befriending her won't be as easy as I thought.

Mr. Scarboro walks in, the heavy door closing harshly behind him. He drags a metal chair with him, the noise sounding like nails on a chalkboard. Most of the class winces, but no one comments.

"You're going to work on getting out of a chair today." There are a few whispered words between the students and the upperclassmen laugh before Mr. Scarboro holds a handful of zip ties up and smiles.

That was the absolute worst class I've been in. I rub my sore and raw wrists after I unsuccessfully broke out of my zip tie. Mr. Scarboro walks up to me and I offer my arms for him to cut the tie.

"You did well, Miss Whittier."

I smile despite myself, and when he frees me, I inspect my reddened skin; wincing when I touch the tender spots. I walk over to my bag, ignoring the set of green eyes that never seem to leave me.

"Come with me." Julien grabs my arm to drag me God knows where, and I yank it free.

Shaking my head, I say, "No."

"You need something for your wrists," he counters.

"I'll survive, or I'll hit up the nurse for medical attention. Don't start acting like you care now. You'll ruin your streak."

A low, irritated growl leaves his lips as he slowly advances on me until I'm backed against the wall. I look around for help, but we're the only ones left. Everyone else is already gone, including Mr. Scarboro.

"Stop being difficult, Princess." He lifts my hand, and it's so gentle and caring, my heart stops for a moment. He inspects the red sensitive skin and when he rubs his thumb over it, I wince. "Shit," he mumbles as he turns my arms over to inspect every part. "Put vaseline on it and keep it covered until it heals."

"Why are you being so nice to me?" I question, my voice barely above a whisper.

He jerks his head up like I've slapped him, eyes raking over my face. I'm an open book. He doesn't need to search hard. And if he asked a question, I'd answer.

"Laconia." He still hasn't dropped my hands and the pulsing current flowing through us has my feet glued to the floor. I couldn't move away from Julien, even if I wanted to. And right now, I don't want to. I can't help but feel this connection to him. Like I know him. I can't shake the feeling. Even when he's being an asshole or trying to scare me away, there's this nagging feeling.

I blink at him, my mind taking longer than it should to comprehend what he's just told me. And when I do, I suck in a sharp inhale of breath. He's finally answered my question from this past weekend. I don't know why, but that makes me happy. Maybe it's because he remembered I even asked the question.

"Hey, there you are," Wesley announces as he walks into the room. Julien drops my hands and walks away, picking up his bag as he leaves. That moment of tenderness, it was so unlike the Julien I've seen. It made him seem…human.

He says something to Wesley in passing and Wes slaps him on the back in greeting as he leaves.

"Ouch." Wesley says, examining the red marks. "Zip ties?"

I nod and give him a small smile, but watch as Julien leaves without a glance back at us.

He kisses the tender skin before collaring my throat, holding me against the wall. His lips come down and I greedily accept them, coaxing his mouth open. He nips my bottom lip and I startle.

"Don't rush me, Hellcat. I've missed you." He says before taking control of our kiss again. My hips move on their own as I search for any sort of friction to help ease my growing need.

"Wes," I moan when he kisses the delicate skin over my racing pulse.

"Tell me what you need, baby."

"You," I moan, wrapping my leg around his hip. He wraps his hands under my knees and lifts me with ease, pressing my back against the cool wall as I wrap my legs around him, clinging to him.

"You can do better than that." He presses his hips against mine and my entire body heats with want. We're in public and definitely should not be doing this. That seems to be our MO though—PDA in public places. It's like that couple at the beginning of this year in the bushes. It feels dirty, but I'm fully aware of how horny it makes me. Fantasies of Zander watching us through the cameras flash through my mind, and I all but whimper. I wonder if there are some in here.

He kisses along my jaw and down my neck. When he bites the spot where my shoulder meets, I squeak. "I want your dick."

He rolls his hips into mine once more and I drop my head back, relishing in the feel of his body. "Where do you want it?"

"Inside of me. I want to come on your cock, Wesley," I moan.

"Fuck me, Riley. You're beautiful when you talk dirty."

He puts me down but reaches between my legs and pulls my panties down. I kick them off as quickly as I can, thankful for once that this stupid uniform is a skirt. He pulls a condom out of his pocket and smirks when I chortle.

With a sexy as sin grin, he slowly undoes his belt, button, and zipper as he teases me. He rolls it on and lifts me, pressing me against the wall once again. He sits at my entrance until I wriggle in frustration and then he plunges deep inside me. No foreplay, but it's not needed. I got wet the moment he kissed me. I was already soaked, so this intensifies it. The corded muscles in his arms and neck strain as he holds me and thrusts into me.

"You'd better come quick, baby. I want to feel you milk my cock, and if we get caught, I'm taking it out on your ass."

He fucks me hard and fast, but it's not the right angle. I know we have limited time because anyone could walk through that door at any minute. It excites me, but I can't concentrate. "Wes, I need more."

He pulls out and places me on my feet and spins me. But before I can protest, he is angling me how he wants me. I press the palms of my hands against the wall. His hand comes down between my shoulder blades and he grabs my hip, holding me in place, pressing into me once more.

Deep. He's so deep that I moan and bite my arm to keep quiet.

"I'm going to ride your ass, Riley, and you're going to come for me. Do you understand?" I nod, lost, feeling every nerve ending fire. He collars my throat, pulling me toward him, my back still perfectly arched to accommodate his size. "Answer me." He growls and tightens his fingers, cutting off my air.

I suck in a labored breath, but I need more. My vision blackens and dots around the corners. It should terrify me. He could do some serious damage, but I feel nothing but a euphoric high. I've never had this feeling in my life. It's as if I'm floating. I barely recognize my voice as I whisper "yes" and he reaches around me and rubs my clit. I clench down so hard on him and my knees all but give out as I come.

"There's my good girl," he coos as he finds his own release moments later. I press my face against the cool wall as he pulls out of me and tosses the condom. I don't have it in me to move. He slides my hair off my shoulder and kisses it gently. "You take my cock so well, beautiful." He picks up my discarded panties and helps me back into them. "Come on, let's get out of here."

I'm the literal definition of stars in her eyes right now. I have never had an experience as thrilling as that in my life. And as I'm relishing in my high, the thought hits me. I really know nothing of importance about him. He's from New Jersey and his brother died when he was seventeen. I know from social media he's a playboy, but the more time I spend with him, the more I know it's all an act. I take a steadying breath and ask, "Will you tell me more about you? The real you, not the social media playboy."

He's silent as we walk and I'm afraid he won't answer me, but then he says, "You don't want that man, Hellcat."

TWENTY-THREE
WESLEY

No one ever wants to get to know me. I screw and chew. It's the best I know how. I don't even know where to begin. Talking about myself is such a foreign concept. The only time I've come remotely close to telling Julien and Zander my sordid past is when I was piss ass drunk on my brother's one year death anniversary and I started punching a wall.

Julien pulled my arms behind my back, holding me in place as I spewed word vomit. I'm not even sure how coherent my rant was, but after that, things were different. That's when my playboy persona came out. I knew I had to hide my pain in order to make it through Pointebreak—to climb to the top of the food chain. And that's exactly what I did. I buried my brother deep within the recesses of my mind, never to show the light of day. Just like his cold, dead body buried six-feet under.

"I want all of you, Wes," she says, looking up at me like I'm some fucking hero.

"Come on, let's get some lunch," I say, changing the subject.

She huffs in annoyance, but follows me out of the room and into the quad. I take her hand in mine, needing to feel her. I always want to touch her or be near her. Something about Riley's soft voice and steady gaze always manages to settle my anxieties. The only other person in the world that used to make me feel that way was my mom. Well, until Elias's untimely death. Zander and Julien are my found brothers, and I would do anything for them, but Riley is my heart. She makes me feel complete.

I know I'm not going to be able to push this conversation off. If there's one thing I have learned about Riley in the short time of knowing her, it's that she lacks patience. She's going to be in for a world of hurt if she can't control that. Julien's on his own timeline. To hell with anyone else. And Zander knows nothing but patience. He watches until he has every angle figured out. That's why it's no surprise that he caught wind of Riley coming to Pointebreak even before her father announced it on his campaign tour. Thank God he did. I think Julien would have attacked her if he had been surprised when she stepped from the car.

I've seen the video. Riley's shocked and hurt face when she heard the news will forever be ingrained in my mind. I felt for her that day. The one person she thought she could trust to have her back turned on her without batting an eye. Then she broke a little more this weekend when her dad lied on TV about talking to her. I was watching her from the door and heard the audio from her phone before making myself known.

I would know that prick's voice anywhere. I've heard it enough over the last three years when Julien told us the plan to get his old man out of jail.

Riley's playing with the food on her tray instead of eating. I know she has at least one more class today and then she normally spends a few hours in the library doing her homework. I usually give her space at that point and Zander makes sure she's safe from the video monitors. When Zander's home, he's tuned in to everything she does. Every conversation, and every place she visits on campus.

That's how he knows Ava and Nick have been seeing one another behind his back. He's letting it go for now, after some convincing on my part, but it won't be long before his protective side comes out again. He doesn't want Ava anywhere near this life. But he also knows unless he kills his old man, there's little he can do to save Ava. She'll be married off as a pawn. It's not uncommon for arranged marriages to happen in our world. It's a business acquisition. A way to unite families with common interests.

"I'll meet you outside the library tonight after you finish. We will go somewhere private where we can talk."

Her head snaps up, and she looks deep into my eyes, waiting for the catch. "No one needs to hear my fucked up life." I let a humorless chuckle slip free. "Most of us here have some kind of sad story. No use spreading it around for others to exploit."

Riley offers me a warm smile and nods her head. "Okay. I'd like that."

Nervous energy flows through my body and I can't stop pacing outside of the library. The evenings are getting chilly even though it's only mid September, but before long the ground will have a frost on it. I run my fingers through my hair and tug at the ends, needing to get a hold of myself. It's a crazed mess, but I don't care. This is insane.

"Hey," Riley says from behind me.

I stop my pacing and scoop her into my arms, kissing her

warmly. She sighs contentedly into my embrace, the scent of her hair filling my senses, and I feel myself relax. I take her bag from her and the two of us walk across campus. I know our conversation will remain private because these buildings —excluding the gym—should be empty. Julien was at home when I left, but Zander ran out of there without so much as a hi.

We stop in the middle of the quad, where I've set up a blanket and a small spread of fruit, crackers, and cheese. She looks at the blanket and back up at me, her eyes sparkling with amusement. I help her sit and hand her another blanket to place over her legs. Her fingers trace the soft edge of the fabric as she waits, her gaze distant and unfocused. The sun is setting, and before long, it will shield us in the cloak of darkness. Exactly how I want it.

"How much do you know about my family, Hellcat?" I know she's looked into all of us. She'd be a fool to not, and comments in passing have made it clear she has.

"Not much. I've only found your socials. I looked up your brother after getting his name from you, but the information I found is…lacking. From what I know of you and where you come from, I assume it's by design."

"Yeah. All for good reason. It's easy to keep things out of the press and offline with enough money thrown at the situation." I take a deep breath.

"My father is Christos Bastian. He's heavily known for his dealings in skin."

Her eyes widen. "Like sex trafficking?" she asks.

I nod and continue. "Girls, and sometimes boys, depending on the client, weapons, and drugs are the most lucrative businesses. You'll find most families at Pointebreak have their hands in these trades." Riley nods, which gives me the confidence to continue. "I've never liked it, but that's my reality. I learned early on what we do and to keep my emotions out of it. When I turned fourteen, my dad gave me a girl as a birthday present to use."

I still remember it. I lost my virginity to a drugged out girl who couldn't even tell me where she was. She was so high on whatever the hell they gave her. Her name was Mallory. That was about all I got from her before she undid my pants and climbed on top of me and rode me until I came. I was fourteen and horny. It's not my proudest moment. I didn't know her age, how long she'd been held captive, or anything else. I know she did that job like a pro, like someone who knew that was their fate and she had accepted it.

Dreams of saving her flitted in and out of my head for the next few weeks. When I asked my father about her, he smiled and assumed I wanted another girl to fuck. Not that I wanted to save the one whose lost brown eyes had already taken root in my subconscious.. He was almost proud of me. I felt disgusted with myself and my family. I confided in Elias and he told me it's just the way things were. My mom doesn't know, I never told her. She knows the type of man my father is, but never stopped him.

"Anyway, after that night, I knew I wanted nothing to do with my father's business or his clientele."

"And what about your brother?"

I give a mirthless laugh. "He was the golden boy, and my father's shining star. Elias was following in his footsteps like the prodigal son he was. But a lot of what he did was to protect me. We may have the same parents, but we were very different. My dad got his claws into Elias at an early age and molded him to be a carbon copy of himself. Elias knew as long as he took over, I would be free to do what I wanted. And in a way, I'll always be indebted to him. I'm more like my mom when it comes to people. She cares too much for them."

"How does that work when your dad sells people like animals? Doesn't it bother her?" Riley's getting heated. The blanket is being crushed between her clenched hands.

"Not much you can do when you're forced into a marriage, Hellcat. She hates it, I know she does. But she can't do anything about it. She focused her energy on us instead. She was always offering a shoulder and a hug whenever we needed to feel loved."

"She sounds nice, Wes."

I nod. "Yeah, she was."

Riley scrunches her face. "Was? I thought she was alive."

My fingers find my hair, and I run them through again. "My father blamed me for the death of my brother," I pause and swallow hard, "and in a way, he's not wrong. I was at a party that night. I was seventeen, hanging with my friends, and things got a bit more exciting than usual. Drugs and alcohol were flying around like candy thrown at a parade. It wasn't my scene, but my friends were too high to go anywhere. I wanted to leave, but I was drunk and knew I couldn't make it home safely." Taking a deep breath, I push it out before I continue. "Elias was making sure there were no issues with a shipment that night while my parents were at a charity event. It's not the first time, as dad was doing it more and more frequently."

I snort. Ironically, they attended a human trafficking awareness event. I think it was my dad's sick way of getting his kicks in. Knowing he was the one responsible for a lot of missing persons. But it was also an easy way to keep the target off his back. Who would ever suspect the man who donates hundreds of thousands to a cause that exists because of evil men like him?

"I called him and asked him to come get me. He was a good brother, would do anything for me, and handed the responsibility of handling the shipment to his right-hand man, Marcus."

I don't enjoy talking about this, about Elias. I want to claw my heart out. It's my fucking fault. Riley must sense my hesitation because she crawls over to me and sits on my lap, rubbing my shoulders.

"Hey, it's okay. If you don't want to tell me, that's fine. You've shared so much already. Thank you." She kisses my jaw and molds her body against mine. Her warmth seeps into my bones, a comforting shift to the dead I feel inside.

I want to stop. I can't tell her it's my damn fault he's dead. But she deserves to know. She needs to hear my darkened truths, even if it drives her away from me. She'll never be free of me, even if she doesn't know that yet.

"Someone was tailing him. Elias was so intent on getting me out of that party that he forgot to keep tabs on the surrounding cars." I shake my head, the memories flooding back like a dam broke. "Shortly after hitting the highway to bring me home, a car rammed into us from behind, sending us spiraling into the guardrail. If the impact hadn't thrown him through the windshield, we both would have survived."

She covers her mouth with her hands and shakes her head in disbelief. "Oh, my God. I'm so sorry, Wes. I don't even know what to say."

She hugs me tight as I rub her back, hoping the feel of her will ease some of the anxiety trembling through me. "My dad blamed me for his death and my mother shut down. That was almost four years ago."

"How old were you?" she asks.

"Seventeen. Pointebreak was always in the cards, but I couldn't wait to come. I couldn't wait to get away from my father's wrathful words and my mother's vacant expression. She died the day he did. I remember hearing her wail when they arrived at the scene and the cops had to tell her he was dead on impact. My father held her up and glared daggers at me the whole time. When we got home, he beat the shit out of me with no regards to my injuries."

I smile like it's no big deal, reverting to my carefree persona, but she doesn't let me.

"He's a monster, Wes. Who would do something like that?"

"Christos." I deadpan. Her arms tighten around me, a comforting pressure that makes me tremble, and I hug her back tightly. "Thanks, Riley." I kiss her shoulder, and then her neck, before slowly finding my way to her lips. I want her so damn much it hurts.

"I need you, Riles." She grinds down on my lap, slowly working her hips back and forth over me as she attaches her mouth to my throat. Her quiet moans of pleasure stirring my growing desire for her. "I don't have a condom."

I didn't expect this turn of events when I left the house. This isn't how I pictured her reacting. "I'm clean, though."

"And I'm on birth control," she groans as she fumbles with my belt between us.

My abs clench with the thought of feeling her bare. I've never fucked anyone without protection, but with Riley, I want there to be nothing between us. I want to feel every bit of her and I want to come deep inside her. My dick jumps at the thought of my seed deep inside her, dripping out of her and down her thighs. I could get used to that.

I lean back and give her the access she needs to undo my pants and free my aching cock.

TWENTY-FOUR

RILEY

My belly flips with a mixture of excitement and nervousness as I anticipate the feel of Wesley bare inside me. We're outside, where anyone could walk by, and that adds to the thrill. I scoot down his legs, taking his throbbing dick inside my mouth, and he rubs the back of my head in gentle strokes.

"Such a dirty girl, Riley. You want me to fuck this pretty face of yours?"

Oh God, yes. His words are like molten lava to my pussy, and wetness pools between my thighs. I still can't believe he told me everything about his brother. My heart aches for him and I want him to use my body to repair the parts I shattered by making him open up to me. I nod the best I can as I plant my fist at the base of him and he jerks his hips up.

He gathers my hair in his hand and helps me set the pace he wants as he works himself in and out of my mouth. I want him to come down my throat. I want to taste him as I swallow him. Thoughts of Julien throat fucking me ricochet through my mind and the moment he made me swallow his come. And instead of pulling me out of the moment, all it does is make me latch on to him and suck harder.

Thoughts of another man shouldn't turn me on more, but they do. Just like when I knew Zander was watching in the cameras at the gym. It turned me on so much knowing he was witnessing my pleasure. And deep down, I hoped he got off just as hard as I did.

Wesley's heavy breathing infiltrates my senses, and he pops me off him.

"Come sit on my cock, beautiful."

I waste no time as I crawl back into his lap, rubbing my clothed core against his hardened length. I sit up on my knees, pull my panties to the side, and position him at my entrance. Then I stare into his eyes as I slowly sink down on his length. The stretch burns, especially from earlier, but it feels so damn good. His tortured groan in pleasure is all I need to hear to urge me on.

I also figured sex without a condom wouldn't be very different, but boy, was I wrong. A wave of electric tingling, a thousand tiny sparks, shoots through my body as my synapses fire. He almost feels bigger somehow. He lays back and places his hands on my hips, helping me ride him.

"Ride it baby. Take your pleasure, because when you're done, I'm going to fuck my come deep inside of you. I'll own you, Hellcat."

I squeeze around his cock in response to his filthy mouth and do as he asks with my hands on his chest for balance. The tantalizing sensation of our bodies moving together sends waves of ecstasy through me as he hits that sweet spot, making me gasp in pleasure. My heady pants are so loud if there is anyone around, I'm sure they'd be enjoying the show. But if I'm being honest, the thought of someone seeing us in such a compromising position has my orgasm racing to its brink.

"Wes, I-I'm close," I pant.

"That's it, Riley. Fuck yourself on my cock. You're taking it like such a good fucking girl," he grits. He clamps his mouth shut, the muscles in his jaw and neck strain as he tightens the grip on my hips, holding me still. His abs contract and he pushes a heavy breath out of his nose.

I hear the footsteps he's probably already heard to my right and I slow as I wait for whoever it is to leave the area. I look around me, but Wesley angles my face to focus on him again.

"Don't worry about them. It's dark now. They won't know it's us," he reassures.

He's right. I look around once more and push the thought out of my damn head. When he thrusts up into me, rattling my body, I know I'm as good as gone. My orgasm comes back in full force.

"That's it, baby. You're squeezing me so damn tight. I can't wait to come deep inside you."

A pair of legs comes into view and when I look up, Zander's dark eyes are staring down into mine. I suck in a deep breath and try to scramble off Wesley, who holds me in place.

"Come for him, Luna," he commands in his deep, husky voice.

My eyes travel down Zander's body, and they stop on his hardened length. He's straining against the zipper on his pants and my mouth salivates, wanting a taste. Wesley squeezes my hips and thrusts up into me, my whole body rattling as I come. Oh, lord do I come. As I'm still working through my intense orgasm, Wesley flips us so I'm on my back and pounds into me, extending my own delicious release. Zander kneels down next to us and I focus on him. I can't help it. Wesley may be fucking me, but my body yearns for Zander as well. When I reach my hand out toward him, he leans forward and sucks my index and middle finger in his mouth before popping off them.

"Rub that pretty little clit and come again," he demands.

Wesley slows his pace, and I slide my fingers between us, doing exactly as Zander wants. My focus bounces between both muscular men, unsure who to give my attention to. Wesley doesn't stop moving in me, but he also doesn't seem to care that Zander's here watching. Have they done this before? Wesley seems overly calm with his best friend watching him have sex.

"She's in her own head, Wes. Better change it up if you want her to come again."

"If you hadn't shown up, she would have come all over my dick again by now." He retorts with a grunt as he continues to snap his hips into me.

How the hell are they carrying on this conversation like it's nothing?

Wesley pulls out and slides my panties down my legs before helping me to my knees, facing away from him. He slides back in, pulling my back flush with his chest. Zander is directly in front of me now, his dark eyes focus on my face, examining me like I'm a science project.

"Kiss her, Zan. She needs you."

It's unnerving how true those words are. I need Zander. I need to feel his warm body, feel his hard dick that's straining in his slacks. Zander takes my chin between his thumb and forefinger and brings his lips close to mine, barely brushing them as Wesley continues to slide in and out of me.

"Daddy," I whisper as I flutter my eyes closed and rest my hands on his shoulders. That one word is enough to force him to press his lips against mine and his tongue to invade my mouth as his hand slides down to my throat. I whimper into him as Wesley uses my body, working us both up to perfect pleasure. I'm floating higher and higher. It's too much, all too much.

I gasp, so close to finding my release. "I-I," I pant against Zander's lips. He squeezes and I wheeze, trying to catch my breath around his large hand.

Wesley moves faster in me, my body bouncing while Zan holds me in place, never letting up on his kiss. Wesley groans as I come with him, my whole body shaking with the force of it. He angles my face away from Zander and kisses my neck and jaw, whispering praises into my ear as I slowly come down. When I finally open my eyes, Zander's nowhere to be found. I look all around. Did I imagine it? I touch my beard burned lips and know it was real. The vulnerability of the moment leaves me feeling foolish as Wesley withdraws, his come dripping out of me just like he wanted. Even though I smile, a feeling of loneliness washes over me. I've never experienced something like this in my life, but not having Zander here after what just happened is doing strange things to me. I almost feel abandoned. And where did he come from, anyway?

How could Zander show up like that and then run away without so much as a goodbye? Does he hate the fact Wesley and I are together? Have Wes and Zan shared before? Both men seemed oddly comfortable with one another. I haven't had enough time to process what's going on with him. Zander's hot and cold. The minute I think I understand him, he does a one-eighty and I second guess myself all over again.

"Come on, Hellcat. Let's get you back to your dorm."

It's on the tip of my tongue to ask to sleep at his place instead, but I know going the needy route will probably get me pissed on. Julien would see it as a sign of weakness and exploit it. Probably tell the school I'm sleeping with all three of them for real. Which is the last thing I need because I already hear the snide comments when the Kings aren't around. The girls are jealous as hell, and the guys can't wait for the Kings to drop me to have a piece. I've basically become the campus slut and I've only had sex with one person here.

Now's not the time to get weak and let sex go to my head. It's no big deal.

Wesley helps me back into my panties and smirks when I wiggle my hips.

"What?" I ask, picking up my bag as he finishes packing up everything.

"Nothin'. Just picturing my come dripping down your luscious thighs." He gives me a shit-eating grin, then takes my hand and pulls me against him, sealing his lips over mine for another kiss. "Thank you, Riley. You don't know how special you are." He drops his forehead to mine and we stand like that for another moment before he tugs me with him toward my dorm.

Tonight was…loaded. I have *some* answers but more questions.

"Just so you know, no one else would have seen you tonight. I had a few guys keeping the area cleared for us. Zander and Julien were the only ones allowed to get past."

That tidbit of information surprises me. I'm grateful knowing that not anyone would have seen us, but now I want to know what Zander was doing out there. Wesley walks me up to my room and gives me one more kiss before wishing me sweet dreams and leaving me alone. I open my door and all the lights are off. *Hmmm, I guess Ava's still out with Nick.*

I flip the switch and light floods the space. I stop dead in my tracks and look around at my destroyed room.

"What the hell?" I ask out loud, taking a step closer to my scattered items. My clothes lay strewn around my room, as if someone had been searching for something. Ava's side is still as neat as it was this morning when we left. The bedding lay in a chaotic heap, the once-fluffy pillow discarded on the floor. I pick it up and drop it on the bed, and sit down, letting my eyes roam over the damage.

My first thought was to call Wesley—or hell, Zander. He's the computer wiz, and I'm sure he could tap into the cameras and get a recording on who came and would do this. My eyes well with tears and I take a shuddering breath. I feel dirty—violated. Having someone go through my belongings is more than I bargained for.

Who do I even tell about this? I doubt the administration is going to care. They don't seem like the type to interfere. *Or maybe they will?* Has anyone ever brought anything like this to their attention before? Has something like this ever happened? Or is this some sort of hazing? The students here are from different backgrounds, but that doesn't mean that they don't all play similar games. I seem to make more enemies than friends after all.

Then my gaze lands on some vaseline and gauze sitting perfectly in the center of my desk, and my blood boils. Every cell in my being shakes with rage as the puzzle pieces click into place.

Julien. That motherfucker!

There's no other explanation for this. The gears in my head spin as I work to piece together what could have happened. Of course, he would leave Ava's side alone. Zander would probably kill him if he touched her stuff or messed with her. But me? I'm free game.

I growl and scream into my pillow. I want to punch him, or scratch his eyes out or something. This is the last thing I need to be dealing with after what has already been a confusing night.

I hate him.

Julien Azarian can kiss my ass. I'm not backing down from this. He can't bully me any more. I'm not going down without a fight.

Once more, I glare at the vaseline and gauze again and chuck them straight into the trash bin. I want nothing from that asshole. I change out of my uniform into a pair of sweatpants and a t-shirt and put a pair of headphones in to blast music, as I pick up the mess. All while wishing terrible, horrible things upon Julien.

TWENTY-FIVE
RILEY

Within an hour, my room is back to normal, and Ava still has yet to return. I know I'm not her keeper, and it seems she can use some freedom, but I hope she's being careful. It's easy to get carried away when you don't have someone watching your every move. Not that I didn't have freedom, I did…kind of. James was almost always there. Bodyguard and chauffeur. I never felt as if I was stuck in my life, though. I get the sense Ava has more going on than she's willing to share, but if Zander is any indication, she was under lock and key.

I almost wonder if she was under house arrest, or if she could have friends.

I smile down at my phone and shoot her a quick reply to be safe.

While cleaning, I took the time to plan to catch Julien off guard and be able to get a few words in. It has to be tonight.

If I wait, or say nothing and ignore this, he'll think he can do this again and again. I may not be from his world, but that doesn't mean I don't know how to fight for myself. Pair that with the almost daily training I'm getting from Wesley and I should be able to get a few kicks in.

My mouth pops open when a thought smacks into me. Were Wesley and Zander accomplices in this? Did they set me up? Keep me out and away, so he had time to do this? I shake my head in disbelief.

No.

Wes wouldn't do that to me. He wouldn't let Julien mess with me for the hell of it.

Why not though? It's not like I've known him for long. He could be just as cunning as the rest of them. Disbelief floods me and I refuse to believe either of them had anything to do with it.

But I've been here less than two weeks, and neither of them is pushing me around like Julien is. Maybe that was the plan all along. Make me feel safe—secure with them, make me let my guard down. Wouldn't that be funny? Get me to fall for them and then turn around and use it as a cruel joke.

My stomach sinks at the thought, even though my heart is screaming at me to not listen to my traitorous brain. Rage blinds me as I pace around my small space. Everything seems to be accounted for. I had my laptop and phone with me in my bag, and other than some clothes, I didn't bring many personal effects from home.

I think about texting my dad to ask him to find out more about Julien, but then think better of it. After the crap he's pulled and the lies he's been spewing, I can't trust him. I rub my aching chest as that thought guts me. He's the last person I have, and I can't trust him anymore. He's tossed me aside like I'm nothing.

Yet I still find myself dialing his number. It rings...

rings…rings. I expect it to click over to voicemail, but his familiar voice comes through the phone.

"Hey sweetie, how's school going?"

Tears fill my eyes at his happy, familiar tone. This, this is the man that I know and love. The one who calls me sweetie and smiles as he talks to me.

"Daddy," I say with a breath.

"Riley, is everything okay?" His voice changes in an instant, like he's on alert.

I swallow past the lump in my throat. "Y-yeah. It's going okay."

"I miss you. How are classes?"

"I miss you too. Classes are okay. My roommate is great, though." I pause, the actual question I want to ask on the tip of my tongue.

"Good, I'm happy to hear that. You'll come out of there stronger and smarter than ever. You've got a bright future."

Gag. He's talking to me like he's sitting around a bunch of people, putting on a show for them. Or maybe…that's exactly what he's doing. "How come you haven't returned my calls?"

He laughs, and there's some static before his voice is directly in my ear. "Not sure what you're talking about. We spoke the other day."

I shake my head, disappointment filling me. He's using me as a pawn in this game of his. "I hate you," I whisper as my hand shakes and I fight to keep the sob at bay. This is truly a turning point in the relationship I have with my dad and not for the better. Things had been going downhill for a while, but I never pictured cutting myself out of his life. He's my dad.

"I'm sorry you feel that way, Riles."

"Yeah. Don't worry, I won't bother you again."

I hang up and wipe tears from my eyes, not allowing him

to get the last word in, and I block his number. If he won't make the effort, then neither will I. I'm sure he'll send word through James if he really needs to get in touch with me. The thought of also blocking James crosses my mind, but in the past few years since he's come on, he's been more of a father to me than my own. I wonder if he has a wife and kids.

I can't go down rabbit holes right now. Not when I have the chance to make Julien pay for what he did to my room. I throw my phone on my bed and pull my running shoes on, like I'm going for a jog…at night.

This will never work. I know I shouldn't be walking around campus alone. Especially in the dark. I push out a heavy breath and sit on the edge of my bed. A knock on my door has me looking up and narrowing my eyes. Now, who could that be? Not Ava. She would have called out for me by now if she didn't have her key, and not Nick, because he's with her. And that's the end of my friends list. The door handle jiggles, and I can't help how my heart kicks up a notch and my breathing comes out a little ragged.

And now I know I'm paranoid. This is stupid—*I'm* being stupid.

"Who is it?" I push an exasperated sigh past my lips. *Get a grip.*

No one answers. I grab the closest thing to me, which is a desk lamp, and hold it, ready to bash someone over the head with it. I slowly wrap my hand around the door handle and apply a death grip to it before I take a soundless breath and pull the door open with force.

Derek stands on the other side of the door and jumps back at the sight of me. He eyes the lamp I'm holding above my head and looks back down at me, waiting for me to put it down. It's times like these that I wish I were taller. Being able to look down on someone would be more threatening.

"What are you doing here?" I put the lamp on the floor but refuse to move away from the door.

He puts his hands in front of him, like he's looking at a dangerous animal he doesn't want to spook. "I'm here to tell you that you're in danger. Those guys, the Kings, aren't good for you." He holds his splinted hand up as a reminder of what happened to him because I kissed him. "They're ruthless, and are going to use a nice girl like you."

A few weeks ago, I would have bought that, but now… I'm not so sure. Yes, Julien still wants to watch me fall, but not Wesley. And I don't think Zander wants to either. My phone rings and I turn to look at it. It's too far away to see who's calling. Probably Zander, because I know now he watches those fucking cameras like a hawk and I'm sure he's seen who came to visit.

"I have something I want to show you. It will prove to you they don't care. Do you trust me?"

No, I sure as hell do not. Repulsion runs through me, making my skin crawl. The hairs on the back of my neck stand at attention as I look at his outstretched hand. My mind is screaming "get the hell out of dodge". I start to bend to pick up the forgotten lamp, and he tuts at me as I freeze in place.

"Don't even fucking think about it." He switches an impressive sized knife blade open, the light glinting off of the shiny metal, and points it at me. The tip looks sharp enough to slice through flesh with little pressure. Derek's willing to do a hell of a lot of damage by the looks of that thing. The only thing I brought to this knife fight is a lamp, and I can't even grab it.

I slowly stand to my full height and do my damnedest not to shake in fear. A feat made nearly impossible because of the adrenaline coursing through my veins. The blood rushing between my ears deafens out any other sounds, and I feel like

I'm trapped in a small bubble. I know if I can keep him here and keep him talking, Zander will show up eventually. Or at least one of the guys. My phone goes off again, but this time I don't look at it. I don't need to make this easier for him.

"Why don't we talk inside?" I take a step to the side to allow him room to pass, but he doesn't take the bait. Instead, he grabs my wrist and pulls me close to him. A shrill scream leaves my lips until the tip of the blade presses against my racing pulse. I snap my mouth shut and shudder as my eyes fill with tears.

"Looks like you're already dressed to go out. Move."

"Please, Derek, don't do this," I plead, being careful not to move too much.

He shoves me forward, through the door, and down the hall, keeping the blade trained to my throat and his hand firmly around my arm.

"Derek, listen to me," I try again, but he presses the knife closer to my skin. I can feel the cold metal and the bite as it nearly punctures my flesh. I pull my bottom lip between my teeth and bite hard, keeping my trembling chin under control. Tears run down my cheeks and it's getting harder to breathe out of my nose.

"Shut up," he demands.

As we make our way down the stairs and out of the building, a thought hits me. Why is there no one else around? The halls aren't usually completely empty. He pushes me forward, and I put my hands up to open the door and he's not alone. Not that I thought it would be, but I hoped he was. It was already going to be an unfair fight, but now it's worse, much worse. There are three other masked men standing around, and their conversation stops as soon as they see us. I may have had a sliver of a chance if it was only one, but four? I'll never be able to fight them off. Stopping short, I press my body back into Derek's—the lesser of the evils right now. He bands his arm around my chest tighter and presses the knife a little until a sharp pain pricks through my senses.

My hand immediately flies to the wound as blood descends on my sweatshirt. *Fucking bastard!* It's on the tip of my tongue to say something, but I wipe the wetness coating my finger on his shirt instead. Here's hoping it's enough to mark him if I don't make it out of this alive.

"Get her outta here."

He shoves me forward, and I stumble, not expecting the force, into the arms of the tall, broad man in front of me. I immediately try to dodge his grasp, but he holds me tight. So, I do the next best thing, and drop like dead weight and let out the loudest, high-pitched scream I can muster. Someone had to have heard it. I look at the windows that face the parking lot, but I can't make out any faces. No one is watching. A hand clamps over my mouth and rough hands pull me upright and flush against his firm body.

"Shut the fuck up," a deep voice echoes in my ear. His voice is unfamiliar, but harsh.

These are not the men to mess with. I can't overpower them, and I know I can't seduce them like in the movies. And if I give up and give in, I'll die. My options aren't looking so good and my panic attack is settling in. My breathing shortens to breathy pants. There isn't enough oxygen in my lungs, and it burns trying to suck in a breath past his rough hand. My heart is pounding like I just finished a marathon and sweat coats my body.

I'm going to die.

I know it. There's no way out of this.

I stare at Derek with wide, pleading eyes, and he won't even look at me, his eyes trained on the ground.

"Look at me," I shout from behind the man's hand, but it's too muffled to be understood. Tears fall with abandon down my cheeks, and on to the ground below. "Please,

Derek," I say, pulling in a deep breath. What's his angle in all this? And where the hell are they taking me? A strangled noise escapes me—half sob, half gasp, and I'm shaking so hard I feel like I might snap in half.

I fight. I kick and wrestle, trying with all my might to free myself. If I can just get out from under their grasp, I can run. Adrenaline is coursing through my veins so strongly that I can hardly feel anything. Physically and mentally, I am shutting down, and I can't. I focus on only one thing.

Freedom.

I have to get away from them. In movies, when the subject gets moved to a secondary location, it never ends well. I've got to believe that's true in real life kidnapping as well. Victims hardly ever get found, and when they do, it's months, or even years later, if at all. And knowing the clientele that goes here, it wouldn't surprise me if I was going to be sold off. Or used for blackmail against my dad. Wesley told me his dad trafficked people.

What if this is all a setup? What if the Kings were working with Derek all along and this was their plan? I know Julien hates me, but would he really have me kidnapped? Deep down, I don't believe it, but my fear is overpowering any other rational thought. I hate them. I hate all three of them and my dad. If I had never met them, this wouldn't be happening now.

One man grabs at my legs and I kick out with all my might, catching his knee and he buckles when he puts weight on it.

"You'll pay for that, bitch," he groans and rights himself again. He limps and I internally high-five myself. I tug and pull, trying with all my might to free myself from their grasp.

The cocking of a gun is the only thing that makes me pause. My heart barreling in my chest as the realization hits me like a freight train.

Students can't have guns.

Panic settles deep. It radiates from every pore on my body. My palms sweat, my heart races, and I can't think straight. I know if it pulls me under, I'm as good as dead. Whoever these men are won't care if I cry or beg. They are here to do a job, and nothing will get in their way. The fight leaves me in a whoosh as one of them trains the barrel between my eyebrows.

I turn to look at Derek and grind out, "Why?"

Derek holds up his hand, showing off Julien's handy work. A single splint is the only thing amiss with him. "Your boyfriends need to be knocked down a few pegs. What better way to do it than through you?"

I shake my head back and forth, trying to understand. What gain does he get out of this?

"I never wanted you to get hurt, Derek," I plead as the men drag me toward a white plumber's van. With the gun to my head, I don't fight. The back door slides open and the one holding me backs up into it, dragging me with him in his arms and forcing me inside.

Derek places his phone to his ear. "It's done."

TWENTY-SIX

RILEY

They shackle my arms above me, securing handcuffs around each wrist and settle in nice and close—one man on either side and one in front of me. The men rip their masks off as soon as the door shuts and the driver heads toward the edge of the property. I'm right. Definitely not students. These men are easily in their mid thirties and rough looking. The students here look like prep-school kids in comparison.

My shoulders jerk, shaking against the restraints as the metal clangs together. My head hangs low, tears streaming down my face, blurring my vision as I fight to breathe. I'm not cut out for this crap. I half expect someone to jump out and yell "surprise" and tell me I failed a test I didn't even know I was taking. Everyone would get a good laugh at my expense. And honestly, right now, I wouldn't care. I'd laugh with them. You fooled me. Ha. Ha.

Except I know that's not what's going to happen here. I know it from the way the men leer at me.

"Where are you taking me?" I ask, keeping my head

lowered. "You know my father's going to be looking for me. Michael Whittier, the Governor?"

The men exchange a curious look, but they don't seem bothered by the information. In fact, the one to my right, his eyes light up like a tree and he licks his lips as his beady eyes travel the length of my body, stopping at various spots.

I've never wanted to vomit more in my life. "Who do you work for?"

No answer. Not that I actually expected one, but a girl can hope. The van slows, and I know we must be at the front gates now. This is my last chance before we're off school grounds. The driver rolls down his window and says something to the posted guard.

"He—" I yell and the man across from me with the gun smacks it across my cheek, my head snapping to the side from the force of the blow. Pain brands my skin as I struggle to take a deep breath. I turn my face into my shoulder as the tears flow in rivulets down my cheeks. I think he broke something. My face is numb and throbs all at the same time. *Son of a bitch, it hurts!*

"You don't know when to stop, do ya?" he whispers in my ear. "I'm going to have fun breaking you. Boss never said anything about no stops along the way."

I shake my head, hoping to wake up from this nightmare. "No, please," I say quietly as my crying picks up. My entire body wracks with sobs.

The van pulls forward again, and I know that was my last chance. Unless I can escape, I'm at their mercy; and no amount of fighting is going to put me on top. These men easily have eighty pounds or more on me. And being restrained, I don't have a chance. They are going to do whatever they want to me, and I won't be able to stop them.

I don't have my phone. No one knows where I am, or who I'm with. And I only know that someone turned off the cameras. Which means Zander is probably the one who was calling me before Derek dragged me out of my dorm. I know how much he watches those things.

The van jostles us and the men carry on a quiet conversation, as if I don't exist. I listen, hoping for any useful information. Because I'm damned sure I will find a way out of this, and these fuckers will rue the day they messed with me. I'm not going down without a fight.

The van comes to a sudden stop and I lift my head, trying to look out the windshield to see where we are. It was already dark when they kidnapped me, which means I can't see a damned thing outside the headlights. Plus, I have no idea where we are. How far from campus did we get on the short drive? Was it actually longer? My sense of time has flown out the window with each sense on high alert.

I say nothing. I know it won't do me any damn favors, and I don't need my face bashed in more. The front door opens and closes, and then the driver slides the back door open. It stops with a final bang and I jump in my spot. I glare daggers at him as he squats down, so he's directly in my line of sight.

Dark hair and eyes, some face scarring that looks like acne caused them. He's covered from head to toe in black, which covers any distinguishing marks, like tattoos, on the rest of his body. I file as much as I can to memory, hoping it will serve me well.

"You know, it's been a long time since we've had merchandise as pretty as you." Merchandise? So I'm being sold off. That answers that question. He drags his finger down the side of my cheek that I know is probably turning a deep shade of purple, then gives it a slap. Under normal circumstances, it wouldn't have hurt, maybe just a slight sting, but with the bruise, I cry out in pain.

"I like when they fight. Makes me hard as a fucking rock."

I glance between his spread thighs and then back up to him. "You're sick." I try to sound as disgusted as I feel, but it comes out scared. I'm terrified. My body shakes involuntarily and I know the three of them see it.

He smiles, but it doesn't reach his cold, dead eyes. "All part of my charm." He looks at the other men. "Let's play a game, boys." He opens his hand and holds up two small white pills. "Open your mouth."

I shake my head quickly. "No," I whisper. He laughs and puts the gun against my temple. "I said open. Your fucking. Mouth."

My heart pounds in my chest and I can feel it pulse in my throat. Whatever that drug is, if I don't calm down, it's going to take hold of me a hell of a lot faster than it should. When I make no move to acquiesce, he squeezes my cheeks together and forces me to, then shoves the pill between my lips and holds my mouth closed. The sharp taste of medicine assaults my taste buds and I try to spit it out.

"Swallow it. Now!" he screams in my face, pushing the barrel harder into my forehead and covering my nose as well, cutting off my air supply. "Or I'll crush it and force you to snort it."

I hope I can throw this thing up. My tears start up again, a steady stream down my cheeks. I work hard to swallow them with the little spit I have. My mouth is so damn dry, it feels like cotton. He removes his hand from my face. I'm going to die or be raped by the end of this anyway, and I don't want to feel like the timid thing I feel like right now. I want to go down swinging. To be more of a brat, I open my mouth wide and stick out my tongue, showing him I took it. I see the flash of desire cross his eyes and bile rises in my throat.

"Get up."

I stand, and someone unlocks the handcuffs from the bar and slaps it back down on my wrist. The only thing I can be thankful for is they put them in front of me and not behind. "You've got five minutes and then we're hunting." He grabs my sweatshirt and pulls me close to him. His breath smells of stale tobacco and I twist my face up. He pulls a knife from his pocket and rips my sweatshirt down the middle, exposing my bra. My skin breaks out in a cold sweat.

"Run!" He screams in my face. I trip over my feet, trying to get away from them and fall in the dirt. The men laugh behind me as I scramble to stand and take off. My feet pound on the soft ground of the woods as I trample on fallen leaves and vegetation. It's nearly impossible to see with only the light from the moon above me. Some low branches catch on my hair and the fabric of my sweatshirt as I keep up a steady pace. My vision swirls and I know whatever that pill was is going to catch up with me sooner than later.

I need to find a road, or a clearing, or something. There has to be someone around. But even as I think about it, I know the chance of me being close to anything familiar is slim. I don't know if those men know the area, but I have to assume they do.

My foot catches on a fallen log and I grind my teeth as I twist my ankle. I stop myself from falling by falling against a nearby tree, but I know I can't keep up the same pace. I wince as I place weight on my foot and hobble along until it feels marginally better.

"Come out, come out, wherever you are," their taunt comes. They still sound far away. I listen for a moment for crunching leaves, knowing time isn't on my side, but don't hear anything. My head spins and I shake it, warding off the vertigo it causes. I turn around in circles, trying to determine the best way to run.

How did my night turn from one of the best to one of

the worst in the blink of an eye? If I had just gone with my gut to confront Julien straight away instead of cleaning up, I may not have been in this mess. And who the hell is Derek working with? A sob breaks free and I slap my cuffed hands against my mouth, stifling it as I frantically look around me. I don't know which way to turn or where to go. I'm in the middle of the woods. The only people crazy enough to live out this way are hermits.

The temptation to give up and lay down to close my eyes weighs heavily on me, but if I roll over, I'll never survive it. Those men are going to more than rape and sodomize me. They're going to sell me to the highest bidder and I'll never be free again. I'll never see Leah and Ava again. Will Wesley and Zander mourn for me? Julien? I know he doesn't like me, but would he feel bad about what happened or feel responsible? As much as I'm on the outs with my dad, I know he would stand up for me and fight to find me. Even if it's just to protect his public image. I take a few steps in one direction and stop again. Everything is getting fuzzy and my body is sluggish.

Is that…is that light? Off to my left, I swear I see light coming from just over the hill. I race that way, stumbling every few as my mind screams at my body to fight whatever the hell they made me take. When he told me I only had five minutes, I knew throwing the pills up wasn't an option.

Get to the light. It's a chant I repeat over and over as I get closer. And just over the crest of the hill, I see it. A small ranch style home in the middle of the woods, and there are lights on inside. Somebody is home. Someone who can call for help.

I pant and wipe tears from my eyes as I focus on making it to the house. My mind is the driving force behind getting me to take step after torturous step. I hear rustling behind me, but I'm too focused on my task to give it more attention.

The house is a few yards away now. I'm so close I could cry. My ankle is giving out, but I trudge on, my pace slowing with each step. I climb up onto the small porch and fall in front of the door, my legs no longer able to support my weight. I don't even have the energy to reach out and knock on the door.

I lay my head down and focus on my breathing. I reach my arm up but miss the door by a couple of inches. But it doesn't matter. Quiet footsteps infiltrate my ears and the click of the lock on the door tells me it doesn't matter that I missed knocking. Whoever lives here knows I'm here now, and they are coming for me. The door swings open and light pools around me.

"Miss Whittier?"

I smile before everything goes dark.

LEAVE A REVIEW

If you enjoyed this book, please consider leaving a review on your favorite platform so others can find me too!

THANK YOU!

Wow, I can't believe this book has finally come to fruition. For the past year, I have dreamed about this book, and to see it finally in print feels unreal. There are many people who have made this possible.

First and foremost, thank you to my husband, Dan. You've been there for all of it and have been a sounding board when everything seemed impossible. Even when I thought I couldn't do it, you were there reminding me I could. Plus, I needed a new release, otherwise I couldn't keep going to book signings!

Katie Huminick- You will always be Katie to me, no matter how many people now call you Kate. My bestie since high school, I couldn't have done this without you! Thank you for letting me bounce ideas off of you and for taking me away for a writing break. I swear that's the reason this book was finished on time!

Jamie Buck- Thank you for being with me since the beginning. I'm not even sure how you found me, but you have been around since my first release, Sugar and Spice. Even when I was gone for three years, having babies, you never lost touch with me. Thank you for always being there and for letting me bounce ideas off of you. Also, thank you for agreeing to be a beta reader and telling me when something wasn't working for you in the story. Your friendship means a lot to me. Thanks for not giving up on me and for sticking around!

Cass Michaels- We've been pocket friends for way too many years and I wouldn't change it for the world! My Tumblr fanfic days are fond memories and a lot of that is because of you! Thank you for all your feedback on the story and for taking the time to read it and give me your thoughts. I am so happy with how this book turned out and a lot of it was because you pushed me to write it and how it needed to be written. Thank you for your encouragement!

Vicci Hine- Thank you so much for everything you do! You took a chance on me at the first RomantiConn event and I am forever grateful for you and our friendship! Thank you for reading some of the story and providing feedback. Your positive comments made me excited to continue, and I knew I was on to something great! You're always a pleasure to be around, and one of the most thoughtful people I know. Thank you so much for being you!

To the readers- Thank you for taking a chance on me! Whether you're a new reader, or have my full backlist, your support is unparalleled! You're the reason I keep going, and writing stories. Thank you for everything!

ABOUT THE AUTHOR

Cara Wade is an emerging author of young adult thrillers. This is Cara's first book.

Just kidding. None of that is true, but it's what the formatting program thought would be a fitting statement.

Cara Wade is a daydreamer and a lifelong teenybopper. Boy bands forever! She would love to spend the day in the kitchen baking up sweet treats but hates doing the dishes after. When she is not writing (or suffering writer's block) you can find her reading, hiking, or relaxing by the water. She lives in southern New Hampshire with her husband and children!

ALSO BY CARA WADE

Sugar and Spice

The Publicist (Hollywood Lust #1)

The Playboy (Hollywood Lust #2)

The Starlet (Hollywood Lust #3)

Ever After: A Dark Suspenseful Romance

Infatuated (Black Stallion Ranch #1)

Enamored (Black Stallion Ranch #2)

RISE: A Sin and Secrets Novella

High Rise Secrets (Sin and Secrets #3)

My New Forever (Falls Village Collection)

Darkened Truths (Kings of Pointebreak #1)

COMING SOON

Darkened Desires (Kings of Pointebreak #2)

Darkened Hearts (Kings of Pointebreak #3)